CONTROL

Hugh Montgomery is a professor and the director of the UCL Institute for Human Health and Performance at University College London. A distinguished physician, he is known for his pioneering genetic research. Outside the field of medicine, he was a founding member of the UK Climate and Health Council and is an endurance expert, who has run three ultra-marathons, scaled the world's sixth highest mountain, jumped naked from a plane at 14,000 ft and holds the world record for underwater piano playing.

CONTROL

HUGH MONTGOMERY

ZAFFRE

First published in Great Britain in 2019 by
ZAFFRE
80–81 Wimpole St, London W1G 9RE

A CIP catalogue record for this book is
available from the British Library.

ISBN: 978–1–78576–743–2

Also available as an ebook

1 3 5 7 9 10 8 6 4 2

Typeset by IDSUK (Data Connection) Ltd
Printed and bound in Great Britain by Clays Ltd, Elcograf S.p.A.

Zaffre is an imprint of Bonnier Books UK
www.bonnierbooks.co.uk

To Oscar and Fergus

PROLOGUE

NOVEMBER 1987

Kash gulped down the last spoonful of microwaved macaroni cheese and pushed the plastic container across the little table, savouring the peace and quiet. Well, relative quiet. The noises of a bursting-at-the-seams general hospital – the bangs and crashes, the raised voices, the occasional screams – were always faintly discernible in the background, even when he was back inside his hospital flat with the door firmly shut. But it was still an oasis of calm by comparison, and after another frantic shift on the wards, lurching from one emergency to another until he could no longer see – let alone think – straight, it felt like paradise.

A compact version of paradise, for sure. There was a tiny sink and hob in one corner, the latter largely redundant since the electric kettle and microwave together were sufficient to provide for all his nutritional requirements; a bookshelf crammed with medical textbooks; the table he was sitting at; two kitchen chairs; and a boxy little armchair covered in an unidentifiable orange fabric, which he largely avoided. A tiny bathroom and dorm-like bedroom just big enough to accommodate the bed and a single narrow wardrobe completed the picture.

It was cramped and uncomfortable and lacking in the remotest sense of homeliness.

Kash loved it.

He'd learned that being a junior doctor was a lot like being a soldier in action: if you found an opportunity to eat or sleep you took it, whatever time of the day or night it was, never knowing when the next one would come. So the first thing he'd done was to quickly shovel down some carbs with a garnish of E numbers, and, hunger satisfied, his mind and body were now crying out in unison for sleep; in fact, he knew all he had to do was shut his eyes, even sitting as he was now, straight-backed (in case you're watching, Mum) at the kitchen table, to plunge instantly into a slumber so profound it would approach the medical definition of coma. But brain-achingly tired though he was, there was something else even more important that he had to do before he could sleep. Stifling a yawn, he reached for the writing pad and took the top off the gold fountain pen that lay beside it, reading the inscription for the millionth time with the same mix of pride and embarrassment: *Dr Kash Devan: who would have thought!* He tapped the bottom of the pen against his teeth for a few moments and began:

Dear Mum,

Sorry for the long time since my last letter. Yes, as you will have guessed, I have been very busy. I don't think I knew what busy was until I started working at the hospital. But that is no excuse. I will do my very best to write more regularly. And, you can rest assured, even when I am not writing, I am thinking about you. And Dad, of course.

In answer to your first question, no, I am not making any money. Not yet! In the fullness of time, of course, I expect to have a Harley Street clinic where I will charge exorbitant fees for the most cursory examination in between trips to the golf course and the opera, but for now I am – despite my grand title which you are so proud of – a mere slave, at the beck and call of every sick person who turns up at the hospital. But, please be reassured, I am happy. Tired, occasionally frustrated, but happy. I am doing what I always wanted to do – what you and Dad worked so hard for me to be able to do – and the worst day here, when everything goes wrong, is still better than any other I could imagine. Like working in Uncle Terrance's accountancy firm, for instance. But let's not go there! Really, please, let's not.

In answer to your second question (I may have been a very inattentive son – please don't pretend to disagree – but I still know exactly what you are thinking), yes, I have 'met' someone. Please do not say 'finally' in that tone. As I think I mentioned, I have been busy saving lives and whatnot with precious little time for socialising. You may be surprised to learn that they do not hold tea dances at the hospital where it is possible to meet eligible young ladies. (Do I even know what that means? Not really.) Instead, at the end of an exhausting week, we all go the nearest pub and (feel free to put your hands over your ears at this point) get so drunk that even if I were to spend the evening conversing with the most beautiful, charming and – yes – eligible, girl you could imagine (and I know you have imagined a fair few), the next morning, I would not remember anything about it, and neither would she. I can see you shaking your head and you are right, it is not a very good system. But somehow in the midst of all this mayhem and amnesia, I have managed to find a girl whose name I can actually recall from one day to the next, and who, even more remarkably, can recall mine – and I dare to say even with a modicum of affection as she does so. What is she like? Hold your horses: I haven't told you her name yet—. Oh blast.

* * *

'Beep-beep beep!' Loud and grating, his bleep screeched beside him on the table. Not the more common 'someone-wants-you-please-look-at-the-number-on-the-screen' alert, but a crash call. Kash was already on his feet, pager in hand, as it spoke. 'Cardiac arrest. Mr Trenchard's office, outpatients department. Cardiac arrest. Mr Trenchard's office, outpatients department. Cardiac arrest. Mr Trenchard's office, outpatients department.'

Kash sprinted down the corridor and shoulder-barged the fire door at one end, its handle smashing into the plaster of the wall beyond. Twenty metres on, and someone was following behind, the same crashing noise now punctuating his progress, his confusion. *A cardiac arrest*, sure, but *in Mr Trenchard's office*? It didn't make any sense.

He hurtled down the corridor. Another turn, and now into the doctors' mess, and out the other side, careening through a set of screen doors, startling relatives waiting anxiously outside the emergency department. Then down the long hall between departments, rain beating a tattoo against the skylights above. Losing his balance as he turned a corner, he slipped and fell, his bumbag spilling a tourniquet, his *Oxford Handbook*, four syringes, two green needles, a collapsing patellar hammer and a handful of coloured biros. As he scrambled to retrieve them, a strong hand reached down to heave him back up and he looked up to see Max, a young doctor famous for his lopsided grin and terrible jokes.

But he wasn't joking now.

Kash got to his feet, thanked him with a curt nod and together they took off again.

Outpatients was normally deadly quiet at this time of night, but as they approached, they could hear an unaccustomed buzz of activity at the end of the basement hall. Kash saw light spilling out of the open doorway to Trenchard's office, then something weird – the unmistakeable sound of

Holst's *Planets* – it was 'Mars, the Bringer of War' – blasting out at maximum volume. Kash had heard it playing in the background in Trenchard's office so many times it would pop unbidden into his head at the strangest moments. It was, he thought, almost like Trenchard's theme tune: powerful, commanding, smashing through any obstacles in his way. Kash heard it and thought, yes, that's what you have to be like to be a successful surgeon – a *really* successful surgeon like Mr Trenchard. He slowed down, for the first time starting to feel apprehensive about what he was going to find. Max overtook him and then one of the night sisters appeared out of nowhere, carrying the portable crash-box and defibrillator, rekindling Kash's urgency. His jaw set, he hurried after her into the room.

Almost instantly he stopped, took one look at the scene before him, put a hand to his forehead and said, 'Jesus H Fucking Christ.'

The group around the figure on the floor turned as one. No one had ever heard him swear before.

1

THREE MONTHS EARLIER

The Victory had once occupied palatial grounds on the edge of parkland in South-East London, but now it sat at a conflux of roads, surrounded by a looping flyover and a motorway bridge at which the traffic was already stacked at 7 a.m. On a number fifty-nine bus, caught squarely in the middle of the traffic jam, Kash squinted through a window on the top deck and wondered if the grimy behemoth he could see below could really be the end point of all his hopes and dreams. No more studying, no more exams, no more rehearsals. This was the real thing. The end of the line. He would finally be able to say, 'Trust me, I'm a doctor,' even if he couldn't quite believe it himself.

Pressing his face to the glass like a kid outside a sweetshop, Kash imagined himself purposefully striding down the corridors, perhaps with a couple of juniors trailing behind, as he did his ward rounds, tossing out brilliant diagnoses as he went. The bus suddenly lurched forward as the lights changed, and his forehead banged on the glass. As the Victory disappeared from view, Kash realized he was about to miss his stop, and had a momentary panic that if he did so, the bus would just keep going, faster and faster and the Victory, along with all his hopes and dreams, would gradually melt like a distant mirage.

He leaped to his feet, pushed the bell, and squeezed his way past a heavyset woman to reach the lower deck. At first the driver appeared to ignore him, eyes fixed on the road ahead, before violently decelerating and swerving toward the roadside. The doors wheezed open, and Kash felt himself being propelled onto the pavement by the press of eager commuters behind him. He put a hand out to steady himself, but stumbled and snatched at the air, falling and banging his knee painfully on the concrete. He let out a cry of anguish, not so much because of the pain, but in fear that he had fractured his patella and would make his first entrance into the Victory being carried on a stretcher into the A&E department, rather than proudly walking through the front entrance.

As the pain receded he let out a sigh of relief – his big day was not going to be a disaster after all – only to see the handful of personnel forms he'd been clutching starting to blow away in the bus's exhaust fumes. He had a sudden, odd sensation, as if he'd been in this exact situation before, or would be again in the future, when he felt a gloved hand close over his. He looked up. The woman who was bent low next to him, her other hand grasping the personnel forms before they could tumble over the motorway bridge, looked like a kindly ageing mother, but her eyes suggested she had too often seen things she might wish that she hadn't. It took Kash a moment to realize she was wearing nurse's whites under the grey woollen coat, which was fastened with a silver brooch.

'You're Devan,' she said, matter-of-factly. 'Kash Devan. No, don't look so surprised. It isn't magic. I've seen your face pinned up on the ward rounds board. They do it for all newbies. Helps us old warhorses know who's coming.' She stopped, mildly amused that he was still crouching down in the gutter, squatting as if about to empty his bowels. 'Well, come on, Kash. You can't loiter here all day. People to see. Patients to save. Blood pressure and bedpans, and all that; I'm sure you know the drill. I'm Sister Vale, by the way.' She reached into her coat to look at her watch, a silver timepiece that hung from the pocket of her uniform. 'And soon, we'll both be late. I don't imagine Mr Trenchard will be very pleased about that.'

* * *

To look at it, the Victory was anything but special. Built by subscription after the First World War, and bombed to oblivion in the Second, it had risen from the ashes, less phoenix than half-pecked city pigeon. Outside, its face was weathered and cracked, its windows blind with grime. Inside, the obligatory coats of 'hospital green' paint were peeling like eczema from the weeping walls, trickles and stains the inward signs of blocked gutters and pipes. But none of this mattered to Kash. It was a central London teaching hospital; what it looked like wasn't the point. So, here he stood at the entrance to the Victory – with its stained lino, dented doors and blown bulbs, smelling of blood, sweat and air freshener, his home for the coming year and the launch-pad to a brilliant future.

Up the stone flag steps, past a vacant reception desk and on down the corridor, and Sister Vale stopped. 'What were your orders?' she asked. 'Or was it just "work it out on the day"?'

'Pretty much,' he admitted. 'Apparently the last houseman left his bleep and a handover list in a pigeonhole in the mess. I'm supposed to pick it up, and meet the registrar on the ward.'

Sister Vale looked at her watch again. 'OK. Quickly then.' She bustled on, pointing out key parts of the hospital as they went. Pharmacy was in one direction. Outpatients was down there alongside a set of other offices. He noted the Hospital Friends' Coffee Shop, the canteen – and, at last, the Doctors' Mess. Sister Vale pushed open an old oak door, weirdly out of place amid the general shabbiness, suggesting that some magic kingdom lay beyond. Inside, however, was nothing but a wasteland of pizza boxes, discarded crusts and crushed plastic cups, with a smattering of yellow rice on the thread-bare carpet.

Sister Vale held the door open, but made no move to enter, whether out of disgust or lack of entitlement Kash couldn't tell. Across the room, beside a bar counter, were some pigeonholes. In one, he found an A4 sheet with 'Kash/ Mr Trenchard H/O' written on it, wrapped around a pager and held in place by two elastic bands. Kash seized it, returned to Sister Vale and waved it triumphantly.

'Trenchard? Oh, yes.' A fact, as if some reality had only now become crystallized and concrete. She seemed paralysed for a moment, before recovering. 'Right, come on. Let's get you to the ward. You can meet the registrar there for his 7.30 ward round.'

When they reached the ward, Sister Vale pointed towards a door. 'Doctors' office. There's probably a spare white coat in there somewhere – and you can get a new one from the laundry later. Sort yourself out, then head onto the ward. This is where I leave you for now. I'm boss on this ward for a few months more, but then I move to fourteen as Matron. I think you have your second six months there too, so we'll be seeing a lot of each other.' She reached out a hand. 'Good luck, Kash. If you're unsure, just ask. You'd better hurry. Trenchard is a stickler for time.' She paused. 'Oh, and, Kash? You seem like a nice chap. Mind your back.' She turned on her heel and briskly marched away.

Mind your back? Of all the things that had been keeping him awake at night before this moment, worrying about that wasn't one of them. He shrugged and entered the office.

The doctors' office – *his* office, he thought – was best described as utilitarian. A long desk surface. Two telephones, some biros, an almost bare stationery rack, and a metal desk-top stack, each drawer filled with a different sort of form. Three straight-backed chairs. A notes trolley, bulging with patients' files. A faded 'Cardiopulmonary Resuscitation' poster held at three points to the wall with yellowing tape. Behind the door, a number of white coats hung limply. He selected one which lacked a name badge, filled its pockets with *Handbook*, note-book, *British National Formulary*, tape measure and pens, then passed a red and white pin (for neurological examina-tion) through his lapel. He clipped the bleep to his belt, bur-ied the tourniquet deep in a trouscr pocket, dumped his bag and, with the patient handover list folded into his top pocket, opened the door and looked out onto the ward.

He stood there, savouring the moment, like a diver poised on the edge of the high board, at once fearful and excited. He took a deep breath and plunged in.

Uncertain where he was actually supposed to be going, Kash advanced towards the nurses' station. Behind it, some-one was busying herself with an observation folder.

* * *

'Hi. I'm Kash. Mr Trenchard's new house officer. I was told to come here to join his ward round?'

The nurse looked up, and immediately smiled, her brusque pace slowing. She extended a hand.

'Hello, then, new boy. I'm Claire.' She was slim and efficient-looking, with chestnut hair tied back in a neat ponytail. 'Don't worry. I've only been here three months myself. You'll soon get the hang of things.' She was about to continue, then stopped in her tracks, her whole body stiffening to attention as she caught sight of something or somebody over Kash's shoulder.

Kash turned and saw a tall man in a dark blue pin-striped suit approaching. He must have been six feet four, with swept-back grey hair and piercing blue eyes, that would have made him stand out in any gathering. But what actually struck Kash most forcefully was his air of total focus and calm. In a place where everybody seemed to be hurrying, he was utterly relaxed, as if the most dire emergency would wait for him until he decided he was ready. Feeling his own pulse racing, his mouth dry, and a trickle of sweat between his shoulder blades, before he'd even come face to face with his first patient, Kash envied Trenchard's air of impeturbability. That's how I want to be, he thought with sudden clarity: the eye of the storm, the unmoving mover, like God himself.

A rich baritone, deep and musical but with an edge of something harder beneath, jolted him out of his reverie.

'Dr Devan. Nice of you to join us.' He lifted his sleeve from his Rolex, and raised an eyebrow. Kash felt himself flush.

'Got yourself a white coat, I see. Well, white-ish.' He eyed it up and down. 'Laundry opens at nine. Best trade it in for a clean starched one. Reputations are hard to gain and easy to lose. Looking the part is more important than you might think. And so is timekeeping.'

With that, he strode smoothly to bed one on Nightingale ward, where Sister Vale was waiting with a clipboard in hand.

'Good morning, Mr Trenchard.'

He gave an almost imperceptible nod of acknowledgement. 'I was just telling Dr Devan here about my passion for punctuality.'

'I'm afraid that was entirely my fault. I tripped getting off my bus and your man here stopped to help me.'

Kash was taken aback. Sister Vale had no need to lie for him, and yet here she was, putting her own reputation on the line just to save his blushes.

Trenchard gave her an appraising look but she held his gaze. 'Then I don't need to introduce you two, then.' He nodded towards the rest of the team, who had been waiting patiently on the other side of the bed. 'Alexa. Staff Nurse Wright.' Alexa nodded, holding on to the notes trolley with both hands as if afraid that someone was about to rip it away from her. Then, 'Dr Aldiss, Samantha. Your fellow house officer. You know each other, I assume?' They both nodded. Samantha had graduated from Oxford with a first in English, before sidestepping into medical school. She could discourse equally fluently on Burton's *Anatomy of Melancholy* and *Grey's Anatomy*, and could drink Kash under the table – not, he would be the first to admit, much of a feat. 'Angela Warner, our senior surgical registrar, would also normally be here, but she's been up all night and is just finishing a case.' Trenchard smiled, and Kash wondered if he was just imagining a hint of admonishment in his tone, as if Angela might have organized her patients a little better. Trenchard then turned his smile on Sister Vale.

'I know Sister Vale doesn't like me to dawdle. We'd better get on.'

Trenchard led on, pausing at each bed like a bee seeking nectar, as all around stood tense in fear of stings. At every stage, the staff nurse went ahead to straighten the sheets and retrieve the observations clipboard from the end of the bed. 'Normally,' said Trenchard, 'you'll present the cases, Dr Devan. But for today, you can listen and learn, if that's all right with you?'

Kash wasn't sure if he'd been asked a question, so simply nodded.

As they made their progress down the ward, he glanced back to see Sister Vale watching them. He gave a quick smile to signal his thanks for her standing up for him, but she didn't seem to see him. Her eyes seemed to be fixed on Mr Trenchard with an expression he couldn't read.

2

By the time the ward round was finally over, Kash had developed a headache from trying to commit every word Trenchard uttered to memory. What he needed was a glass of water and a lie-down in a darkened room, but although he knew he wasn't going to get that for a good few hours, he was still taken aback by the way the hospital seemed to pick him up and whirl him from department to department like a rag doll. The sense of being rushed off his feet was compounded by not knowing who anyone was or who to ask. Angela Warner had clearly moved straight from operating overnight to operating by day, or was committed in the outpatients department. Wherever she was, she wasn't around to show him the ropes. The nursing staff were pleasant enough, but made it abundantly clear that they were as busy as he was and were not prepared to cut him any slack. Maybe at some point they'd trust him enough not to call him for every drug chart. Maybe they'd flush the odd intravenous line. But until they got the measure of each other it was all going to be strictly by the book. He felt like a pinball, bouncing from bleep to bleep, ward to ward, task to task. And all the time, he was trying to get to see every one of the patients officially under his care. That, he knew, was a matter of survival. Not for them, but for him. The tables would soon be turned and he'd have to present the patients to Mr Trenchard tomorrow. He had a feeling it would not be a good idea to fluff his lines.

* * *

Six o'clock came, and he'd survived the day on one cup of coffee from the patients' drinks trolley – the brown liquid so scalding that it had melted the cup and given it a sagging waistline. His own, he suspected, would soon look like that too: his only other sustenance had come from a pocketful of boiled sweets. He'd been bleeping for a porter for an hour without response, and was now wondering if he should take the blood samples to biochemistry himself and, if so, where the hell that was. He ran his fingers anxiously through his hair.

Suddenly, the door flew open. It was Claire. 'You're needed. Bed four,' she said quickly – and then she was gone.

Kash leaped to his feet and hurried after her. The urgency in her voice was clear. Welcome to hospital life, he thought: just when you felt you had no more in the tank, worn out by a hundred humdrum procedures, that was when the real emergency hit.

Just up the ward, the curtains were drawn around a bed space. Patients stared silently like spooked antelope, heads up and alert, trying to identify the danger. As Kash approached, he could hear Claire saying, 'Mrs Connell? Mrs Connell? Can you hear me?'

Kash slipped through the curtains. Inside lay an elderly woman. Eighties? *Older?* However old she was, she hadn't been there an hour earlier. She was dressed in a surgical gown, which had risen up to reveal her genitals, and also the lower inch of a surgical dressing.

Sister Vale was fixing an oxygen mask over the old woman's face. Claire glanced round. 'Alice Connell. Eighty-four. A-P resection for colon cancer. Long op – on the table for four hours. Back from theatres thirty minutes ago. Drowsy when she got here. But now she's unresponsive . . .'

Kash approached and felt for a pulse. It was there, but a little slow. 'BP?'

'Ninety on sixty. Was one-two-five on eighty-five when she got here. Respiratory rate is only six.'

'Diabetic?'

Sister Vale and Claire glanced at each other.

'Sister Vale, could you do a quick BM for me and tell me the blood sugar?'

He moved to the other side of the bed. 'Let's sit her up a bit. I don't want her vomiting and aspirating. One . . . two . . . three!' Together, they pulled Mrs Connell up on the sheet, and further onto the head rest. 'Can you put a Guedel in, if she'll tolerate it?'

Claire put the airway in.

Kash was fast and methodical. The patient was indeed unresponsive. Both pupils were pinpoint in size. 'She's either had a pontine stroke, or a lot of morphine. Has she had any here?'

'Not here. But probably in theatre? We haven't seen the anaesthetic chart yet – they left it in recovery.'

'OK. Can I have one ampoule of Narcan?'

Sister Vale had returned, and was pricking Mrs Connell's finger to test the blood sugar levels. 'Do you want some help?'

Kash paused for a fraction of a second. 'No. Let's try that first. If there's no response, we'll call Angela or the med reg.'

Claire glanced at Sister Vale, who gave a subtle nod.

With that, Claire exited, returning two minutes later with a small syringe and an empty ampoule. Together, they read it. 'Naloxone hydrochloride four hundred microgrammes per millilitre. One millilitre.' They checked the expiry date.

She showed him a second syringe and ampoule, this time of saline flush. Kash tried hard not to show that his hands were shaking as he uncapped the intravenous cannula, injected half the Narcan, flushed it in, and put the cap back on.

Forty seconds later, Mrs Connell's eyes fluttered and opened. Twenty seconds after that, she was moaning in pain – the effect of the morphine she'd been given had been reversed.

Sister Vale smiled. 'Well done, Kash. Spot on. You and I are going to get on just fine. Claire – could you call the anaesthetist? They left the mess on our floor. They can come and clean it up.'

Claire smiled, leaned in and whispered, 'Well done.'

Kash tried not to grin. Despite his shaking hands and clamouring heart, he hoped he was exuding a Trenchard-like calm, even though inside he was manically fist-pumping. He'd been tested, and had passed. He stepped out onto the ward, where the approving looks of all the patients greeted him. He breezed past them as if it was nothing, nothing at all.

*   *   *

Nine o'clock. The incessant bleeps had slowed long enough for Kash to have seen the remaining patients, write in their notes, and file the blood results. He'd found all the X-rays which Mr Trenchard might want to see in the morning and made a mental note to come in early to write the blood forms. But for now, he was done. He'd bleeped the new on-call house officer, who was palpably relieved that Kash wasn't handing over a huge list of incomplete tasks.

'Cheers, mate. Everything all right? To be honest, I'm shitting myself.'

'You'll be fine,' said Kash, getting a buzz from suddenly being treated as the grizzled veteran. 'And look, my bleep is on and I'll be around for a while. Shout if you need another pair of hands.'

'You're sure you don't want to go out to get pissed?'

What Kash actually wanted, now that he thought about it, was to listen to a bit of Mozart with a cup of camomile tea, but he decided not to let on. 'Maybe tomorrow.' With that, he hung his coat on the back of the door, remembering with a sigh that he hadn't managed to get a clean one and hoping that Mr Trenchard would understand that he'd had more important things to do.

He was walking down the corridor, wondering if he ought to get some proper food inside him, when he heard the squeak of trainers behind him. He looked round to see Claire, who had just finished the nursing handover and was now dressed in a dark-blue tracksuit with a fawn raincoat over it.

'You did all right in there today. How did you know?'

Kash smiled. 'The benefits of ignorance. If you only know two causes of bilateral pinpoint pupils, it has to be one of them.' He paused. 'And if it had been the other one, she would have been a goner, and so nothing to be done but call the family.'

'We'd already done that,' Claire grinned. 'They were a bit surprised when they rushed in to find Mum the picture of health.'

Kash smiled back. 'Good thing no one had a heart attack. Next time I'll make sure she stays on the critical list.'

Claire smiled again. 'You'll make a top surgeon yet. So, you coming?'

'Coming where?'

'The Balti, Kash. The nursing staff's second home. Anyone not actually unconscious or dead will be there. You're sure no one mentioned it in the mess?'

'I haven't seen another doctor all day, to be honest, and I last passed through the mess a lifetime ago.' He glanced at his watch. 'Well, fourteen hours ago.'

'High time you had a drink, then.'

'Well, I . . .' Kash felt like a rabbit in particularly dazzling headlights. Despite the fourteen hours of mayhem she must have been through, Claire looked as fresh as a daisy and as pretty as a . . . well, something very pretty. And she wouldn't stop smiling at him.

Despite his fatigue, the prospect of a drink with nurse Claire Barker was really very appealing. But there was something else he really needed to do. A letter he had to write.

'Thanks, but I think I may already be technically unconscious. I wouldn't be very good company. Another time, yes?'

She gave him a sad look, testing his resolve, then shrugged and walked away.

3

A week had somehow passed and Kash was slumped in the mess. Never had a room been so appropriately named. His soggy Chesterfield had long since been swamped, and bobbed at an impossible angle amidst the flotsam and jetsam of a takeaway tide.

Kash sighed. To him, it felt like seven months, not seven days. But paradoxically it also felt like seven minutes, the warp speed of ward life creating some weird quantum effect that compressed events together so they seemed to happen simultaneously. Surely it wasn't physically possible. He had lurched through a lifetime in the mere launch time of a career. He was still struggling with bursts of anxiety – usually in the quieter moments rather than during an emergency. Imposter Syndrome. He didn't deserve to be here. He needed somehow to acquire Trenchard's Zen-like calm, but suspected that came with years of experience, the hard-won sense that the hospital couldn't throw anything at you that you hadn't seen before. There were no short cuts. Unless, of course, people like Michael Trenchard simply experienced time in a different way, like hummingbirds who lived life so fast that every second felt like a minute to them. Didn't top sportspeople describe a similar feeling – the ball coming at you over the net in slow motion? What did they call it: *being in the zone*? Well, Kash had never been any good at sport, and he certainly didn't have the physique of a hummingbird, so perhaps he was destined forever to experience time as a mad, downhill rush where everything fell out of his pockets. Which reminded him, he needed to get a new bumbag to put everything in. He shook his head and took another bite of his stale cheese and onion roll, looked quizzically at the grey froth on his coffee (known colloquially as 'flat shite'), but took a gulp anyway to lubricate the fossilized crust.

'Don't you need to be somewhere?'

He looked up, almost choking on his mouthful of roll, and instinctively started getting to his feet.

'Gotcha!' Angela Warner plonked herself down opposite him, sweeping her mass of dark curls behind her ear with a broad grin. She was five years his senior at twenty-nine years old but with the fragile look of a teenager who had grown up in a war zone. She'd got through medical school by the age of twenty-two, and had been the first of her year into specialist surgical training.

Kash sighed, settling back in his chair. 'Aren't you supposed to be mentoring me? You are the senior surgical special registrar.'

Angela waved a hand dismissively. 'Sink or swim, that's my motto.' Kash couldn't help noticing the sharply defined muscles of her forearms. Surgery, he was beginning to appreciate, was sometimes just bloody hard physical work.

She pointed at his half-eaten roll. 'You want a scalpel for that?'

'I was thinking more of a bone saw,' Kash replied with a smile, pushing his plate to one side. 'So what's going on with you?'

Angela shook her head. 'Where do I fucking begin?'

'Anything I can help with?'

'You could shoot that Mr Greengrass on twelve for me?'

'Isn't there some sort of regulation against that?'

Angela shrugged. 'Not regarding Mr Greengrass specifically, no. I've checked.'

Kash smiled. 'In that case I'll try and make it as painless as possible.'

Angela shook her head. 'Don't do that. I want the bastard to suffer.'

'Maybe we should keep him alive, then.'

Angela sighed. 'Fair enough.'

It had taken Kash a while to get used to Angela's humour, and to realize that it was just the flipside of her almost super-human dedication to the job. It was hard to imagine a surgeon who cared more or worked harder for her patients. Even the incorrigible letches like Mr Greengrass, who, though handicapped by a ruptured spleen, the product of trying to teach his motorcycle to fly, still insisted on treating physical exams as a two-way process.

'So how's it going with Mr Trenchard?'

He blew out his cheeks. 'What can I say? I feel immensely privileged to have him criticizing every last little thing I do.'

'You should. He's one of the best you'll ever meet.' She paused. 'In fact, *the* best. You don't know how good he is.'

'I'm beginning to get a sense of—'

Angela held up a hand to interrupt. 'Let me tell you a story. I was on-call, got bleeped by the emergency department. Turned up to find this big bearded bloke on the trolley. Mid-fifties, looked a hundred. Porcelain white, ice cream cold, face ashen, beaded with sweat, his breath coming in shallow gasps through his oxygen mask. Snatching breaths, thousand-yard stare. You know the sort.' She paused. 'Anyway. Two nurses running bags of intravenous fluid into him. The oxygen sats monitor alarming that no blood oxygen saturation could be recorded. ECG monitor screeching because the leads kept coming off with the sweat. Blood pressure flashing and pinging at sixty-two on forty.'

And then she was there again. Living it.

After a few moments, Angela refocused, and was back in the room with Kash.

'Someone said "shit" very loudly. They had a tourniquet tight around the guy's arm, and were slapping the skin to raise a vein. All eyes turned to me, the newbie. Was I any good? I look at the patient, then at the monitor. Hypovolaemic shock. Acute. No blood in a bowl or smell of melaena, so it's not a GI bleed. Must be a Triple A.'

Kash nodded. Abdominal aortic aneurysm. 'Go on.'

The abdominal aorta is the main artery which carries blood to the body from the heart. If it expands – an aneurysm – its wall weakens and then bursts, like the blow-out of a tyre. Death can follow soon afterwards. Unless someone repairs the hole, or replaces the tyre's inner tube.

'I ask the doctor – Dave, I think his name was – if we had an anaesthetist. Not yet, he says. So I ask one of the nurses if she'd mind crash-calling one. We slap a line in . . .'

Typical understatement from Angela, thought Kash. Most people couldn't find a vein in a patient like that without explosives and a digger.

'. . . and and then I said, "Look, Dave, we're running out of time, here. We'd better get ready to push him round to theatres." So I'm taping his venflon in place, and Dave's attaching the oxygen mask to a portable cylinder, before disconnecting the monitor, when the anaesthetist turns up. Harry Adams, his name was. Anaesthetic SpR. So we all introduce ourselves and I tell him we've got a leaking triple A, we've just got a line in and we need to get to theatres. He looks at me a bit sceptically like the Big I Am. Snooty fuck. "And we know this how?" *Fucking anaesthetists*, I think.

'I want to say, "Because we went to medical school." But I keep my cool and say – because Dave has given me the whole story – "Mr Craig McDougall. History of hypertension. Abdominal pain through to his back. Pulsatile mass.

Hypovolaemic shock." Harry isn't impressed. "Has he had any imaging? Plain films? CT? What do the bloods show?" I'm getting pissed off, now. "We've only just got a line in," I tell him. "He's not fit for a trip to Radiology. And the results won't help." I look at Dave. "Good to go?" Dave looks like he's not entirely sure, but nods anyway. We're about to get moving with the trolley when Harry stands in front. "Slow down, *doctor*. Just started? Right? Your first on-call?"'

Kash leaned forward. 'Was it?'

Angela shrugged. 'I was right. He was wrong. Then he says, "Let's just pause for breath, for a moment, not get carried away." *Arsehole*. So I think, fuck that, no good telling the bloke on the trolley to pause in the middle of his leaking bloody triple A while we have a nice civilized conversation about it. I kicked the brakes off and start pushing the trolley out of the bay and down the corridor. Harry can't believe what a silly bitch I'm being. "But theatres aren't ready!" he says. I keep pushing. Dave's fully on board now, and helping me navigate the foot end around the corners. But Harry decides it's time to put his foot down. "We need to stop. *Now!*" he shouts. He even puts a hand on my shoulder. I'll be honest, at that point I began to wonder if he was right. Maybe I'd just got carried away.'

She stopped for a moment, lost in the memory.

'And?' Kash asked.

She turned to look at him. 'Suddenly I heard this voice. Not loud, but it got my attention. Sort of low and fruity, like someone doing King Lear.'

Kash's eyes lit up. 'Trenchard.'

'"If anyone is going to lay a hand on my SpR, Dr Adams, it will be me." I looked round and he was smiling, as if he found the whole situation rather amusing. Then he nodded at the trolley. "Keep pushing! So?" Dave started to explain what was going on, but Trenchard held up a hand to shut him up. "Angela?" I remember it was hard to speak. I had this big lump in my throat. "Leaking triple A. I thought we should get to theatres." He gave me a look. "Where no one is ready. And we don't have the diagnosis confirmed." I didn't have an answer to that.

'Then he puts a hand on McDougall's arm, feels for a radial then a carotid pulse. Slips his hands onto his abdomen, just for a moment, then gives a little grunt. "We do now. Straight in, please." So we push McDougall down the corridor and into the anaesthetic room of theatre two. Trenchard looks at Dave. "Get volume in, please. I see you have O-neg blood. Use it. Mr Adams? Morphine, please. And get ready to intubate." Harry goes white. Literally. "Mr Trenchard? You can't be . . ." I remember Trenchard's suit jacket looked like some kind of fancy cashmere blend, but he just kicks it across the floor, together with his yellow silk tie – funny the things you remember – like it's an old bin bag. He tears McDougall's shirt buttons open, and pulls down the waistband of his trousers before emptying a bottle of pink chlorhexidine disinfectant over his abdomen. He sloshes more over his own hands and forearms. He rolls his sleeves up, snaps on a pair of sterile size-eight gloves with a little flourish, like he's a magician about to pull a rabbit out of a hat, then picks up a number eleven scalpel, holds it poised for a moment with its tip over McDougall's abdomen, just below the ribs in the midline, and turns to Harry, who's sort of frozen to the spot. "Come on, catch up.""

Angela stopped for a moment, smiling at the memory.

Kash put his hand on her arm. 'And then?'

'So he just starts operating! Arse to tit incision, grabs a mass of gamgee swab, and plunges his fist deep into the wound, his arm straight and his full body weight leaning through it. He smiles up at me and says, very matter-of-fact, "Like any bleeding, press on it hard enough and it will stop." I sort of nod but I must have looked as if I was going to say something because he then says, "Oh! Infection?" I think he actually laughed. "You can always treat an infection with antibiotics. But not, of course, if the patient's already dead.""

'Blimey,' Kash said.

'You can say that again,' said Angela. 'You might even go so far as "crikey" or possibly "good heavens". So we finish up, and then Trenchard strolls casually back into the anaesthetic room, picks up his coat and drops it into a yellow clinical waste bag for incineration. "You can never get blood out of wool," he says. "Trust me." I couldn't help glancing at the waste bag and he just shrugs and says, "It's only money."'

'And Mr McDougall?'

'Complete recovery. I still get a Christmas card. It's Mr Trenchard he should be thanking, though. I still can't quite believe what I saw him do.'

'What? Throw away an expensive jacket?'

Angela picked up the remains of the bread roll and threw it at him. 'You know what I mean.'

Kash nodded. 'Yes, Angela, I think I do. Good thing this isn't wool, by the way,' he added, brushing himself down.

4

The next time he saw Mr Trenchard was on ward fourteen. Not Kash's favourite part of the hospital, if he was honest. Fourteen was the long-stay ward. Not that all of its patients necessarily stayed long; it was just that once they'd arrived there, they didn't go anywhere else. Not back home, anyway. At best, *a* home. But usually the choice was more teak or pine. Fourteen was sometimes referred to as 'Professor Whitley's Waiting Room', Professor Whitely being a histopathologist, which meant he performed all the hospital post-mortems. Kash looked around at the old, exhausted faces. It was definitely quieter than the other wards. Breakfast had come and gone. Bedpans had been emptied, soiled bedsheets removed. Most of the patients seemed to have lapsed back into a semi-comatose state. The expression on the faces of those that had not was one of resignation. They knew that once they put you on ward fourteen, you were just waiting for the end.

He was beginning to wonder why Mr Trenchard had asked to meet him here, when he spotted him by the nurses' station, leaning casually on the desk. Trenchard crooked a finger, and Kash trotted over.

'If you ever fancy a bit of peace and quiet, this is the place to come, eh, Kash?'

Trenchard was wearing a lavender shirt with a bright red tie. He didn't exactly look as if he was in search of peace and quiet.

'Er . . . yes, Mr Trenchard.'

Trenchard grinned, clearly enjoying Kash's bemusement. 'Right.' He pointed across the ward to a white-haired old lady propped up on her pillows, taking delicate sips from a cup of tea gripped in a shaking claw. 'That's Liz. Liz Murray. Admitted eight months ago after suffering a stroke at an old folks' ballroom dancing class. What we charmingly call "domiciliary support services" looked after her until Christmas, when her son's family were asked to do their bit for three days – which was three days too much, apparently. They took the traditional approach to unwanted things you get landed with at Christmas: immediate re-gifting, parking just long enough to dump her in the emergency department, before legging it back to Penge. Nobody's seen hide nor hair of them since. Of course, once she was in our clutches we gave her a battery of blood tests – which revealed her chronic lymphocytic leukaemia. Already pretty end-stage. Must have had it for years. When Dr Carney put it in layman's terms and told her she was dying, she shrugged her shoulders and told him, "I'm ninety-one. Tell me something I don't know." Well, now she's ninety-two. Let's introduce you.'

As they crossed the ward, Kash tried to work out what this was all about. Despite what Trenchard had just told him, there must be some medical mystery about Mrs Murray, some puzzle he was supposed to solve. He felt a bead of sweat forming on his forehead.

'Liz? I'd like to introduce a young colleague of mine, Dr Kash Devan.'

Liz put her teacup down carefully on the bedside table and gave Kash a mostly toothless grin. 'Pleased to meet you, Kash,' she said in a surprisingly steady voice. 'You haven't seen my glasses, have you?'

Trenchard chuckled. 'Don't worry, she asks everyone that. We'll ask a nurse to have a rummage in a minute, Liz. Now, I'm going to ask Dr Devan here to examine you. Is that all right?'

Liz shrugged her bony shoulders. 'I'm ninety-two, and I've got blood cancer. That's quite enough to be going on with, so if you find anything else, Kash, I'd be grateful if you could keep it to yourself. Unless it's my glasses, of course,' she added.

Kash smiled. 'Sounds good.'

As Trenchard watched, he gave Mrs Murray a thorough examination, paying particular attention to her breathing and heart rate. But for the life of him he couldn't find anything you wouldn't expect in a ninety-two-year-old cancer patient. In fact, she seemed in remarkably good nick, all told. He blinked away a drop of sweat. What was he missing?

'Well,' she said, 'have I passed my MOT?'

Kash smiled warily. 'A bit of wear and tear, but mechanically sound, as far as I can tell.' He tensed, waiting for Trenchard to tell him the obvious symptom he'd failed to spot.

'Jolly good,' Trenchard said affably, steering Kash back towards the nurses' station. 'Thanks for your time, Liz, and I'll be back to have more of a chat soon. I'm sure Dr Devan will be popping in from time to time from now on, too.'

Kash smiled over his shoulder and Liz gave him a little wave, before turning to pick up her tea.

'So,' Trenchard said, once they were out of hearing.

Kash was sure whatever he said would be wrong. 'So, I missed something?'

'As a matter of fact, you did. I was asked to review her because of a change in bowel habit and a microcytosis on top of the anaemia from the leukaemia.' Small red blood cells – microcytosis was a common sign of iron deficiency – usually meaning chronic blood loss. 'She's got a low rectal carcinoma. But you'd not have found that without doing a rectal examination. And no, Kash. I didn't tell her. She's right. The leukaemia will get her long before the cancer. But that wasn't the point, Kash.'

He raised an eyebrow.

'Since you don't seem to have grasped the point, Kash, let me ask you a question. What do you think is the commonest cause of death in this hospital? And don't try and be clever and say heart failure.'

'Well, infection, I would imagine, must be—'

Trenchard loomed over him. Kash thought he was about to get a slap.

'Unhappiness!' he boomed. 'Why do you think Liz Murray, ninety-two-year-old stroke victim and cancer sufferer, is clinging on to life so tenaciously? Why do you think I am willing to bet a week's wages – mine, not yours – that she will outlast every other patient on ward fourteen, and possibly several of the staff to boot? *Because she enjoys being alive.* Look at the sparkle in those eyes. She probably extracts more pleasure from a dollop of that slop we call tea than you would from a glass of vintage champagne. Do you see what I'm getting at?'

Kash nodded tentatively. 'I think so, Mr Trenchard. I suppose you're saying it's no good operating on patients and then just leaving them lying in bed being miserable. We need to make sure they have, um . . . stimulating interactions with, er . . .'

Kash stopped. Trenchard was literally rolling his eyes. He put his hands on Kash's shoulders.

'I'm not talking about the *patients*, Kash. I'm talking about *you*. All work and no play. I've seen your type before. You might think what you need is sleep, but you're wrong. What you need is some fun. Otherwise you'll be the one having stimulating interactions with Mrs Murray – from the adjoining bed. *Carpe diem,*' he added, with a meaningful look.

Kash looked confused.

'If your Latin's a little rusty,' Trenchard explained, 'that means if a pretty young nurse invites you out for a drink, you bloody well say yes!'

5

The consultants' offices were buried like a bunker deep in the outpatients block, and had a sense of sanctuary after hours. It was only here, of all the thousand corners of the Victory, that the ordinary chaos of hospital life leeched away with the light at the end of each day. Kash sat behind the desk in Mr Trenchard's office, a tower of papers and patient folders teetering at his side. He was working on an audit of surgical waiting times across all major surgical specialities. Trenchard wanted three months of work audited from across each of three years, and Kash was determined to complete the task quicker than Trenchard expected. Perhaps he was putting more pressure on himself than was sensible, but at least the seclusion of Mr Trenchard's office meant he could lose himself in the work, and the truth was that compared to the pressure of making instant life-or-death decisions on the wards, this was almost like a rest cure for his frazzled brain. It was a part of doctoring that took Kash back to that golden first year as a student, when his head was happily lost in his books and everything seemed possible. He'd had to put up with some ribbing from his fellow students for never going anywhere without a book in his hand and for having mastered the art of reading while walking, eating or watching TV (not that he did much of that), but he knew that really they were jealous, frustrated that their powers of concentration and mental stamina couldn't match his. He'd never felt that he was missing out: what was the point of going out and having fun when you could use the time to learn? Wasn't that what they were at medical school for? You'd have the whole of the rest of your life to watch movies and eat over-priced meals in noisy restaurants. But the truth was he preferred to get his teeth into a tasty medical textbook. And he felt genuinely sorry for students for whom it was a chore, or even a form of painful torture to be endured rather than enjoyed.

Still, Mr Trenchard's advice had made him stop and think. Did all work and no play make Jack a dull boy? He'd always been proud of being a bookworm. Didn't knowing things make you more interesting? Now he wondered if, in fact, it was in danger of making him boring.

A firm tapping at the door derailed his train of thought. Who would come here this late looking for Mr Trenchard? Outpatients was closed. When the door opened he was surprised to see Sister Vale. She was wrapped up in her grey woollen coat, fastened with its silver brooch, a look of matronly concern on her face.

'I thought I'd find you here. Don't you have a home to go to, Kash?'

He might have asked her the same question. Kash checked his watch. 'I've got a couple of hours left in me yet, Sister . . .'

'You young men think stamina's an endless reserve. Well, Dr Devan, I'm here to tell you it's not.' She came further into the room, and perched on the edge of Mr Trenchard's desk. Kash was momentarily taken aback, knowing she would never have done that if it had been Mr Trenchard sitting behind it, and Sister Vale smiled at his embarrassment.

'I know you admire Mr Trenchard, Kash. And so you should. I've never known a talent to compare to his. He's not the only good surgeon in this hospital, of course. Not the only good doctor. There's Dr Carney, for one. Quite brilliant in his field, a ground-breaking researcher, but he never quite had the . . . flair of Mr Trenchard.' She smiled wryly. 'And, of course, he's acutely aware of it. That's why he's not top dog, and there's nothing he can do about it.'

Kash nodded. 'How long have you worked for Mr Trenchard?'

Sister Vale's expression changed, and Kash wondered if he'd made a mistake, like he'd asked her how old she was.

'I'm sorry, I didn't mean . . .'

Sister Vale laughed. 'Oh, I've known Michael a long time. I used to work for him down here, in outpatients, long ago. I learned very quickly how he hates powdered surgical gloves, or when the lights go out on his sigmoidoscope. I know what he loves as well. A decent biscuit, a tape measure on a trolley. The little things, I suppose, but they can be important sometimes.'

She stood up and gave Kash a look he was very familiar with; an expression of maternal concern with a glint of steel underneath.

'I know you want to impress Mr Trenchard, and by all accounts you're doing a good job, but it's no good if you spend all your time when you're not on the wards doing his paperwork, when I'm sure you have plenty of your own.'

Kash nodded towards the pile of papers on the desk. 'But Mr Trenchard's snowed under, Sister. If I can—'

'Oh, *snowed under*.' Sister vale gave a little snort. 'We're all *snowed under*. But do you know why he hasn't got time to finish his own patient records? Because when he's not here, he's seeing private patients, Kash. I'm not saying he doesn't work hard. But he's being paid handsomely for it. And he relies on faithful junior doctors like you to tidy up after him. He flatters you. But it's all about control in the end.'

Kash frowned. He might be dull, but he wasn't naive. Of course Trenchard did private work. They all did. But at least he was treating patients. It wasn't as if he was playing golf while Kash was slaving away in his office.

'Sister, you don't need to worry that I'm being exploited. Maybe I'm doing all this to impress Mr Trenchard so I can get promoted, and then I'll be able to do my own private work.'

Sister Vale smiled wryly. 'I don't believe that for a moment, Kash. I could see you ending up in a refugee camp somewhere, maybe, working for nothing, but not in some plush Harley Street clinic. Still, suit yourself.'

She turned away with a shrug, then stopped with her hand on the door, as if she'd just remembered something.

'Oh, Kash, there was one more thing. The real reason I came down here. You see, about an hour ago, a young nurse left the Victory with a spring in her step. I'd let her leave early so that she could miss handover. Not something I'm in the habit of doing. But she said something about . . . a date with a handsome young doctor? She was beginning to think he'd never ask. Maybe he was just too shy. Or perhaps he was just . . . snowed under? And then suddenly, out of the blue, he asked her if she'd have dinner with him. She seemed rather excited. He must be quite something, I thought to myself, if Nurse Barker's interested in him. I wonder who—'

'Oh my gosh!' Kash leaped up, almost knocking over his chair. Sister Vale opened the door and stood back smartly as he flew past her and down the corridor.

'Have a lovely evening,' she called after him.

6

When he entered the restaurant, Kash wasn't sure which he was more afraid of: that she wouldn't be there, having long since decided to cut her losses and go home, or that she would be, quietly fuming and looking forward to giving him a piece of her mind. When he caught sight of her sitting alone at a table near the back, toying with an empty wine glass with a look of icy fury on her face, he decided that this was definitely the worst-case scenario. Part of him wanted to turn tail and return to the hospital, put a white coat over his hastily ironed shirt, rip off his one nice tie and roam the wards looking for medical emergencies. That way he could plausibly pretend he'd been helping with a life and death situation and forgotten the time. But before he had a chance to slink away, she caught his eye and he knew he was going to have to take his medicine. The walk from the entrance to her table felt like the longest of his life.

'Claire . . .' he began, not knowing where the sentence was going or how it would end.

She put her glass down on the white tablecloth, her lips a tight line. She raised an eyebrow, inviting him to continue if he dared. She was wearing a light-blue dress with a pattern of yellow flowers. He couldn't help noticing how well it went with her hair.

'I . . . er . . . I forgot,' he stammered.

She cocked her head to one side as if waiting for more. When she spoke, the sing-song lilt he found so charming now seemed suffused with sarcasm.

'And . . . that's it?'

He nodded, his mouth dry. He found he couldn't swallow.

'Well,' she said, 'I suppose I should give you some marks for honesty.'

'Claire . . .'

She held a hand up. 'Don't. I'm fairly certain you'll only make it worse.'

She really is lovely, Kash found himself thinking. Even with her mascara smudged and looking at him as if he was a particularly toxic piece of medical waste. Is it just the eyes? Or the eyes and the mouth? The combination. With the cheekbones, of course. Ah well. It didn't matter any more. He just had to get through this awkward moment, however long it lasted, apologize a few more times until she got tired of hearing it, and then they would never speak again; she'd walk straight past when they met in the corridor, perhaps give him a curt 'Dr Devan' without making eye contact. Eventually – or perhaps quite soon – she'd take up with someone else and make sure he heard about it, and he'd go back to his books, his paperwork, burying himself as deep as he could in patient files, emerging only to curse himself for being such a fool.

For being so dull.

'Oh sit down, for God's sake, will you? Everybody's watching. And then you can order me another glass of wine. I won't tell you how many I've already had. I started with a small glass of the house red, then the glasses got bigger and the wine more expensive. I think I'm on the fancy cabernet sauvignon if you're taking notes.'

As if by magic, a waiter appeared, his exaggeratedly blank expression feeling to Kash like the jab of a scalpel in his ribs.

'Um, a large glass of the cabernet sauvignon for the lady, and, er, I'll just have water.'

The waiter nodded gravely. 'Still or sparkling?'

'Sparkling,' said Kash.

'A glass? Or perhaps a bottle for the table?' the waiter persisted. Kash wondered if he was planning to be there all night, feeding off his pain like an emotional vampire. It was probably more rewarding than tips.

'Yes, a bottle. A large one,' Kash said firmly.

The waiter nodded and drifted away. Kash sat down, a hollow feeling in his stomach. He recalled the hours of research he put into selecting this restaurant. Not too fancy, as if he was trying too hard to impress her. But not cheap and cheerful either, as if he was hedging his bets. Fun without being noisy. Cosy without being overtly romantic. An interesting menu without being pretentious. Yes, it looked as if he'd got it all absolutely spot-on. But now he wouldn't be able to eat a mouthful and would never come here again.

'So, you forgot,' Claire said, bringing him back to the moment. 'Well, do you know what I forgot?'

Kash sat down, shaking his head warily.

'I forgot how mortifying it can be, sitting alone in a busy restaurant, while everyone else is smiling and laughing and having a good time. The waiters becoming super-attentive as soon as they realize you've been stood up, the way we are with terminally ill patients. Then probably placing bets on how long you'll sit there before the humiliation becomes too much – or whether you'll slap the bastard who stood you up when he arrives or just chuck a glass of wine at him.' Kash flinched involuntarily. 'Not that it's happened to me very often. Only once actually. Before this, of course.'

Kash found himself nodding, leaning slightly forward, like when a patient was telling him their symptoms, trying to look interested when he already knew what the problem was (obstructed bowel from faecal impaction came into his head for some reason) and what to do about it (get the nurse to give them an enema) and just wanted to get on to the next patient, hoping for something more challenging.

'Anyway. I won't forget again. Not for a long time. I think the whole experience is now indelibly etched in my memory. Indelibly. Is that the right word, doctor?'

'Yes, yes, indelibly,' Kash nodded furiously, happy to be agreeing about something.

Claire gave him a long look, then dabbed at her eyes with a napkin. 'I must look frightful. Like one of those mad old biddies on ward fourteen.'

'No, no,' Kash started. 'You look—'

'Don't,' she said firmly. She wiped the last of the mascara away and took a quick breath. 'Right. That's over, thank God. I do hate scenes like this. It's like being trapped in a bad play with only dreadful clichéd lines to say.'

Kash looked astonished. 'You mean you're not going to . . .?'

'Chuck a glass of wine over you? I'm not sure. The night is young. You probably ought to be on your guard, just in case. It depends if you're planning on doing anything else stupid.' She looked at him earnestly. 'Are you planning to do anything stupid, Kash?'

'No, no, I'm going to do my very best not to.'

'Good.'

'Does that mean we're staying? I mean you're staying? I mean, we . . .'

She smiled for the first time that evening. 'Yes, Kash, we're going to sit here and have a lovely evening.'

Kash shook his head in bewilderment. He couldn't quite believe what he was hearing. 'You're a very remarkable person, Claire. I really deserve to have a glass of wine poured over me. And the slap as well.'

Claire made a dismissive sound. 'You're a junior doctor. I should probably count myself lucky you turned up on the right night.'

'No,' said Kash, meaning it. 'I'm the lucky one.'

She shrugged. 'We'll see. Now, tell me all about yourself. I'm sure you've been rehearsing some grand stories for me. Ah, thank God, here comes my wine.'

* * *

Kash hadn't prepared any stories. The truth was, he didn't really like to talk about himself. And what was there to tell, anyway? Ever since his parents, back when they lived in a one-bedroom flat in Leicester – the same one they'd rented when they'd first come to the country – had put the idea of being a doctor into his head, that was all he'd really thought about, and the whole of his existence had then become books and exams and interviews until, well, here he was, a doctor. So he told her about his parents – especially his mother, because his father, to be honest, had always been working; that was all he could really remember about him – that he was some-where else, he never knew quite where, working himself into an early grave. Whereas his mother was a constant presence. The light of his life really, even now, he wasn't ashamed to say. A woman with no education who'd taught herself to read and then absorbed what seemed like the entirety of English literature so that she was forever quoting Dickens and Jane Austen and Thomas Hardy at him. 'It's a very strange feeling, knowing all these books that I've never actually read. And music. She had an old gramophone and there was always something playing in the background – Mozart, Beethoven. Classical. Only ever classical.'

'She sounds like a wonderful person. And it sounds like a wonderful childhood.'

'It was,' Kash agreed. 'We didn't have much, but I never felt I was missing out on anything. Not anything important, anyway. But what about you? Tell me about your family.'

Claire took a deep breath and gave him what was clearly the short version of a story she didn't particularly like telling: how she'd been adopted shortly after birth, had always known – or at least couldn't remember ever not knowing – but never found out any more than that; that 'the family' as she referred to them, her adopted family, was a big Irish brood of brothers and sisters and cousins and aunts that she loved dearly, even though she'd grown up feeling a little bit like a cuckoo in the nest, an olive-skinned, dark-haired girl in a pack of flame-haired girls and boys with pale skin and freckles. 'I've always felt a part of the family, you know? But at the same time I've always known I was different.'

'And you never tried to find out who your birth mother was?'

'When I was sixteen I had a go. But my heart wasn't in it. I think I thought, well I'm happy enough, maybe finding out will spoil everything. And maybe there was a little bit of feeling bitter. I thought maybe my mother was thinking, one day she'll come looking for me and then we'll fall into each other's arms and everything will be forgiven, and I suppose I didn't want her to have that satisfaction. Selfish, really, I suppose. Cutting off my nose to spite my face. But there it is. And I didn't really think about it. But then the clock started ticking, and, well. Things changed.' She took a gulp of wine and pushed a strand of hair behind her ear. 'Right. Enough of the serious stuff. Tell me something stupid.'

'I think I promised not to do that.'

'No, that was *doing* something stupid. There's a difference.' There was a mischievous twinkle in her eyes. 'Come on.'

Kash thought for a moment. 'You mean like a joke?'

'Uh-uh, no jokes. Especially not medical ones.'

Kash had a brief reprieve when the waiter appeared to take their order, looking slightly disappointed that their disastrous evening seemed to have taken a turn for the better. Claire ordered quickly, having had, as she put it, 'ample time to memorize the menu', and Kash just ordered the first thing he saw, amazed that he could even think about eating once again.

'Um, okay. This was something my mother told me which always stuck in my mind. You know Little Nell, the character from *The Old Curiosity Shop*? The Dickens novel? The little girl who dies?'

'Well thanks, I was going to read it but I won't bother now.'

Kash smiled. 'Sorry. Anyway, she was this impossibly cute little girl with a heart of gold, and she's basically dying, wasting away, and Dickens' readers are all on the edge of their seats, desperate to know whether she survives.'

'Why didn't they just flip to the end?'

'Ah, that's because he was publishing it in a magazine, so you had to wait for the next issue to find out what happens next. There was no end – yet.'

'Right.'

'So my mother told me that when a steamship arrived in New York, sailing from London, as it was coming in to dock there was this big crowd and they were all shouting, "Is Little Nell dead? Is she dead?" Because the ship was carrying the latest issue of the magazine.'

Claire looked quizzical. 'And?'

'Well, I mean, a whole crowd of people desperate to know whether she lives or dies, when she doesn't actually exist. I mean, how stupid is that? I think it only really hit me when I became a doctor and started dealing with the real thing.'

'Do you think that was what your mother was trying to tell you? That caring about non-existent people is silly?'

'No, actually I think she was trying to tell me the opposite: what a wonderful thing literature is, that a writer can make you care so much about someone they just made up in between breakfast and lunch. But I just thought . . . how stupid.'

Their food came, a mushroom risotto for Claire and some sort of chicken in a creamy sauce for Kash. While they ate, Kash reflected on how little he knew, really, about people, and how they could surprise you. Especially women. Or maybe it was just Claire. She really was something special. The rest of the meal flew by; they both had crème caramel for dessert, and then coffee. The conversation, that had meandered amiably through trivialities, settled back to life and death.

'You know what you were saying, Kash, about doctoring – or nursing – being the real thing? I know what you mean, obviously. I feel the same way. Even if you've had the shittiest of all shitty days, you've at least been trying to help people. And I'm sure the idea of being a surgeon seems like the most important way you can help people. I mean, what could be more important than saving a life?'

'Nothing,' he agreed.

Claire started to twirl a wisp of hair between her fingers. Kash guessed it was something she did when she was think-ing seriously. 'Well, I'm not so sure. My flatmate, Tiff, for instance. She's a nurse at St Luke's in Peckham.' Kash looked puzzled. 'You won't have heard of it. It's not a hospital. It's a hospice. They don't save any lives there. At least not in the way we've been talking about. Palliative care only. And Tiff, she might look a bit crazy – you'll see when you meet her – but she could have stuck with being a regular ward nurse, or even retrained to be a doctor, I reckon. She's smart enough, certainly. But she chose this – maybe just because most of us don't, I don't know. She doesn't talk about it much. But I think it's harder, what she does, caring for people with no hope of getting better, no hope of ever going home. No . . .' She checked herself. 'Sorry, I'm rambling. I've had too many glasses of wine – too many *large* glasses of expensive wine. Would you mind if I got a taxi home? It's been a lovely evening, Kash. Horrible, then OK, but finally lovely.'

Kash smiled. 'No thanks to me. Well, the horrible bit was thanks to me, but the rest is all down to you. Thank you, Claire. There was a point I thought this was going to be the worst evening of my life. I honestly did. Now I think it might turn out to be the best.'

She frowned. 'Steady, Kash. I think that's just the fizzy water talking.'

Kash called for the bill and insisted on paying. He left a generous tip, and they went outside to wait for a cab. 'Right, this is me,' she said briskly as one pulled up. 'Thank you again, Kash, and see you tomorrow.'

As the cab eased its way back into the traffic with Claire safely inside, the rain started to fall. Kash was relieved she hadn't suggested sharing the cab, that the awkwardness of saying goodnight on her doorstep, not knowing whether a peck on the cheek was in order or just a handshake, had been avoided.

'Thank you, Claire,' he said quietly, pulling the collar of his coat up around his ears. Not that he minded getting wet. He didn't mind at all.

7

Without really thinking where he was going, Kash found himself walking back to the hospital. He was tired, but he knew he wouldn't be able to sleep, so there wasn't much point in going back to his flat. He considered returning to Trenchard's office and picking up where he'd left off with the paperwork, but he doubted he'd be able to focus properly. He felt as if he'd been on a rollercoaster ride through the full gamut of human emotions, from abject terror through utter despair to hope, joy, and . . . was it love he was feeling now? Kash didn't have much experience of such things; not enough to know if it was real or just a reaction to all the adrenaline coursing through his body and then draining out of him in a rush. But could the effect of her eyes, her mouth, her smile, the way she twirled her hair, be explained by chemistry? He certainly hoped not. This was one phenomenon he would rather leave a mystery.

The Victory was in its usual state of chaos as he trudged, zombie-like, through the wards, a faint, slightly bemused smile on his face. Suddenly, his pager started to blast at his hip. He wasn't on call. But someone obviously thought he was. He saw the number flashing and pressed the button to mute the noise. He found a phone in the corridor, and dialled.

'Kash, it's Ange. Where is he?'

Kash was momentarily thrown. 'Where's who?'

'Trenchard. Weren't you with him?'

With him? Why would he be with him? Did she mean was he in Trenchard's office?

'Kash?'

'No, no Ange,' he stammered. 'Mr Trenchard wasn't—'

'You'd better get to the ED, Kash. I'll meet you there.'

'Me? I'm not on call.'

She paused. 'Are you sober?'

Well, that might not be the best word to describe how he was feeling right now, but technically, yes.

'As it happens.'

'Then I need your help. We had a locum booked for the evening – Sam is sick, as you know – and he hasn't turned up.'

Kash sighed. He was exhausted. But then, Ange would know that. And she wouldn't ask unless she had no other choice. He dropped into the ward and grabbed his white coat, before jogging towards the emergency department.

When he got there, he could see it was getting busy. He crossed to the nurses' desk.

'Ange?'

The nurse looked up. 'Major resus. Bed four.'

Kash nodded. A bed in the resus bay of the 'major injury' section: whatever it was, that meant it was bad. He pushed through the swing doors and slipped behind the curtains surrounding the fourth bed.

Ahead of him lay a fourteen-year-old boy, as gangly and slight as Kash had been at that age. At first, Kash could not see his face – the bedside was crowded, another doctor – Marcus Something? – and Ange bent low over him. When he moved closer, he saw the boy was pale, his eyes fixed on the ceiling. His breathing was fast and shallow. A woman – his mother? – was mopping the sweat which beaded his forehead.

Kash had seen some very sick people since he'd been at the Victory, but this boy looked like shit. He lay there completely still. A spider of intravenous lines sprouted from the back of one hand and from the forearm above it. Ange was running through two of gelo stat – and the monitor by the bedside showed his blood pressure at 60/40. His mother held on to the other line-free hand, consoling herself by repeatedly telling him he was going to be fine.

Ange caught Kash's eye. Ordinarily, Ange seemed to thrive on the intensity of the emergency department, but now she looked worried.

The mother looked up.

'I'm Kash. Another doctor.' His voice was calm and measured. He smiled. The mother tried to reciprocate. Kash turned. 'Angela?'

Angela straightened. 'This is Edmund. Edmund Chaloner.' She gently stroked the boy's arm. 'Marcus here,' she nodded to the casualty officer, 'called at once because he was worried. Previously well. Bit of asthma. Has an inhaler which he rarely uses. Otherwise fit and well. One-week history of sore throat.

Fevers. Worsening general malaise. Been off school. Missed football, which isn't like him. Two hours of left hypochondrial pain followed by pain in the left shoulder. Pale. Mum put him in the car and rushed him here. BP fifty on thirty on arrival. One litre in so far, and those two.' She flicked her eyes towards the gelofusine on the drip stands. 'But it must be coming out somewhere. BP's still low, pulse one-forty and thready.'

Her examination had been brief. Edmund Chaloner was pale and clammy, his throat raw – but when she'd touched his abdomen, she'd found it hard as a board. No bowel sounds.

Marcus looked up. 'I'll get two more gelo up after those ones.'

'Bloods?'

'Cooking now. Should phone them down in a moment.'

Kash watched the imperceptible flicker on Ange's face. 'We're going to have to move, Kash. But I need the boss in for this one. Can you get him for me? Now?' She turned to Marcus. 'Call theatres. Tell them to prepare for a laparotomy. Then you might as well call the porters, get them to send him straight up.' She turned to the boy. 'Young man, you're going to need an operation. Your belly, it's sore, isn't it? Well, we're going to make that better for you . . .'

She walked from the bedspace, followed quickly by the mother, who grabbed her sleeve. 'He'll be OK, won't he?'

'I'm sure. I don't know what the problem is, but we need to look inside to find out. Then we'll put it right.'

While Ange was getting the consent form signed, Kash made his way to the telephone on the wall nearby. Once, not so long ago, his heart would have pounded at moments like this; now it felt like work, what he did every day. He lifted the receiver, and dialled zero for the hospital switchboard.

'Switch?' he said. 'Can you page Mr Trenchard for this number?'

'Mr Trenchard for A and E resus?'

'Yes please.'

'Coming up.'

Kash replaced the receiver and waited, his eyes fixed on the receiver, while the ordinary emergency room chaos somersaulted around him. He felt like the eye in its storm. One minute later, the phone was still silent. Two minutes later, and Trenchard had not rung. He snatched the receiver, and dialled again.

'It's Kash, in the ED. No news from Mr Trenchard?'

'He hasn't answered yet.'

Kash looked over his shoulder. Marcus and Ange were standing back as the porters wheeled Edmund Chaloner out of his cubicle, his pale-faced mother still clutching his hand.

'Can you put me through to St Philippa's, please?'

St Philippa's was the private hospital up on the river, only a cab ride further east. Kash waited.

'St Philippa's Hospital switchboard. How may I help you?'

Kash breathed deep. He had to be there. He knew Trench-ard was on call for the Victory, so shouldn't be operating else-where, but perhaps he'd just called in to see a postoperative patient from days before. 'Hi, there. My name is Kash Devan. I'm a doctor at the Victory. Could you put me through to theatres, please?'

'Connecting you . . .'

The seconds stretched out. There was too much silence, silence on the other end of the phone, silence as the lift doors closed, even a strange, distant silence in the emergency room around him. Then, at last, a voice broke through the veil. 'Theatres,' it said.

'Hi, theatres. Sorry to trouble you. I'm Kash Devan, Mr Trenchard's house officer at the Victory. I need him urgently. Is he there?'

And there was that stultifying silence again.

'He was here earlier, doing a case. But he left a good two hours ago.'

'Do you know where he went? He isn't answering his pager.'

'Sorry. Maybe he's with you?'

'OK. Thanks anyway.'

He slammed the receiver down, grimacing. If Mr Trenchard was with him, he'd scarcely be calling them, would he?

He took a breath and tried to think. If Mr Trenchard wasn't at the Victory, and if he wasn't at St Philippa's, then he'd be at home. Perhaps he'd slept through his pager? Or it had run out of battery? He dialled the home number.

'Hello?' came a sleepy voice.

'Mrs, er, Trenchard,' Kash stammered. 'It's Kash Devan, from the Victory. I'm a doctor – I work with your husband . . .'

He waited a moment while she seemed to be processing this. 'Yes, of course. Dr Devan. He's spoken about you. Just the other day he was—'

Kash hated to interrupt her but he couldn't wait for her to finish. 'Mr Trenchard. I'm looking for Mr Trenchard . . . it's an emergency . . .'

Her voice soured. 'I know. He called from St Philippa's to tell me. He was heading straight to you.' She sounded wide awake now.

Kash was confused. Perhaps Angela's message *had* reached him somehow? Maybe he'd seen the pager number and come straight over? Maybe he had gone straight to theatres? But, then, St Philippa's had said that he'd left a good two hours ago. He should have been here by now.

'Thank you,' he said faintly.

The phone went limp in his hand. Kash dropped it back into the receiver and, for a moment, froze. Mr Trenchard was *not* in the Victory, he was certain about that. He was not at St Philippa's and he was not at home. And a young lad was about to hit the operating room, with Angela being left alone to manage him. He looked up. For a moment, he had felt as if he was trapped in a bubble, with the emergency room swirling outside. But as the room came back into focus, his thoughts did too. Angela Warner was the best young surgeon there was. She had coped before, and she would cope again. Hell, it was probably just another appendix. Kash had scrubbed up for three of those already and had observed plenty more; given the green light, he could probably fly solo. Or maybe not. The pain was in the wrong place. But common things were common . . .

Angela would need his help. Kash wheeled around, rushed for the lifts. The flickering yellow lights showed them hovering three storeys above, but the adrenaline was already coursing through Kash's veins. He took to the stairs, three at a time.

8

Theatres were private universes. They nestled in the controlled chaos of the hospital, moving to their own rhythms, keeping their own times. In an operating theatre, there was no day or night, just the slow ticking of the clock to mark the passing time. Even when they awoke, they were not the scenes of excitement or chaos depicted on television screens. More, they resembled a factory floor, a busy assembly line where everyone knew their role.

The porters swung Edmund Chaloner's trolley into the anaesthetic room, which connected the main corridor to theatre three. They exited briskly, shutting the two swing doors behind them. Inside stood Jan. She had been an operating department practitioner, or ODP, at the Victory for six years and reckoned she'd seen it all. This case wasn't going to be any different. Most of these 'query appendix' cases were nothing – pelvic inflammatory disease in young women, nothing at all in young men. It was rare that she saw any appendix come out that wasn't lily-white, and even the inflamed ones could usually have waited until morning. But one glance told her that this was not one of her usual cases. Edmund Chaloner was lying far too quiet, far too still. He grunted with each shallow breath. He was less pale than white. Beads of sweat freckled his forehead, coalescing to mat his hair and run in rivulets to soak his gown.

Jan slowed briefly to introduce herself to the boy, checking the name on his wristband against the notes that had come with him. 'Edmund?' The boy made no response, staring fixedly at the ceiling. 'We are going to make you better. Don't bother about me. I'm just going to attach a few wires, and then you can have a decent sleep. When you wake up, Mum will be there, and you'll be fine.' Her voice was relaxed and smooth, and she spoke deliberately slowly. But her hands now worked fast. She pulled the gown, connecting three electrodes to the boy's chest, and then the three coloured wires which descended from the monitor on the anaesthetic machine. Next, she wrapped a blood pressure cuff firmly around Edmund's upper right arm, and hit the automatic measurement button.

As she did so, the doors behind her opened once more. Geoff Wright was the on-call emergency anaesthetist, his haystack bulk in stark contrast to his gentle manner and soft voice. Angela had called him. She had been brisk and to the point, and the lack of social niceties told him everything. Angela was quality. If she was worried, then he needed to be too. One glance at the boy, and his concerns were confirmed. Beside Jan, the blood pressure monitor flashed red and alarmed. Sixty on forty.

'Hello young man,' Geoff began. Perhaps his voice really did have a magical quality, because the boy's breathing momentarily became less ragged. 'Let's sort you out then, shall we?' He reached forward and stroked the boy's left arm. It was icy cold. Seizing two rubber gloves, he knotted them together to make a tourniquet and wrapped it around the boy's left arm. As he slapped it to bring up a vein, Jan handed him a cardboard kidney dish containing an orange intravenous cannula and an alcohol swab. The production line at work. But no vein was going to appear. The boy was just too shut down.

Jan read his mind, and removed the makeshift tourniquet. 'We've got a green and a blue line in on the right.' She held out another pressed cardboard kidney dish containing some labelled syringes.

'Thio, sux, tube, atracurium?' he asked.

'Vecuronium. Chart says he's asthmatic. ET tube? Five or six?'

'Five.' Jan *was* good. She turned to select the right size of tube to pass down the boy's airway to his lungs.

Meanwhile, Geoff worked quickly and calmly. There were some doctors who would mess around all night. Not Geoff. Besides, time had run out some moments ago; you didn't need a medical degree to see that this boy needed an operation now, not in twenty minutes. Cool and efficient, even polite – it was his way of keeping in control – Geoff slid a bag of fluid into a net casing, pumped up the bladder behind it to force the fluid in faster, and quickly checked that the trolley could tilt head-down, in case the kid vomited. Next, he switched on the suction, and put the connecting tube under the pillow. Now, if the boy vomited, he could clear his mouth and pharynx. Then, with a final word of promise to the boy, he turned on the oxygen, and placed the black rubber mask over his face.

'Deep breaths, young man. A few moments and you'll be fast asleep.'

Jan slid past him, taking control of the mask. As she did so, Geoff moved to the drip-arm, connected a syringe, and injected the thiopentone. A barbiturate anaesthetic, thiopentone had the advantage of tending not to drop the blood pressure too much. Dropping this boy's pressure would be near terminal. He breathed a little more rapidly, briefly moved his arms restlessly, then relaxed.

As he did so, Geoff spoke firmly. 'Sux, then cricoid.'

Jan injected the contents of the 2 ml syringe – 'Sux in!'– then turned and pressed firmly on the cricoid cartilage, at the lower part of the boy's voicebox, thus compressing and blocking his oesophagus and preventing any regurgitation of stomach contents into the lungs.

To open the belly of a sick child requires all of the muscles of the abdomen to be relaxed, and to do this requires paralysing the patient. Likewise, to pass a tube through the voicebox south towards the lungs. In an emergency, this has to be done as quickly as possible, and suxamethonium is the quickest agent available. It took only twenty seconds or so for the sux to work. The boy's muscles twitched. His eyelids fluttered; his face winked and rippled. And then, nothing. He was sedated and paralysed. Quite literally; he couldn't move a muscle.

Geoff flicked the grey steel blade of the laryngoscope into Edmund's mouth and, peering in, held out his right hand. 'Tube.' Jan placed it in his hand, and Geoff slid it through the larynx and into the trachea, inflating the small balloon at its tip. 'Cuff up!' He connected the black rubber bag to the tube, and squeezed, listening for air entry into the lungs on both sides. It was there. 'Cric off!' Jan released her pressure on the boy's throat and began to connect the endotracheal tube to the ventilator, as Geoff injected the Vecuronium. Sux was good and quick, but it didn't last long. Vecuronium would last a good deal longer.

The whole business had taken less than a minute.

Kash, meanwhile, had changed rapidly into blue surgical scrubs and white vinyl clogs. As he pushed back out into the corridor, he glanced at Trenchard's locker. Its door was open. It was empty.

Inside the operating theatre itself, Angela was already scrubbed, standing in one corner with gloved hands clasped. She raised her eyebrows as Kash walked in and made his way to the steel trough to wash his own hands.

'He wasn't anywhere, Ange. No answer on the pager. St P's last saw him a couple of hours ago. He's not at home. His wife thinks he's here.' The nursing staff, busying themselves with preparations, paused for a beat. Angela didn't move. Kash continued to wash his hands. 'But . . . ta-dah! You have me!' He assumed a sonorous tone, reminiscent of Trenchard. 'I am a very experienced surgeon, you know. The best. I'm sure that you know my reputation? I have seen three appendectomies. *Three*, I tell you.' He turned to one of the staff nurses. 'Gloves please. Size eight . . .'

Angela allowed herself a half-smile. Kash's cheesy routine was exactly what she needed.

Behind them, the doors from the anaesthetic room opened and the trolley was wheeled in. Jan pushed it to one side of the operating table, and locked the wheels with a flick of her heel. 'On slide. Ready . . . steady . . . slide!' Together with the staff nurse, they slid the patient from trolley to table. Geoff reconnected him to a second anaesthetic machine and hung another litre IV bag to the drip stand. Meanwhile, Jan removed the boy's gown, and swung the theatre's operating lights to focus on his abdomen, another scrub nurse wheeling her trolley of sterile instruments into place.

Geoff looked at the monitors. The boy's heart rate was at 160 – far too fast. His blood pressure was at 64/35, despite that litre going straight in, but at least its oxygen saturation was 99 per cent.

Ange moved into place beside the theatre sister and scrub nurse, as Kash snapped his gloves on and took up position opposite her. She glanced up at Geoff. 'Ready?'

'As we'll ever be. His pressure's crap. He's empty. Jan just went for the blood.'

At the same moment Jan crashed back into the theatre. 'No blood. Lab says no one phoned the sample through. They're doing it now, but it's going to take forty minutes . . .'

Kash felt the gut-punch. *Shit.* Marcus must have forgotten. He watched as Ange's jaw clenched beneath her surgical mask. 'Call them back, please,' said Geoff. 'Explain the urgency. Ask them for ten units ASAP.' Then he turned to the nurse. 'Grab the six O-neg from the fridge. Ange, we can start with those.'

Ange nodded. It was best to give cross-matched blood, but you could give O-negative to most people in an emergency.

She stepped swiftly to the patient's side, picked up the scalpel from where it had been left. Beneath her, the belly was tense and swollen – but there was no point in messing about. No point debating the whys or wherefores, no point even thinking about what might have happened to Michael Trenchard to stop him from being there. While Kash watched, she placed the tip of the scalpel just below the ribcage and drew the blade all the way down to the line of Edmund's shaved pubic hair, only deviating to curve around his umbilicus. A swab soaked up the blood that appeared in the cut. Then in went the diathermy forceps to fry any little bleeding points of the skin. A second sweep took her deeper again, through the thin white layer of subcutaneous fat. Again the diathermy. And now another sweep, this time through the muscle layer and the peritoneum, and into the abdomen itself.

Blood welled up through the wound, a slick red wave which spilled across her hands, cascading across the sterile drapes and flooding the floor. Ange stared at the wound and held out a hand, saying quietly, 'Suction, please.'

She pushed the hard plastic suction tip deep into the abdomen, the clear tubing to which it was connected bucking and slurping in response. 'Kash?'

Kash took the suction from her, as blood continued to well up around it, rich and dark.

'Gauze. Big one. Gamgee.'

Just as measured, just as calm as before, Geoff said, 'Pressure's going.'

'Thanks, Geoff.' Ange had wrapped the gauze around her fist, and now plunged it deep into the boy's belly. Her eyes fixed in the middle distance, she slid her fist up the boy's spine, feeling his aorta – the main blood vessel of the body – fluttering feebly beneath. Then she went further up, as high as she could go, until she could feel the diaphragm pressing down against her with each inhalation. Taking a deep breath, she placed her fist over the aorta and leaned down with straight arms, her whole bodyweight pressing below. The pulse was weakening. 'Another gelo stat, please, Geoff.'

'Already running.'

Kash glanced to his left. The clear cylinder to which his suction tube was connected already held a litre. Behind it, Jan appeared.

'O-neg. Six units.'

Geoff glanced at her. They were meant to check each one, but there was just no time. 'First one up, please, Jan.' He glanced again at the blood pressure monitor. 'We aren't picking up. Ange – head down?'

'Head down.'

Geoff kneeled and grabbed the silver handle on the side of the table, turning it fast. The operating table rose at the boy's feet, forcing the blood to flow back into his heart, his brain.

The boy's heart rate was slowing. *160. 140. 80. 50.*

'Atropine! Straight in, Jan!'

It took seconds for Jan to bring the syringe to the boy's arm. As she did so, Geoff disconnected one empty blood bag, connected another and squeezed it with both hands, wrestling it by force into the boy's empty body.

As one, they turned to the monitor. 'Got it.' It was Jan. 'Fifty-five systolic. Better than nothing.' They waited, Ange still leaning forward with all her strength, Geoff discarding another empty blood bag and attaching a third unit. 'Seventy. And pulse back up to one-sixty.'

Angela clenched her teeth. 'The fucking A-team,' she whispered. But there were no smiles, no false bravado. This boy wasn't out of trouble yet.

Kash looked at Ange. 'Any ideas?'

Angela looked back across at him. 'Whatever it is, it's high. Got to be his spleen,' she said. 'EBV? Glandular fever can cause the spleen to rupture spontaneously . . .'

'Yes. It can,' he said uncertainly.

'It'd fit with the one-week history and sore throat.'

'Rare,' interjected Geoff.

Ange pressed firmly on the boy's aorta, the warmth of his body enveloping her forearm. 'Well, that's all right then. He'll be OK, because it's rare. How stupid of us!' She rolled her eyes. 'Bloody anaesthetists.'

'One-oh-two on sixty-two,' said Geoff, eyes still on the monitors.

'Movin' on up. Nothin' can stop us now . . .'

Angela maintained the pressure while the last two units of O-neg went in. 'Where's the cross-matched blood?' she breathed.

* * *

'Still twenty minutes away,' said Kash, 'but we've got colloid to keep us going . . .'

'Rate's down to one-twenty,' said Geoff. 'We're catching up.'

Ange nodded, caught Kash with a steely glare. This was it. Time to take a look. 'Jan,' he said, 'can you move the lights? We'll need them pointing in and up, if it really is the spleen . . .'

Once the operating lights were in place, Ange looked back at Kash. 'I need you to occlude the aorta,' she said. 'Can you manage it?'

Could he? Only one way to find out.

'One fist,' Ange said as she prepared for Kash to take over. 'One fist, but all your weight. Fuck up and he'll bleed to death.' She smiled. 'And then so will you.'

'Sounds fair,' said Kash, with a lightness he no longer felt.

The switch-over happened in a second. He slipped his hand, holding a large swab, over and above hers. Then he made a fist, leaned in and down. Slowly, Ange released her pressure . . . Perhaps this was their one moment of divine intervention because, by some strange mercy, no more blood erupted. Kash concentrated on forcing his weight through his knuckles and nothing else.

For the first time, Ange breathed. 'Ring retractor, please.' The scrub nurse pressed the notched metal ring into Ange's hand. By attaching blades to the ring and slipping these inside the wound, the wound's edges could be pulled apart, giving a clear space in which to operate. She was settling her-self to insert it when a sudden thought occurred: to get it in place, whoever was holding the aorta would have to have their hands inside the ring. A hundred thoughts collided in her mind. They had switched over too soon. 'Kash,' she said, 'we're going to have to switch again. I'll do the aorta. You'll have to attach the blades. Are you up to it?'

Kash nodded. A single droplet of sweat was beading on his eyelashes, distorting his view of the boy splayed open underneath.

Ange moved without hesitation: her gauze-wrapped fist passing through the ring retractor, sliding down Kash's forearm to the place where his knuckles clenched tight. Slowly, breathing in unison with her, Kash released the pressure. He looked at Ange, her face a rictus of concentration. All was fine so far. She could do this. He knew she could . . .

Everything changed in an instant. Kash was still fixed on Ange when the thick smoky blood welled up in the wound, over her knuckles, over her wrists, fountaining out of Edmund Chaloner's belly like a burst water main. 'You've come off the aorta!' he breathed. 'Ange, you've come off the . . .' Words failed him. The blood was dark. It was not spurting. This was not aortic arterial blood. Venous, then? Was it the boy's veins? Below the crimson surface, Ange moved her fist – but the bleeding only worsened. It cascaded down the boy's sides now, pooling on the operating table. A waterfall onto the theatre floor.

'Clamp!' Ange called. 'Clamp, now!'

Kash seized the clamp, plunged his hands in along Ange's own. Beneath the surface, Angela fought to get it up to the aorta – but by now she was flying blind, groping unseen in the crimson surrounds. In a vain effort, she pushed the clamp as high as she could, squeezed it closed – and still the blood welled up.

'Pressure's going fast,' Geoff cursed. 'Jan – fast bleep the porters to get that blood. Group specific will do. Failing that, more O-neg.'

Ange plunged her remaining hand into the boy, right up to his spleen. Kash saw her face drain of all colour. 'That's it,' she said. 'It's the spleen. It's gone. It's like . . . wet cardboard down here.' Her face twitched once again. 'It's torn, Kash. There's an inch-long tear. Clamp!' She paused. 'No pulse here. Geoff?'

Geoff reached for the carotid pulse, paused and shook his head. He glanced at the monitor. There was still an ECG trace. 'EMD.' *Electromechanical dissociation.* It meant the heart had electrical activity but was pumping no blood.

'Crash trolley!' called out Kash. 'Jan, call triple three. We're going to . . .'

Time slowed down. The world closed in. All that was left of it was these four theatre walls, the blood-soaked table between them and the boy who lay upon it, teetering on the edge between life and death. Out of the corner of his eye, Kash saw Geoff disconnecting the breathing machine, ventilating the boy by hand. Jan had already started the chest compressions. The theatre's saloon doors were swinging open and a scrub nurse was hauling the crash trolley through, while another pulled the sterile green towels from the boy's chest and slapped conducting pads onto his bare skin.

Soon, four more doctors and a nurse would crash into the theatre, but by then it would already be too late. The way she was standing now, Ange seemed to know it. The panic had left her, to be replaced with a cold realization.

They would carry on, working steadily, methodically, as they had been trained to do, but it was all pointless.

She seemed to be watching herself from on high, as if her body were not her own, as if her actions, the actions of Kash, Geoff, Jan, were seen through a camera lens. *Retractor, suction, swabs. Retractor, suction, swabs. Adrenaline. Chest compressions. Pulse check. Fluids.* In that way, one minute passed. Two. Five. And all the while she knew. Twenty minutes in, she stepped back, almost unnoticed, and headed for the door, snapping off her gloves and flicking them to the floor.

9

Fifteen minutes later, Kash made his way to the female changing rooms. After knocking gently, he cautiously opened the door and peered round. Ange was sitting on a slatted wooden bench, her head in her hands. She was still wearing her blues. She didn't look up.

'They say you get used to it,' she said, her voice a taut monotone. 'I guess you largely do with time. I've seen a hundred people die, Kash, But . . .' Kash understood. It hadn't happened to him yet, but sooner or later you had to lose the sensitivity. Everyone – doctor, nurse, porter ferrying around the dead – must do, sooner or later. And most people who died were old, at the ends of their natural lives. The young ones were often 'BID'– brought in dead – and you never got to feel for them. But this was different. Different, because . . . 'He died at my hand, Kash.'

Kash walked over and raised his palms. '*Our* hands, Ange. We are a team.'

She didn't respond.

'Look, Ange, I know it isn't my place but . . . it wasn't your fault.'

Ange hung her head. 'Then whose fault was it? The boy? His mother? It was my call, Kash and . . .' For the first time, Ange's voice broke. 'I wasn't up to it.'

Kash took her by the shoulder, turned her around. 'That's nonsense, and you know it.'

He held on to her, not knowing what else to do. In the end, it was Ange who had to pull herself away.

'People like you round here, Kash. You've settled in well. You're going to be a good doctor. And you're trying to say the right thing. But just . . . leave it, would you? Because . . .' She paused, struggling with what to say. 'Because – where was he, Kash? Trenchard's supposed to be here, in the Victory. So where exactly was he? Where is he, even now? Why was it *me* – why was it *us* – in there, doing that, when Trenchard should have been . . .'

Kash heard it in her voice. It wasn't just sorrow. It wasn't just guilt. It wasn't just the terror of knowing that she'd soon have to face the mother – the mother who didn't yet know, false hope still burning in her heart as she paced the corridor nearby. No. There was anger.

Fury.

'What do I tell her, out there? The surgeon who could have saved your boy was absent, so we killed him instead? Is that it? Is that what I tell her, Kash?'

She was about to step through the door when Kash surprised himself by almost shouting, 'You need to stop thinking like that, Ange. You need to stop it *now*.'

He had never spoken to anyone like this, but he could see the adrenaline still pumping through Ange's body, the almost imperceptible twitches in her temple that showed she was wrestling against herself, trying desperately not to break down or scream.

'That mother through there, when she finds out her son's dead, what does it matter if Mr Trenchard wasn't here? It matters to you, but not to her, not now. She needs someone to hold her hand and look her in the eye and tell her we did everything we could. She needs it plain and simple, Ange. Because she deserves it. She needs us now, just like that boy through there needed us then.'

He stood back, surprised at the words he'd just spoken but even more astonished at the deep-seated conviction that seemed to underlie them without his ever having been aware of it until now. Kash kneeled and touched her shoulder, then wrapped his arms around her and, though she could not return the embrace, she did not resist. She made no sound, but he could feel hot tears soaking his chest.

Softly, he said, 'Ange. I'll do it. You go and stitch the boy up. Get him presentable for his mum. I'll go and deal with her now.' He gave her a gentle squeeze, then rose and walked to the door. 'Mess in twenty?'

She nodded. 'Mess in twenty.'

Before he stepped through the door, he looked back. Angela was sitting, staring at her outstretched hands. There was still blood on them.

* * *

Kash paused in the corridor outside the relatives' room. Used mainly by the families of those on the intensive care unit nearby, it only had one occupant just now. Through the glass in the door, Kash could see the distorted shape of Anna Chaloner pacing the linoleum.

He tried to gather his thoughts. There were sentences you could fall back on. *He didn't suffer. Nothing can change this news. It can't matter to you right now, but it may later, and it's important that you know: we did everything within our power to keep him with you.* They ran courses in breaking bad news. Kash had sat at the front of the classroom as he always did, diligently taking diligent notes, filling up his notebooks and repeating the words by rote until they were drilled into his mind. They'd practised with actors, too. But now, here he was, standing alone late at night, his hand hovering ahead of the door, and he knew that this was different. An actor would allow herself to be consoled. An actor stuck to the script. But there was no script for this moment. He took a deep breath and walked into the room.

As he closed the door behind him, Anna Chaloner stopped pacing, her head snapping towards him at once, a smile forming, her eyebrows raised. Kash met her gaze, and walked forward. 'Mrs Chaloner? I'm Kash. Dr Devan. We met briefly earlier . . .' And Anna Chaloner knew at once. Her smile dying as her face became suddenly pale. She sat down abruptly in one of the worn plastic-covered armchairs.

'Mrs Chaloner,' he began. 'May I call you Anna?'

Her hands, which had been kneading each other, suddenly stopped. A stillness had come over her, as if she'd summoned up some last reserve of inner strength. She looked up, and it was then that Kash, incongruously, noticed what a striking woman she was. She had soft green eyes, like Claire's, and for a moment his carefully prepared thoughts scattered. She was still wearing her scarf, as if at any moment her son might come skipping out of surgery and demand to be taken home. Sweat beaded her brow, where the widow's peak of chestnut hair met her skin.

He crossed the room, sitting opposite her on the low coffee table strewn with TV guides, puzzle magazines and celebrity gossip rags.

He reached for her hands but, instead, she grasped his, her thumb stroking the skin at its back. Even now, he thought suddenly, she was the mother, consoling the young boy.

And so Kash began. He tried to follow advice a lecturer had once given him. *Speak with only half your brain. Let one half be compassion. The other has to observe, to edit, to stay detached. Let them have the emotion, not you.* But those things were easier said than done. The trick was to look into her eyes and yet look past them, to some distant place on the other side where all this was just another part of a normal day.

He began with the simple truth. 'Anna, I'm sorry. We did everything we could, but Edmund didn't make it through the surgery.' He paused for her to respond, but Anna said nothing, her silence encouraging him to say more. 'We believe he'd been suffering from glandular fever. It's rare, but in some cases, it reaches the spleen – and Edmund's had ruptured. That's why he got the pain. He needed surgery fast. We called Mr Trenchard, the consultant, but he . . .' Only now did Kash find himself faltering, for the things he didn't say were even more important now than the things he did. ' . . . wasn't going to get here quickly enough. Dr Warner knew that every second mattered, so we took Edmund straight into theatre.' It was all true, all of it, everything except the inference that Mr Trenchard had agreed. 'We couldn't stop the bleeding, Mrs Chaloner. Edmund had already lost so much. I'm so sorry, Anna.'

Kash sensed that, like him, one half of her brain was also computing, comparing the account she was hearing to everything she'd seen in the emergency department, those precious last minutes she had been with her son.

Face turned away, Mrs Anna Chaloner seemed to be concentrating only on her breathing. Her skin was bleached and drained. Then, as Kash watched, a deep frown set in across her face, the lines spreading and setting like shattering glass. So, he thought, her body was finally absorbing the news. He sensed her breathing changing, alternately peaceful and ragged, as her mind caught up.

In medical school they taught you about Kubler-Ross and their stages of bereavement. Drummed into his head in some long-ago lecture, now he could see them so clearly. Stage one: denial and isolation. OK, he thought, seeing her shrinking into herself, that fitted. Then came bargaining, depression – and, finally, acceptance.

Kash paused. He had missed out a stage. Bargaining was stage three. Something came before it.

What was it?

He saw her turn rigid. The way her eyes, which had seemed so distant, were suddenly brighter. The way her hands, which had been clasping each other, had become claws, digging into her thighs.

Ah, he thought, that's right. Before bargaining comes . . . anger.

Quietly, Kash got to his feet and left Anna Chaloner to her pain.

10

The days following Edmund Chaloner's death were frantic, and this was actually a blessing. There was no time to ruminate or to feel sorry for yourself – or anyone else. You had to move on to the next thing, or you'd fall off the rollercoaster and never get back on. If you spent any time thinking about the last emergency, you wouldn't be able to focus properly on the present one. And he could feel himself toughening in a way he didn't like. There was going to be a narrow line between protecting his humanity and losing it. Only now, he'd had to break bad news again.

You could often tell the age of a patient by their name. Pretty much every Violet, Rose or Ivy was over ninety, and every Kylie under nine. This Rose had been eighty-two and a church organist. At least that had made life simpler when he'd had to tell her family the truth. They'd had to 'open and close': as soon as the abdomen had been opened up, it was clear that it was choked with cancer. There was nothing to be done other than close it at once, and start some morphine for the pain. He'd faced the daughter, leaning forward and holding her hands, as a small silver crucifix had swung hypnotically from a thin silver chain around her neck. She'd tried not to cry, but to smile. She had nodded. 'I guess Jesus just wants her now,' was all she would say. But he could hear the sobs now, as he walked from the room.

If Mr Trenchard felt any regret for having gone AWOL, he didn't show it; he was his usual, breezy self, as he sailed through the wards, casting pearls of medical wisdom overboard as the flotilla of junior doctors and other assorted acolytes paddled frantically behind, doing their best to keep up – both mentally and physically. He did give Kash's shoulder a paternal squeeze at one point, but that might just as easily have been because of Kash's hesitation in diagnosing an obvious case of cholecystitis rather than a discreet expression of sympathy for what Kash had been through with Edmund Chaloner. Kash certainly wasn't going to ask Trenchard what he'd meant by it.

He did feel a need to talk to someone about the dead boy, though, but knew instinctively that it was too soon to start sharing his thoughts about the whole business with Claire; that would surely drive her away. And in any case, while they had managed to chat for a couple of minutes a handful of times since the meal in the restaurant, that had only been when their paths crossed during their busy days. Their different schedules seemed designed by some malign administrator bent on keeping them apart for as long as possible, and they hadn't been able to pencil in another evening when they were both free.

As for Angela, since her mini breakdown she had gone into super-professional mode, her face a mask of determined efficiency. She might as well have had a sign around her neck saying 'Don't Talk to Me', and Kash was happy to obey. That left his mother, of course, to whom he would normally pour out his heart about whatever was bothering him. But the one thing he never liked talking about to her was death.

Which left one other person. Liz Murray. If he went and had a chat with her, he'd be following Mr Trenchard's instructions, wouldn't he? Two birds.

*　*　*

Up on ward fourteen, the sense of nobody going anywhere and nothing needing to be done had an immediate calming effect. Of course, in reality, there were plenty of things needing to be done: after all, this was a place where most of the patients were incontinent. And while they might not be going anywhere, it didn't stop them trying, and they often fell out of bed. With the weekly enemas, and monthly injections of Modecate, and all the daily doses of pills in between, the staff seemed to swarm, bees buzzing amongst withered flowers.

But despite all the activity, there was none of the sublimated panic of the emergency department. The worst that could happen on ward fourteen was that you checked out a little earlier than expected. And no one was going to lose any sleep over that.

Kash was taking it all in when Liz spotted him and waved him over with a bony hand.

'You're Dr Kash, aren't you?'

'You remembered.'

She frowned. 'I've still got all my marbles, young man. Most of them, anyway.' She wagged a finger reprovingly. 'That's the problem with being old. One of the problems, anyway. People assuming you're gaga. Just because I'm dying—'

'Liz, come on.'

'Oh shut up, *Doctor*. Just because I'm dying, people think there's nothing going on in here.' She tapped her forehead. 'Lights on, but nobody at home. People talk to you as if you're daft.'

'I'm sure nobody does,' Kash said reassuringly.

She gave a little snort. 'Well, that nice Mr Trenchard didn't, I'll give you that. You know what he also didn't do? He didn't ask me how I am. And what a blessed relief that is.'

'Why's that? It's what we're supposed to do.'

'All right, then, you try it.'

'I'm sorry?'

'Try asking me how I am.'

Kash hesitated. 'OK, Mrs Murray. Er, how are you?'

'How d'you bloody think?' she shot back.

Kash smiled. 'Ah. Point taken. So what *did* you and Mr Trenchard talk about? When he came to see you about your tummy.' He was genuinely interested.

'He asked me what I thought.'

'About what?'

'What people are up to.'

'And what *are* people up to?'

She gave him a sly look. 'That'd be telling.'

He laughed. 'I suppose it would. Well, how about if I told you something first?'

'Something interesting? Is it smutty?'

'No!'

She shrugged. 'Shame. Never mind. Go on then. I'm all ears.' She heaved herself upright in the bed.

Suddenly the idea of unburdening himself to Liz Murray felt ridiculous. And almost certainly against hospital rules. What had he meant to say to her anyway? He glanced at his watch.

'I'm afraid it'll have to wait until next time, Liz. I've got to go.'

She made a clucking sound. 'Away you go, then.' As he turned to leave, she plucked at his sleeve, pulling him back. 'I'll tell you one thing, though.' She beckoned him closer and whispered in his ear. 'Our lovely Mr Trenchard. Not *everyone* likes him, you know.'

*   *   *

'Do you play squash?'

Kash was about to drop his white coat in the laundry and call it a night. Mr Trenchard was wearing his trademark pinstripe suit with a white shirt and emerald green tie. He looked immaculate as usual, his hair swept back, his skin glowing. The only unusual thing was the squash bag over one shoulder, the handle of a single racquet sticking out. But the idea of Trenchard running around on a squash court, grunting and getting sweaty, was almost impossible to visualize.

'Not really,' said Kash. 'I tried it once, but . . .'

'Quite right. Stupid game. Can't think of a better way to induce a cardiac arrest while grinding your every meniscus to bits. Not to mention the strain on your wrist.' He nodded to the flesh-coloured wrist-support protruding from his shirt-cuff. 'Some people you can only meet on a squash court, though. Either there or a golf course – and life's decidedly too short for that.' He grinned, showing perfect white teeth. 'So you're not a squash player, Kash. Good for you. But some form of exercise, aside from walking a dozen miles a day up and down these corridors, is to be recommended. Doesn't matter what, so long as you enjoy it. *Mens sana in corpore sano* and all that.' He laughed. 'More Latin for you, I'm afraid. A healthy mind in a healthy body. Actually, that's not quite right. It's a mistake to think of the mind as being in the body, you see. The mind *is* the body. Not two separate things. Anyway, neurobiology isn't your speciality, so I won't lead you down that particular rabbit-hole, fascinating though it might be to some of us.'

'Thanks, Mr Trenchard. That's the second piece of good advice you've given me.'

'Only the second? Is that all? You clearly haven't been paying attention.'

'No, no. I mean the second piece of . . . personal advice.'

'Ah.' Trenchard narrowed his eyes. 'And how's that been going?'

Kash felt the blood rushing to his face. 'Well, I think. So far. I almost messed it up, but . . . everything turned out OK. More than OK, I hope.'

Trenchard chuckled. 'Good.' He clapped him on the shoulder as he marched past. 'We'll make a surgeon of you yet!'

*　　*　　*

Kash was just opening the door to his flat when his pager bleeped. He sighed. *Really?* It wasn't a number he recognized. Maybe a misdial, then. Easy enough to do in an emergency. He wasn't on call tonight, and sleep had never seemed so enticing. He considered ignoring it for a moment, but knew that wasn't really an option. He went inside and reached for the phone by the door.

'Kash?'

'Ange?' It sounded like her voice, but slowed-down, distorted. He imagined her with the phone in one hand, a glass of red wine in the other. 'Is that you?'

On the other end of the line, he heard what sounded like a sigh of relief.

'I'm not on tonight, Ange. I was—'

'I need to see you, Kash.'

'Ange, what's going on?'

'No emergency, Kash, I just need to talk. You see, I know where your brilliant Mr Trenchard was that night. I know it all. And you need to know it too.'

11

It was a wild wet walk to the Balti, and Kash was cold and irritable by the time he arrived. It was midnight, and the staff were cashing up at a corner table. A few customers remained. In one corner, Angela sat alone nursing a near-empty pint glass. Several empty bottles of Cobra sat nearby.

'This had better be good, Ange. I'm whacked.' He softened his tone. 'If I don't get some sleep soon, I don't know if I'll be able to get through another day.'

Ange signalled to a waiter for another glass and two more bottles of beer. They sat in silence as she poured. Then she leaned forward. 'Doesn't it bother you, Kash, what happened to the Chaloner boy?'

'Every death bothers me, Ange, but we're doctors. We're going to see a lot more of it before—'

'I don't mean that. I mean Trenchard. I mean – where was he that night? And why hasn't anybody asked?'

She had a point. He certainly hadn't heard anybody mention it. Because he is who he is, Kash supposed. And would the outcome really have been different if he'd been there?

'Mr Trenchard is a great surgeon. A great *technical* surgeon. The best I've ever worked with. That's why I wanted him there. That's why I called him. But he's also a charmer.

People think he's perfect, that he can do no wrong. But he can. And when he does, the shit splatters those around him while he remains Teflon-coated.'

Kash thought about what Liz had said. *Not everyone likes him.*

'Ange,' he said, putting a hand on her arm. 'You're upset. You've had a few beers. Why don't we both get some sleep and then tomorrow we can talk about this properly?'

Ange put down her glass with a thump. 'Do you want to know where he was, the night Edmund Chaloner died?'

Kash sighed and looked at the untouched pint in front of him. 'Tell me.'

'Michael Trenchard wasn't out on an emergency that night, Kash. He was having dinner with Hilary Williams.'

'The anaesthetist?'

Ange nodded.

Hilary Williams was a widow with two teenage sons, but had that classic 'English Rose' look that seemed to defy time. She also had a reputation as the best anaesthetist the Victory had. Kash remembered being slightly daunted by her.

'That's not exactly a crime, is it?'

Ange snorted. 'I don't imagine his wife knew about it.'

'They're colleagues,' Kash said, beginning to feel frustrated.

Ange leaned across the table. Kash could smell the alcohol on her breath. 'He took her to his club in Mayfair; not exactly the sort of place you'd go for a chat about best practice in the operating theatre.'

'Who told you?'

'She did, of course.'

'But why? If Hilary and Trenchard are . . . if they were . . .'

Ange smirked. 'Having an affair?'

'Yes, if they were there in secret, why would she tell you about it? It doesn't exactly make her look good, does it?'

Angela slumped back in her chair. 'They weren't having an affair. That's the point.'

Kash looked confused. 'I'm sorry, I don't get it.'

'Hilary's on her own. Her husband didn't leave her much, apparently. Some bad investments, and I think he liked to gamble a bit. And she . . . well, you know what she's like. She likes to keep up appearances. And the boys go to some posh private school, apparently. Anyway, Trenchard knows all this, and he's being all sympathetic about her situation, saying how he'd like to help, and then he asks if she'd like to do some private work for him. Much better pay than at the Victory, obviously. As many hours as she wants.'

Kash was having difficulty following. 'So they're not having an affair, and he asks her if she'd like to do some private work for him. What's the big deal?'

Ange shook her head. 'For a smart boy, you can be fucking slow, sometimes, Kash. The deal was, she could have all the work she wanted, if she fucked him.'

Kash took a moment to process this. 'And presumably she said no, given that she's telling you all this.'

'Oh, she didn't just say "no". She was so fucking furious, she picked up her fork and stuck it into Trenchard's hand as hard as she could. It's not flattering to be thought of as a prostitute, Kash. He's lucky she didn't kill him.'

12

Kash bailed out unusually early and, by six, was making his way to the bus stops south of the Victory bridge, where a cluster of patients crowded, identifiable by the green paper prescription bags they carried. They were already spilling from the pavement onto the road. Please don't fall in front of a bus, Kash thought, and make me do CPR for half an hour while the ambulance is stuck in traffic on the flyover. He was sure that something was going to prevent him from getting to Claire's flat. The fact that they both had time off and he wasn't on call was miraculous enough. He clutched a bottle of mid-priced shiraz in one hand and a bunch of white tulips in the other, feeling that his plans for the evening were embarrassingly obvious and hoping that the gods, if they happened to glance down and recognized some easy prey, would choose not to play any more tricks on him. Trenchard had already dumped another load of patient files on him once at the last minute (whatever happened to 'all work and no play', Mr Trenchard?), and every patient on Nightingale seemed united in a malign conspiracy to frustrate him. Drips 'tissued'. Relatives appeared and demanded his attention. Wounds broke down. Patients had fits. And – he almost had to laugh – Richard Marshall in bed three had stood on his own urinary catheter while standing up in the bath. He couldn't help but wince and reach for his own groin when he'd been told.

But despite all that, incredibly, here he was. He'd been on call the night before, meaning that he'd now had no sleep for thirty-four hours, but weary though he was, he wasn't going to waste the opportunity that had presented itself. Sleep could wait. He looked at his watch. Claire's flat, overlooking the hospital where she had first trained in Denmark Hill, was only a half hour's ride away. He looked at his watch. If a bus ever came, of course.

* * *

By the time Claire opened the door, the tulips were looking bruised and battered from their ordeal on the crowded bus and Claire wisely reached for the bottle of wine first.

'You made it!'

She led him by the hand up the narrow, musty stairs. 'It's a bit grotty round here, as you can see, but inside's quite cosy. And there are some advantages to living above a newsagent.'

'Easy to keep up with current affairs?' Kash quipped.

Claire laughed. 'That, of course. But more importantly, you only have to pop downstairs if you run out of industrial-grade chardonnay.'

Once inside the living room, which had a tiny kitchenette in the corner, Kash's eye was immediately drawn to the battered sofa where Claire's elfin flatmate, Tiff, was curled up barefoot. Kash couldn't help staring at her mop of bright purple hair and array of piercings. Her toenails were painted black.

'You must be Kash.'

'And you must be Tiff.'

Claire found a bottle opener in a drawer under the sink and began uncorking the wine.

'A cork,' said Tiff, arching an eyebrow. 'Fancy.'

Kash found himself at a loss for a rejoinder. Could it be he was such a stuffed shirt that he was thrown by dyed hair and nose-rings?

'Yes,' he said.

'Don't mind Tiff. She's going to her room,' said Claire, brightly, handing Kash a glass.

Tiff uncurled from the sofa. 'I know when I'm not wanted.' She gave Claire a playful look. 'But I'll be on call. If there's an emergency,' she added with a wink.

Claire threw a dishcloth after her as she disappeared down a narrow corridor and into her room. 'Don't mind Tiff. She may look like a demented pixie, but there's a heart of gold beating in there somewhere.'

'I'm sure,' said Kash, as they sat down next to each other on the sofa.

'No, really,' Claire insisted. 'You should hear some of the locums at the Victory talk about her. They all say she's the most dedicated and knowledgeable of all the nurses at the hospice.'

'So how did you two meet?' Kash asked.

'Oh, it was one of those 999 parties.' Claire saw the bemused look on Kash's face. 'They invite police, fire, and nominally doctors. But mainly nurses. Tiff got talking to me. Found out I worked at the Victory, was looking for a flatmate. We hung out. She bought me a drink or two. Later, she was dancing with a fireman, six feet eight and built like an ox, and he was all over her, getting much too close for comfort, and . . . well, she just kneed him in the balls, cool as you like. He went down like a sack of spuds, and she grabbed my hand and made a quick exit. We ended up spending the rest of the night in a café by the bus station. I said I couldn't believe what she'd just done. I'd have been terrified. She just shrugged and said she'd had plenty of practice. That's when she told me all about it, the year she'd lived on the streets, after she ran away from her foster home. We were still sitting there talking when the brickies and cabbies came in for their breakfasts. I'd been looking for a flat to rent and now I knew I'd found my flatmate. Two weeks later we moved in here.'

'And how long ago was that?'

'Almost a year ago.'

'And you haven't fallen out? I mean, it sounds like a bit of a whirlwind romance.'

Claire gave him a look.

'I didn't mean . . . it's just, you hadn't known each other very long, and living on top of each other . . .'

She gave him another look, and Kash felt the blood rushing to his face.

'We just seem to be suited,' Claire shrugged. 'And to be honest, with her hours and my hours, we're not "on top of each other", as you put it, all that much.'

'She certainly seems to be very protective.'

'How do you mean?'

'I don't know, I just got this sense that she wasn't too happy about my being here.'

'It's nothing personal, Kash. She just tends to suspect the worst about men until she gets to know them. I guess it's because of the experiences she's had. And she knows I like you, so you must be halfway decent.'

'That's good to know,' Kash said, meaning it. 'So no boyfriend of her own, then?'

'Ah, she has a mystery man.'

'Oh? Who is he?'

'That's the point of a mystery man, Kash. He's . . . a mystery.'

Or he's not a man, Kash thought to himself. Or he doesn't exist.

'Talking of mysteries,' Kash said, 'Ange told me where Trenchard was, the night of the Edmund Chaloner op.'

'Really? Where? I assumed he was tied up with one of his private patients. Sneakiness and charm in equal measure, that man.' She paused. 'Smarm. Or he'd been out to dinner and had a couple of glasses too many, despite being on call.'

'Well, according to Ange, who admittedly was pretty drunk herself when she told me, Hilary Williams told her that *she* was with him.'

Claire raised an eyebrow. 'And?'

'Well, here's the bit I'm not sure I believe. Trenchard supposedly propositioned her – said he'd give her private work if she slept with him.'

'Seriously?'

'And she stuck her fork into his hand.'

'I suppose it's hard to knee someone in the balls when you're sitting in a restaurant.'

'She's hard up, apparently. She could definitely have done with the work.'

Claire chewed her lip thoughtfully. 'Mr Trenchard's usually pretty good at getting people to do what he wants. The puppet master where usually no one even sees the strings.'

'What do you mean?'

'Oh, come on, Kash. You know what they say about Trenchard: "You have to learn to take the smooth with the smooth." I bet his amazing success rate as a surgeon is half down to the fact that his patients don't want to disappoint him by dying. "That lovely Mr Trenchard." As for the nurses . . .'

'What about the nurses?'

She rolled her eyes. 'Most of them are mooning after him like a character in a Mills and Boon novel. And he takes full advantage. Not that the doctors are any better. They all want to be his best student. Look at you.'

'That's not fair, Claire,' Kash said, stiffening. 'Not every junior at my stage gets the chance to assist in theatres and do outpatients . . . and audits. If I do a little clean-up for him here and there, what's the big deal? Anyway, I've only been at the Victory three months. It won't last forever. And I'm not doing his paperwork tonight, am I?'

Claire was about to reply when they both heard the click of the front door closing. Tiff had obviously just been teasing when she told Claire she was planning on staying in for the evening. Or perhaps the mystery man had called. Claire turned to Kash with the sort of smile that he had seen all too rarely in his life. She moved closer and gently touched his knee.

'Yes, you're here with me, Kash. Just the two of us.' She sighed. 'And the telly's on the blink. What on earth are we going to do?'

13

'Jesus H Fucking Christ.'

Kash stood in the doorway to Mr Trenchard's office, his mouth gaping. It felt as if a moment ago he'd been writing a letter to his mum, the taste of stale mac and cheese still in his mouth, and now he was in another reality.

Everyone looked at him for a second, then turned their eyes back to the figure on the floor behind Trenchard's desk. Geoff, the anaesthetist, was kneeling over the body. 'Give us a hand, will you?'

Kash willed his legs to move. Trenchard was lying with his trousers around his ankles, his genitals bulging out of a pair of tiny black panties. His chest, thick with wiry hair, was exposed through a tight bra, his head thrown back. Max was already at his head, slipping a noose from over his neck. Deep, guttural snores rolled up out of his throat, his pharynx obstructed. Geoff kneeled behind Trenchard's head and used one hand to pull the jaw forward. The snoring stopped. He turned to the nursing sister, who was already rummaging in the crash box. She passed Geoff a Guedel airway, which he swiftly inserted over the tongue. 'We'll need a collar. We can't be sure that his neck isn't broken. Until then, the head stays in neutral.' He looked around.

Everyone nodded.

Kash kneeled down, his mind beginning to work properly again. He reached his fingers into Trenchard's groin, feeling for his femoral artery. 'Pulse good and strong . . . but slow. Less than fifty. Good God, what happened to him?'

'Autoerotic asphyxiation, I'd say,' Geoff replied. 'He's certainly dressed for it. And' – Geoff waved a hand at half a dozen magazines scattered on the floor – 'he seemed to be keeping on top of the literature.'

Kash stole a glance. Leather, whips, things he had no name for.

'And he had a noose around his neck.'

Geoff raised Trenchard's eyelids. The eyes were staring straight ahead, the pupils tiny, the white sclera speckled with myriad red marks. 'Yup. Petechial haemorrhages. Might have done his pons in. The pupils are pinpoint.' He looked round. 'Will somebody turn that bloody music off?'

The night sister carefully lifted the needle from Trenchard's record player, as if worried that he was about to berate her for scratching the vinyl. A thick silence settled as they all surveyed the scene. There were magazines everywhere. Kash picked one up between thumb and forefinger before dropping it back on the floor. It was simply too much to take in. He took a deep breath and pulled off the bra Trenchard was wearing before attaching a set of sticky 'dot' electrodes to the skin of his chest wall. As he hooked them up to the monitor-defibrillator the night sister had laid on the floor, he noticed his hands were shaking slightly. Then he caught sight of Chris, the Victory's medical registrar, crashing through the door, flushed and panting.

'Jesus,' he gasped, taking in the scene.

'The next person who says that . . .' muttered Geoff.

'Sorry.' Chris kneeled beside Kash and quickly assessed what he was seeing. 'Autoerotic asphyxiation. Too tight a noose. Signs of strangulation – petechiae, rope burn. Larynx intact. No crepitus or stridor. Breathing on his own, but the pupils are one millimetre and fixed.'

'Brainstem?' Geoff asked.

'Looks like it.' Chris's eyes flicked to the monitor. 'Bradycardic, thirty-five,' he said. 'Looks nodal or a high bundle escape. Six hundred of atropine please.' He moved to Trenchard's side as Kash passed him a preloaded syringe. 'Glad you got a line in, guys. But next time, make it a venflon, not a butterfly, will you?'

All eyes turned to the butterfly needle, neatly taped in place, and the syringe attached to it, and then to Geoff. 'Hey, I'm fast. But not *that* fast! He must have been using. Ideas?'

Kash stood and looked around. 'There!' He pointed at a glass ampoule, scarcely afloat in the sea of pornographic pages.

Chris picked it up. 'Morphine, ten mg.' Nearby was a plastic bag and gauze. He sniffed it hesitantly. 'Poppies, poppers and porn.'

Kash bristled. How could he be so flippant at a time like this?

Chris turned to the nursing sister. 'I think we can manage for now. Would you mind heading to the emergency department and grabbing a collar and a scoop?' A scoop was an aluminium clip-together stretcher, and each half could be slid beneath a collapsed patient before joining them together. 'We'll need to move him shortly I think. Oh and mum's the word, eh?'

He removed the syringe from the butterfly and passed it to Kash. 'Best save that for toxicology.' Then, connecting up the atropine, he pushed in half the dose while staring at the monitor. 'Four hundred mics of Narcan, please, Kash.' He flushed the line, injected the Narcan, and then repeated the process to give the remaining atropine. 'That's better. Heart rate ninety-six. Looks like sinus rhythm to me?' Kash nodded. 'Pupils?'

Geoff raised the eyelids again. 'Still pinpoint and unresponsive.'

At Trenchard's head, Geoff intubated him. Once Trenchard's airways were secure, he connected the ambubag, squeezing it to augment Trenchard's ragged breaths, which came in waves of increasing depth and frequency before receding again.

'What have you got up there?' asked Chris.

Geoff looked again. 'Pupils still pinpoint. No corneals, no gag when I intubated him, no doll's eyes.' Geoff rubbed his knuckles firmly against Trenchard's breastbone. 'No response to pain. Cheyne Stokes breathing if you haven't seen it before.' He nodded to Kash. 'Goes with the brain-stem. Or lack of it.'

* * *

'Lights are on, but there's nobody home,' Max chipped in.

'Pontine, then,' ventured Chris.

Geoff grimaced. 'My guess is that it's global. That noose was bloody tight. He's got petechiae all over his face, his eyes, his palate.'

Chris got to his feet. 'OK. Thank you, everyone. A job well done. We need to move him, and fast. Max, run up to the ICU. Tell them we're coming up, and tell them who it is. Remind them about confidentiality. We need to keep this one between ourselves for now. Go! Kash, call for the porters. We'll need a trolley, obviously, and an oxygen cylinder too. Make it clear we want the cylinder *now*, and not in an hour after the dinner trolleys have been taken back to the kitchen. Obviously, he doesn't move until that collar is on. Treat him like an unstable spine. And Kash! Snap out of it! I know it's a shock, but this probably isn't the worst thing you'll see this month.'

'Sorry, it's . . .' He couldn't finish the sentence.

A loud bang, and the nursing sister arrived, carrying the stretcher and collar. She was panting. Together, she and Chris stacked the magazines to one side and helped put on the collar to immobilize the neck. With Geoff controlling the head, they slipped the two halves of the stretcher beneath Trenchard. Moments later, two porters appeared.

'Not a word of this to anyone please, gentlemen.' Chris's voice was firm.

They didn't seem to have heard him. 'Christ! Is that . . .?'

'Yes. So we need to load him up and get to the ICU, and fast, please. Geoff? Good to go?'

Geoff nodded. 'Soon as the oxygen is on.'

Kash stepped back as the trolley was wheeled into place and Trenchard was lifted onto it. Kash took the foot end, but was working automatically, his thoughts whirling. He let go as the porters gently nudged him out of the way and watched the trolley move quickly down the corridor towards ICU, feeling as if life as he knew it was disappearing along with it.

He knew there was nothing more he could do. For a few moments he just stood there, not knowing where to go. He needed to find a quiet place to think about what he had just seen, and . . . what? *Deal* with it? Come to terms with it? No, something more concrete than that. He needed to work out exactly what he *had* seen.

Then another thought occurred to him.

He took off, hurtling up and out of outpatients, towards the theatres.

14

His heart was heaving by the time he got there. The theatre changing rooms were dark and silent. Lockers stood in rows behind the slatted wooden benches. Most were empty, doors ajar, ready for whoever was operating the next day, but at the centre of the wall stood the locker that had been Mr Trenchard's and his alone for as long as anyone could remember. Another sign of his special status within the hospital. Kash approached it tentatively, his heart rate only just finding a steady equilibrium. He fingered the door, expecting to find it locked – only Mr Trenchard had the key, so far as he knew – but, at his gentle touch, the door squeaked open.

'*Jesus*,' Kash said under his breath. These things . . . he had never . . . Handcuffs and silk ropes, a gag made of studded black leather, contraptions whose use even he – having seen every surgical instrument in existence, designed to open and clamp and restrain and penetrate – could not imagine. A black latex mask whose features, even hanging flaccidly here, seemed somehow to be the features of Mr Trenchard himself, looking down at Kash in that fatherly, yet amused, way he had.

He thought he could hear footsteps. Probably it was some theatre nurse. Although time seemed to have stopped for

Kash, the world inside the Victory had not stopped turning, after all.

Instinct seized him. There was a holdall in the bottom of Mr Trenchard's locker. He lifted it out, spilling more magazines he dared not look at, packets of condoms and a single used syringe, which he crammed back in hastily, together with the rest of the locker's contents. His heart hammering, he hoisted the bag over his shoulder, turned and hurried away.

Back through the swing doors, up and out of theatres, he kept his head down, certain somebody was watching him, certain he would stumble over his own feet and send everything in the holdall cascading over the floor. By the time he reached the stairway leading up into the hospital apartments, his chest was burning. He stopped to compose himself, heard footsteps following behind, and pressed on, desperate to get to the safety of his flat. Mr Trenchard would be in the ICU by now. No doubt he was hooked up to a ventilator. They'd be getting an arterial and central venous line in by now.

Kash reached his door, fumbled for a key and almost fell inside. He didn't want to look in the holdall, let alone examine its contents. Not knowing what else to do, he crammed it under the bed. He'd think about what to do with it later.

Suddenly there was a hammering on the door. He froze. Someone had seen him take the holdall and followed him to his room. Or worse, they had alerted security. How was he going to explain himself? Maybe he should just keep quiet, pretend he wasn't there and hope whoever it was would go away. But what if they knew he was in there? If he didn't answer the door he really would look as if he had something to hide. He swallowed hard, and with a trembling hand opened the door. Claire stood framed in the doorway, a look of concern on her face.

His first reaction was relief – followed by panic. She was the last person he wanted to see the unspeakable contents of Mr Trenchard's holdall. If she thought for a moment that any of this stuff belonged to him . . . 'Kash, you look awful,' she began. 'What on earth's wrong? I saw you running up the stairs like a mad thing, and I . . .' She stopped in her tracks, looking past Kash into the room. Kash turned, following her gaze. The holdall was jutting out from under the bed. A pair of handcuffs could clearly be seen, half dangling over the side as if they were trying to escape, while the corner of a magazine was poking out, a woman's naked torso clearly visible, her face hidden behind a leather mask.

Claire went white. 'Kash, what the . . .'

She wrenched her eyes away from the holdall and its contents and turned on him.

'Is this what I think it is? What the hell have you got in there, Kash?'

He put his hands on her shoulders. 'Claire, no, no, no – it's not what you think, they're not . . . it's not mine!'

'Then what's it doing in your room – under your bed?' She said the last word with disgust.

'I took it from Mr Trenchard's locker. I was trying—' He gripped her shoulders more tightly, trying to get her to understand, but she shrugged him off angrily.

'Don't you dare touch me!' She gave him one final look, a mixture of shock, fury and – most wounding of all for Kash – disappointment, then turned on her heel and marched out.

He started after her, then realized he was better off letting her go. If they ended up having a row in the corridor, that would only make things worse. He had a quick look to make sure no one else was there who might have heard their conversation – if you could call it that – and gently closed the door. With trembling fingers, he shoved the holdall's contents firmly inside and zipped it up, then firmly pushed it as far as it would go under his bed.

He stood silently for a minute or two, waiting for his breathing to return to normal. Although it was out of sight, he felt the holdall's presence, like a malevolent spirit in the room. Muffled groans and maniacal laughter seemed to be seeping from beneath the bed.

Pull yourself together. He sat down at the little table, and saw his unfinished letter to his mother. A letter he would never finish now, the good news – the wonderful news – about Claire having been blotted out by the scene of horror in Mr Trenchard's office.

Dear Mum, he imagined writing. *Sorry for the interruption. I had to go down to Mr Trenchard's office – remember my boss, I told you about him – and guess what? He was lying there in women's underwear with a noose round his neck and a needle in the back of his hand. He's now in ICU but I don't imagine there's much hope for him. He told me I needed to chill out, have more fun. Well, now we know what his idea of fun was. Just shows, you never can tell with people, right?*

He put his head in his hands. But Trenchard *was* a great surgeon, wasn't he? Had been? This doesn't change that, surely. He saved lives. People admired him, loved him. I wanted one day to be like him. But now? Is all that undone, erased, gone? His reputation will certainly be destroyed, however many lives he changed for the better. And what about him? The man, the person. What will be left of him?

He shook his head like a man trying to rid himself of a troublesome insect. What had he been thinking? Why hadn't he left everything in Mr Trenchard's locker where he found it? He'd been trying to protect him somehow, he supposed. But from what? Once the news spread, a few more sex toys and fetish magazines here and there wouldn't make any difference, would they? But something had made him do it. Something he didn't yet quite understand.

And now he'd paid the price.

15

There was nothing more contagious than a secret, even in a hospital. Hospitals were generally very good at keeping secrets from those outside. Celebrities came and went, and many inside knew. But the press rarely ever did. And when they did, the leak usually lay outside the Victory's walls. But *inside*, it would have been easier to keep cholera confined – because, in the next twenty-four hours, there wasn't a person in the Victory, from lowly porter to respected oncologist, from ward sister to radiologist, who hadn't heard the sorry story of Michael Trenchard's bizarre night of misadventure. Chris's admonishment to the porters about confidentiality had a Canute-like quality to it in retrospect. Did he really expect them to keep a piece of gossip as juicy as this under their hats? In any case, plenty of people must have seen the trolley on its way to ICU and even if they hadn't recognized Mr Trenchard lying on it – or simply hadn't believed what they were seeing – word would soon have got out.

Not that you would have had to rely on the hospital grapevine for all the gory details. The next day, there it was, splashed across the front page of every newspaper, from the most sensationalist tabloid to the most serious-minded broadsheet. Mr Trenchard had timed his indiscretion

particularly badly, as there seemed to be no more substantial or attention-grabbing news to fill the front pages,
and the Trenchard story expanded to fill the vacuum. Not
that much expansion was needed. After a brief paragraph
outlining his eminence in the medical profession, all the
papers took varying degrees of pleasure, from unashamedly gleeful at one end to morally outraged at the other, in
describing every last detail of his fall from grace. If he had
been a celebrity or a politician, a household name, perhaps
it would have been a bigger story. But then, if truth be told,
it might have actually been less shocking. Unusual sexual
shenanigans were, at the end of the day, what you expected
from such people. For a doctor, on the other, hand – a surgeon who dedicated himself to saving lives, a paragon of
virtue toiling away in the bowels of the NHS (at least for the
most part) – to botch his own autoerotic asphyxiation in
the very hospital where he had performed his miraculous
cures, that was truly bizarre.

In the doctors' mess, there was a feeling almost of being
under siege from the outside world. Geoff had been phoned
at home and offered a substantial sum of money in return
for a first-hand account. Max had been stopped on the street
and offered the same. Security had to be called when it was
revealed that two journalists had tried to sneak onto the
ICU, claiming to be relatives. One – a woman – was even
sobbing convincingly. A third had brazenly appeared with

a white coat and stethoscope, thereby demonstrating that his knowledge of hospitals came mostly from TV, as nobody wore a white coat on the ICU any more. The discovery that Mr Trenchard had once operated on a minor royal only seemed to make the papers' thirst for first-hand accounts of his demise even more frenzied.

And the journalists weren't the only ones pressing the medics for their stories. The police had quickly become involved, led by a cadaverous detective called DI Lambert, and everyone had to be interviewed, or 'interrogated', as Max put it. How well did they know Michael Trenchard? Had they been aware of his sexual predilections? Had there been any previous incidents of this kind of behaviour? Kash had had his own interview, of course, and as far as he could tell gave the same answers as everyone else: 'not very well', 'no', and 'I have no idea'. As one of the first responders, they'd dwelled on him longer than most – and all the more when they learned somehow that he'd been Trenchard's 'protégé', a charge – or it seemed like a charge, from the way it was put to him – that he denied. It was a blur now. He couldn't really remember what he'd told them. Still working through that same night covering the wards, it had frankly begun to seem like a bad dream. And life – or, rather, life and death – went on without pausing to take in the news. Mr Trenchard might not be operating, but others had taken that work on, and Kash still had to care for the patients.

'What about you, Kash?' Geoff said, with a grin. 'All those nights you were slaving away in his office. He never came back and whipped you if you hadn't finished his patient studies?'

Kash felt the blood rush to his face. Less than a week ago, they wouldn't have dared to joke about Mr Trenchard. Now, it seemed, he was fair game for every kind of bad-taste quip imaginable. He got to his feet.

'Don't be ridiculous. You're talking about him as if he's dead. He's still here, in this hospital.'

But if Michael Trenchard wasn't actually dead, what other word was there for the condition he was in? To his shame, Kash had not been to see him since the drama in the outpatients basement.

'Christ, Devan,' Max said. 'We're only pulling your leg. Come on. Sit down. Finish your coffee.' Kash slowly unwound, and seated himself. 'Still, you have to say, it doesn't look too pretty.' He picked up a tabloid from the floor beside him, and opened it to the double-page spread in the middle. There was a picture of Trenchard, obviously taken at some charity bash, immaculate in his pinstripe suit, smiling for the camera, his arm round a woman in a demure black cocktail dress who Kash assumed was his wife, Isabelle. On the facing page, a charming tableaux had been arranged: a noose, a black silk bra and panties, a syringe and a magazine, the cover of which had been mostly blacked out, but which still clearly showed a naked man on his knees being whipped by a woman dressed from head to toe in black leather.

Were these the actual things he'd been found with? No, surely they'd be in a police evidence locker somewhere. Kash went cold, thinking of the holdall still under his bed, untouched since he'd put it there. He didn't even know everything that was in it. Perhaps it, too, was evidence.

He should never have taken it.

But since he had, should he now hand it over to the police? What would he say, though? How could he explain himself without getting into worse trouble?

No, he'd worry about the police later. Right now he had to worry about Claire.

16

Michael Trenchard wondered where he was.

All around him were astonishing blooms of iridescent colour, bursting into sudden life, then just as quickly fading away, against a backdrop of emptiness as black as pitch. After a while (though he had no sense of time) the fountains and flashes died and didn't return. He was left swirling inside blackness, detached from his body, adrift in the vacuum, his only sensation one of boundless space and emptiness.

A thought occurred: perhaps this isn't a 'where'; it's a 'what'. Could this be death, this endless nothing he was drifting in weightlessly, a leaf in the wind?

Well, that would certainly be a surprise. He had always assumed death to be the termination of everything; something by definition that you couldn't experience. And yet here he was, apparently conscious. Conscious enough, at least, to ask himself questions. So he was alive, then.

Cogito ergo sum. *I think therefore I am. Which meant . . .*

He tried to remember where he'd been, what he'd been doing, before . . . before he entered this new state. He recalled music. One of his favourites: 'Mars, The Bringer of War'. Was that the smell of a cigar? Yes, he'd been smoking. Smoking and . . . enjoying a glass of claret. In his office. Sitting back in his chair, feet up on his desk. It must have been evening, then. The end of a long day.

He made an effort to remember more, but nothing else came, and then the rest started to fade: the music, the smell of the cigar, the taste of wine. He was left in the void again.

Not dead, then, he thought. But for some reason he had a feeling he almost had been. That he'd been snatched from the brink. He'd experienced it so many times from the other point of view, sensing a patient under his knife reeling away, tumbling off a cliff top only to be hauled back by a needle in their arm, a flood of some drug or other. There was, unashamedly, a thrill to be had in that – in holding the thread that could lead a person out of the abyss, and back – like Odysseus, from the land of the dead. One little snip and they might go spinning; one little pull and they would come crawling back to life and be grateful, ever after, that you had been there, the only one who could save them, who could grant them the chance to see their loved ones again, never knowing that (if only for a split second) you had wondered what it would take to simply step back, do nothing, walk away, and let them fall. Not that he'd ever seriously considered it. Except once, perhaps. And then the gratitude, the lifelong gratitude. How can I thank you enough, Mr Trenchard? I thought I was going to die, I really did. A smile: it's nothing, really, just doing my job. And now someone, it seemed had done the same for him, had tugged on the thread and reeled him back from the abyss.

Well, thank you very much, whoever you are. I'm alive. In which case why can't I feel anything? Why can't I see anything? Perhaps I'm asleep. Perhaps I'm dreaming. The thought of sleep seemed to suddenly make him very tired. The effort of thinking any more was beyond him. Just the idea of it seemed to weigh a thousand tons. And then he was drifting again, beyond thought, beyond words, a tiny pinprick, awhirl in a sea of nothingness.

17

'Slow down, Kash, for God's sake. I'm not going to run away. And I'm not going to bite your head off, either. Just start from the beginning.'

They were sitting at a corner table in the Balti with two bottles of Cobra and a dish of poppadoms in front of them. Kash's bottle was already half empty. Despite her protests, he was convinced that if he couldn't convince Claire he hadn't done anything wrong here and now, then she would walk out and he would never see her again. Except that he would actually see her every day, which would be infinitely worse.

He paused to compose himself. 'So you know what happened to Mr Trenchard?'

She rolled her eyes.

'Sorry, yes, obviously. The whole world knows. And you know I was there. I got the call. So I saw . . . everything. And then when they took him to ICU I just had this thought – I don't know why – that if he had these magazines and . . . things, then he must have kept them somewhere, and he certainly didn't keep them in his office because I'd have seen them, definitely, so that left his locker in theatres, so, I went up there as fast as I could—'

Claire put a hand on his arm. 'But why?'

Kash frowned, trying to put it into words. 'I'd just seen him so . . . vulnerable, so humiliated. I mean, I was shocked. I didn't really know . . . . But I just thought that if there was more of this stuff in his locker, then I wanted to get to it before anyone else, and – I don't know – stop people from seeing it.'

'To protect him.'

'Yes.'

'Wasn't it a bit late for that? I mean, they found him wearing women's underwear with a noose round his neck.'

Kash frowned. 'Yes, I suppose. It was silly. But his locker was open, which was odd.'

'The whole thing was odd. To put it mildly.'

She took a sip of her beer. Kash picked up a poppadom and started breaking off tiny pieces, making a little pile on the tablecloth in front of him.

'That's the thing. It didn't make sense. I mean, if you're into that sort of thing, wouldn't you do it in private? Wouldn't you do it at home?'

Claire shook her head. 'Not if his wife's not into it, you wouldn't. And if you went to some sort of club, then you might be spotted going in. Or coming out. Or worse, you might meet someone else from the hospital.'

Kash's eyes widened, trying not to imagine Carney, or . . .

'So maybe here was the logical choice,' Claire continued. 'A controlled environment.' She shrugged. 'Except it went wrong.'

Kash thought it through. Logically, what Claire was saying made sense. And yet . . . something still niggled at him.

'Maybe. Maybe you're right. I'll admit I don't know the first thing about this kind of stuff. But at the time I suppose I couldn't quite believe it. And so I was trying to cover for him.' He sighed. 'I know it doesn't really make sense.'

Claire looked at him with a warm expression and he felt his stomach turn over. 'Yes, it does. You're loyal. You liked him. You felt you owed him. There was nothing else you could do for him. You couldn't undo what you'd just seen, so you did the only thing you could. And now you've got a holdall full of kinky paraphernalia stashed in your room.' She laughed. 'Just don't ask me to stay over, Kash. I don't think I could get to sleep with that lot underneath me.'

'I promise,' Kash said. 'And I promise I'll find a way to get rid of it. I just need to work out how best to do that.'

'Cross that bridge,' Claire agreed.

Kash slowly reached out and took her hand. 'So we're OK?'

'Yes, Kash. We're OK. Just, the next time you happen upon an autoerotic asphyxiation victim, promise you won't go rummaging in their personal effects, OK?'

'Promise. Absolutely.' Relief flooded through him. He drained the rest of his beer in one gulp, and suddenly felt light-headed.

'So how is he, Mr Trenchard?' Claire asked.

Kash shrugged. 'Still in ICU. He seems to be stable.'

'That's good, isn't it?' Claire ventured.

'He's alive. Technically. But he's never going to recover, I'm afraid. At least that's what they tell me. PVS. Persistent vegetative state. At best. Not brain dead – his basic life-support systems work – but the thinking parts seem gone. That bit that made him Michael Trenchard.' He paused. 'I hear they're going to move him up to ward fourteen.'

Claire shivered. 'How awful. I mean, to end up there.'

'The end of the line,' Kash muttered. 'Still, that Liz Murray – you know I mentioned her? Crazy old bird but still full of beans. Only met him once, but she loves him.' He smiled grimly. 'Now she can gaze at him all day long.'

Claire had never heard him talk this way. Hospital humour was one thing, but this was properly bitter and twisted.

'Oh, Kash.'

'Sorry.'

'And what about Sister Vale? She was devoted to him, too, in her way. It must have been an unbelievable shock.'

Kash felt bad. He'd been so consumed with his own feelings about Mr Trenchard, he hadn't really considered anyone else's. Sister Vale had told him she'd worked with Trenchard for years. In fact, she must have known him better than anyone. Had she had an inkling, during that time, about his secret proclivities? Or could she even have . . . He had a sudden image of Sister Vale dressed in leather and brandishing a whip. He blinked it away, hoping Claire couldn't read his mind.

'To be honest with you, I'm dreading seeing him up there,' Kash admitted. 'He's not dead, but he's not really alive, either. It's not like you're visiting *him*, spending time with *him*.'

'More like his corpse?'

Kash had a flash of a long-buried memory. He nodded. 'Something like that.'

Claire sighed. 'Well, I'm just a lowly nurse. I just wash them and feed them and give them their medication. I don't ask if they're alive or dead. I leave that to you lot.'

18

Anyone in medicine knew that 1ˢᵗ August and 1ˢᵗ February were the most dangerous days in the health service. For junior staff, it was 'all change', and nobody had the faintest idea what they were doing in their new jobs. For Kash, this had meant moving up to long stay and 'COOP' – care of the older person. And that meant following Sister Vale to ward fourteen.

As he entered the ward, he realized he was more nervous than he had been on his first ward round. Trenchard was on the far side, directly opposite Liz Murray, who seemed to be asleep. Kash took a deep breath and walked over.

A tracheostomy tube stopped saliva running into Trenchard's lungs, but not onto the front of his white hospital smock. It hung in a tenacious column from the corner of his lip; a slick of paperhanger's paste which occasionally snapped and retracted. He breathed, in effect, through a plastic pipe in his neck. A fine-bore feeding tube entered his abdomen and ran directly into his stomach. Connected to it, a growbag of fawn liquid hung above his head. A catheter ran into his bladder, draining orange urine into a nearby urometer. Kash could see that the tip of his penis was already becoming slightly ulcerated where it entered. No doubt someone, perhaps even

Sister Vale herself, had performed what would become his weekly enema, manually evacuating his bowels with long uncomfortable fingers and inadequately lubricated gloves.

Trenchard now sat, propped up but listing to one side, shoulders rounded, in a large Parker Knoll chair. Even in this semi-death, Kash thought, Michael Trenchard was an imposing figure. Like a living Lincoln Memorial: seated, huge, immobile and stately.

And he could live for decades like this, or so they had said – his body was healthy, his heart and lungs strong – if, of course, you could call a persistent vegetative state a life. Kash felt an immense wave of pity, thinking how full of vigour Trenchard had been. How full of energy. A man who always seemed to be on the move, never sitting still for a moment. And now look at him.

He wondered how many of his colleagues would feel the same way, seeing the great man reduced to this dribbling wreck. Would they feel pity and sorrow, or would they think he simply got what he had coming? A man who dresses in women's underwear and puts a noose around his neck and nicks morphine to get his kicks. Would they feel, not pity, but contempt? And disgust? Was this pathetic shell – a victim of his own perverted lusts, as others might see him – the real Trenchard? Or was it the brilliant surgeon, admired by all?

He recalled a long-ago psychology course. What he was currently suffering from in regard to Mr Trenchard was

'cognitive dissonance': he was trying to hold onto two oppos-
ing ideas that both seemed to be true at the same time.

Kash looked into Trenchard's eyes. What was the phrase?
'The windows of the soul'. But Trenchard just stared fixedly
ahead, seeing nothing. No help for Kash there. Kash had to
admit, he didn't know who the real Michael Trenchard was,
but his gut told him that the man he had admired was not a
complete sham.

Anyway, the mysteries of the human soul were not Kash's
area of expertise. He'd carry on, being the best he could be.
And that started with being professional. 'Good morning,
Mr Trenchard. It's Kash.' Absurd as it sounded, he was deter-
mined to treat Mr Trenchard as he would any other patient.
'I've just come to examine you. Nothing special. All routine.
And I'll not be doing anything too undignified or painful.'

He kneeled just to Trenchard's right, and took his hand.
It was warm, and the skin felt smooth from the application
of some emollient or other. The radial pulse was regular and
full, with a rate of about eighty beats per minute. Skin turgor?
Seemed pretty normal. Certainly not suggestive of significant
dehydration. Jugular venous pressure wasn't elevated.

He moved slightly back. The respiratory rate was about
sixteen but its pattern wasn't quite normal. It still tended to
accelerate a little and then decelerate to a short pause – the
Cheyne Stokes pattern not uncommon after neurological
injury, and which he'd first seen on the night all this had

begun. The tracheostomy site itself was well dressed, but a sticky pool of mucus had collected around its margins. He placed a stiffened left middle finger across the upper left chest, and tapped it sharply with the middle finger of his right hand. The resulting sound was hollow. He repeated the process at three points on each side of the chest, before progressing to examine the back of the chest.

Standing in front of Trenchard, he seized his shoulders, and drew his body forwards, allowing him to reach over and behind so as to percuss the chest at the back. As he did so, he noticed a small piece of plastic resting just beneath Trenchard's left buttock. He fished it out with one hand, and his brow furrowed. It was a three-way tap and connector – a common enough piece of kit used on many intravenous lines in the hospital.

But Mr Trenchard didn't have an intravenous line. And nor had he for some time, to Kash's knowledge.

Kash kneeled again, and pried Trenchard's buttock clear of the seat. There was a deep indentation in his skin, red and livid. Left much longer, and the skin would have broken down and a full-blown bedsore would have resulted, which might have taken months to heal. At the very least – if Trenchard could feel anything at all – it would have been exceedingly painful.

On his way out he saw Sister Vale.

'All well, Kash?'

'Yes, thank you, Sister. I've just been to see Mr Trenchard.'
She nodded, her expression unreadable.

'I just thought I'd mention this.' He passed her the tap.
'Mr Trenchard was sitting on it. Skin was breaking down.'

'That's odd. I sat him out myself this morning with Sandra,
and I'm normally meticulous. I guess I must have missed it.'
She dropped it in the front pocket of her uniform. 'Anything
else?'

'No,' Kash said. 'Nothing else.'

He stood for a moment, wondering whether he should have
kept the tap, without being quite sure why. He was about to
say something, but Sister Vale was already on her way down
the ward.

19

Kash's thoughts about the tap faded away as the demands of the night took hold, but whenever there were a few minutes of respite to grab a coffee or gulp down a chocolate bar, his mind returned to the seemingly insignificant piece of plastic. Now it was five in the morning, and Kash made an industrial-strength coffee in the mess.

'Fuck me. Was last night a full moon or something?' It was the orthopaedic registrar.

'It was your fault.' Obstetrics.

'*My* fault? How come it was *my* fault? I wasn't out there breaking their hips. I was in Caesarian Central last night.'

'I know. I couldn't get a bloody anaesthetist half the time.'

'*That's* not my fault.'

He paused. 'You used the Q word.'

In return, she paused, and shrugged. 'OK. It's a fair cop, guv'nor. You got me bang to rights.' She held out her wrists, together. 'Take me away.' It was true. Earlier that evening, she had said that it seemed 'quite quiet'. In a hospital, this was like holding up a lightning rod in a storm.

The registrar plonked himself down beside Kash. 'You all right, mate?'

Kash nodded. 'Sure.'

'How's it going with the lovely nurse Barker?'

Kash looked at him. 'Fine,' he replied in the same flat tone.

'Bloody hell,' the registrar grinned. 'That bad, eh?'

'No, really, everything's fine,' Kash said, trying to inject a bit of enthusiasm into his voice. Not that his relationship with Claire was anyone's business, but even summoning the energy to be annoyed was beyond him. He pulled himself to his feet.

'Right, I'm for my bed. See you later.'

* * *

Nine o'clock, and back in his flat, Kash took a scalding shower, then made himself some more coffee and a piece of toast. Tomorrow – today now – was Saturday, and he was off duty, thank God. But he knew he wasn't going to sleep. Something about the tap refused to let go of his mind. Had someone placed it there deliberately? It was hard to see how it could have got there accidentally. But why would anyone do that? To induce a painful bedsore? Who would be so vindictive? 'Not everybody likes him,' Liz had said. But not liking someone was one thing; trying to cause them pain – even on the vague off chance that Trenchard could feel it – when they were in such a desperate condition spoke of deeper and darker motives. And anyway, Liz might be pretty sharp, all things considered, but a ninety-two-year-old woman in her condition? He probably shouldn't put too much stock in the things she said. Especially when she had nothing to do all day but let her imagination run riot amid the paltry goings-on of ward fourteen. Stick to the facts, he told himself. Stick to what you know. To what you've seen with your own eyes.

With that in mind, Kash decided to replay as accurately as he could everything he'd witnessed that night in Trenchard's office, from the moment he'd first had the call. That would require concentration, which meant not falling asleep, and that meant keeping moving. He decided to go for a walk.

Ten minutes later, he was marching through the winter sunshine, in no particular direction except away from the Victory, his coat buttoned up to his neck and a woolly hat pulled low over his ears. It wasn't much of a way to spend his day off, he had to admit. But Claire was stuck doing a long day. And this was his chance to finally seek out and neutralize the source of the unease which was gnawing away at him. To confirm that the shocking tableaux that had confronted them in Trenchard's office was exactly what it seemed – a kinky solo sex game that had gone tragically wrong. Or . . . that it was something else. He couldn't yet see what that 'something else' might be but he had a terrible feeling that it could be even more shocking.

*   *   *

An hour later, Kash finally stopped walking. He leaned back against the railings of a little park and took a deep draught of the frosty air. He had no idea where he was. But all his vague imaginings had finally come into focus. He didn't have all the answers – not by a long chalk. But he had something. Enough, anyway, he felt, to take to DI Lambert. The police, thank God, could take it from there, and he could get on with his life again.

Two bus rides later, with darkness falling, Kash stood outside the police station off the Walworth Road. It was a nondescript building, barely as imposing as a town hall, and Kash would have thought it had been abandoned, had it not been for the police cars banked up outside, their rooftops beginning to frost over.

Inside the station a duty sergeant took his name, his profession and the reason he was presenting himself. When he mentioned Mr Trenchard, Kash was certain he saw a wry smile flicker and die on her· face. Then she invited Kash to take one of the empty plastic seats and disappeared into the back office.

In the waiting room the walls were drab green, not unlike the Victory's. He hoped someone would come soon, otherwise he was afraid he'd fall asleep. He thought about pacing, but his aching feet told him he'd done enough of that today. He wondered if anyone would come for him. Perhaps DI Lambert wasn't there. It was a Saturday, after all. He cursed himself for not having waited and made an appointment. But he couldn't wait; there was too much he needed to get off his chest.

They seemed to take pleasure in keeping him waiting. More than once, he did fall asleep, his head snapping back in response to its sudden fall forwards. Half an hour must have passed by the time he heard the click of an electric lock. A door opened, and a thin man in a grey suit that hung off his bony frame emerged from the corridor beyond.

'Detective Inspector Lambert,' he said, extending his hand. He sounded bored and mildly resentful that Kash had interrupted his day. 'We've met, of course. I'm guessing that's why you asked to see me personally. Mr Devan, is it?'

'Doctor,' Kash corrected. He remembered Lambert more clearly now; the mournful demeanour and the smell of cigarettes that clung to him.

'Of course, *Doctor*. Well, *Doctor*, why don't we step through here where we can have a quiet chat.'

Kash followed Lambert along a bright white corridor and into a bare room. Inside there was a desk, two chairs, and recording equipment mounted on the wall. One of the walls was mirrored and, in its face, Kash saw himself as the detective must have seen him: exhausted and bedraggled.

Lambert wrinkled his nose. 'I'm sorry about the rather barren office, doctor. Just like the NHS, I imagine. No money in the kitty for paint and pictures, I'm afraid.' He waved to a seat on the opposite side of the interview desk. 'Can I sort you a coffee?'

'That would be great. The NHS runs on caffeine.'

'NHS strength it is, then.'

Lambert slipped out of the door, leaving Kash alone with only his reflection. Just being here gave him the jitters. It was hard to sit in an interview room like this, so familiar from countless TV dramas, without feeling as if you were about to be interrogated. The chairs and desk were attached to the floor, presumably so you couldn't pick them up and hurl them at your accuser. He took a deep, slow breath to lower his heart rate and wiped his sweaty palms on his trousers, aware that he was already showing all the signs of a guilty conscience.

The door reopened, Inspector Lambert using his knee to press down on the handle whilst holding a disposable plastic cup in each hand. He put them down rapidly, then blew on his fingers. 'Bloody cups. Hot coffee turns them to napalm.'

As Kash took a tentative sip of the scalding liquid, Lambert produced a thin buff folder from beneath his arm and began to scan its contents.

'The desk sergeant tells me that you wish to discuss your boss. Is that right?'

Kash nodded. 'Yes. I—'

Lambert interrupted him. 'I've your statement here, Dr Devan. There! Signed in your own fair hand.' He flourished the document as if he'd scored a point, then handed over the sheaf of papers. Kash didn't need to read it. He'd given the statement, just like everyone else, and the next morning, a PC had brought them back, neatly typed, for them to read and sign in black ballpoint pen. Here was Mr Trenchard's downfall in all its banal, titillating detail, and Kash remembered every word.

'I haven't come to change my statement, Inspector. I wanted to see somebody because I've got some concerns about what happened to Mr Trenchard. About the case.'

Lambert sniffed. 'You do realize, Doctor, that there is no *legal* case here, civil or criminal? Mr Trenchard took his indulgences a step too far, some might say, but there was no legal requirement for him to desist from throttling himself with a noose, no legal requirement *not* to dress up in hot harlot panties. Bar finding out how he got the morphine, there's no case to be solved.'

Kash once more took a deep breath, struggling to keep his voice even. 'But surely . . .'

Lambert sensed his distress and took an avuncular tone. 'Look, I understand what a shock this all must have been for you. I'm sure you've seen plenty of blood and guts in your time, even a young and inexperienced doctor like you, but finding your boss, a man you no doubt admired, in that . . . situation, must have come as a blow. For him to finally show his true colours—'

'True colours?' Kash suddenly found his voice again. 'This is what I'm trying to tell you. I'm not sure it could possibly be the way it looks.'

Lambert raised an eyebrow. 'Because he was such a decent, upstanding chap? Take it from me, men like Trenchard, they're good at hiding their ... predilections. Year after year, up to all sorts, and nobody any the wiser. Even his wife probably had no idea. And then one day they get a bit cocky, if you'll pardon the phrase, and hey presto, there's their dirty washing for all the world to see.'

Kash shook his head. 'That's not what I mean. I mean it doesn't add up. Why not do it somewhere more private, for a start?'

'For the thrill of it,' Lambert said, happy to despatch that lazy full-toss to the boundary.

Kash realized he'd strayed badly from the script he'd rehearsed on the way to the station. Lambert was now looking at him almost sadly, as if he was some kind of idiot. 'Take it from me, *Dr* Devan, people like your Mr Trenchard always think they're too clever to get caught.' He spread his hands in a 'who knows?' gesture.

'But the door was unlocked!'

'Maybe part of him wanted to be caught? That's not unusual, either. Trust me.' He started putting the documents back in the file. 'Was there anything else?'

For the first time, Kash felt uncertain. What did he know about the world of sadomasochists, people who got pleasure from pain, from being humiliated, who put nooses round their own necks to enhance their orgasms? Nothing. He was a total innocent in such matters. So maybe Lambert was right. He'd obviously seen this kind of thing before. Maybe Mr Trenchard had got an extra kick out of thinking he might be discovered. It was all so utterly incomprehensible to Kash, perhaps he should just stop interfering and leave it to the professionals.

Then he remembered the reason he'd finally summoned up the courage to come here. He was a professional, too. He might not be an expert on autoerotic asphyxiation, but he knew a thing or two about medical procedure.

'Yes, there is something else, Inspector. The needle in his arm – the butterfly needle. It was in his left arm. Back of the left hand, in fact.'

Lambert started toying with a pen, showing his impatience. 'I've read the reports. So?'

Kash leaned forward. 'Putting a needle into yourself is a fiddly procedure at the best of times. Mr Trenchard was left-handed. That would take quite some dexterity. If he'd put the butterfly in himself, he'd have put it into his *right* hand.'

Lambert raised an eyebrow.

' . . . which makes attaching a syringe of morphine to it really hard without dislodging it. Unless someone has two hands to hold it.' Lambert put the pen down, as Kash continued. 'But it's more than that. Has anyone even asked who called the crash team? Mr Trenchard himself? Unable to release the noose, he makes the crash call . . . and crashes.'

'It's possible.'

'It's very unlikely, surely,' Kash insisted.

Lambert narrowed his eyes. 'Are you suggesting someone else was involved?'

Kash hesitated. He hadn't worked it out. He just knew the evidence didn't add up. It was up to the police to join the dots, wasn't it? That's what he'd imagined: he'd tell them what he'd seen, what it suggested to a doctor, and they'd just say, 'Thank you very much, we'll take it from here,' and Kash would be done with it. But DI Lambert didn't seem to be interested.

'Look,' Lambert said, placatingly. 'I'd put it to you that this wasn't the first time Mr Trenchard had indulged his baser instincts. Maybe Friday night was his *special* night, every week? We policemen are like you poor doctors – we only see it when it goes wrong. So maybe your Mr Trenchard liked a gamble. He's that sort of man. He's a surgeon. He's in theatre every day. An ampoule of morphine is easy enough to lift from a hospital theatre. And as for that needle in the left arm? Well, manual dexterity – isn't that what makes a top surgeon? Who cares? Choose an arm, any arm!'

'And the phone call?' Kash insisted. 'What about the crash team . . .'

'Even you agreed that it was possible.'

'Unlikely.'

'Unlikely in your eyes, but still possible. He's gone too far. The noose is stuck. Faced with a choice of life or death,

Doctor, most of us tend to opt for life, whatever the situation. That's human nature. Trenchard was no different. His last conscious act was to dial 333.' Lambert folded his hands in front of him. 'I think you'll find that all hangs together, to coin a phrase. Don't you think, Dr Devan?'

'No. No . . . I don't,' Kash said, surprised at how vehement he sounded. 'I think' – he swallowed hard – 'he had help. He didn't do this to himself. Someone did it to him!'

There. He'd finally said it.

Lambert just looked at him for a moment, then the corners of his mouth creased into a smile and he started to laugh.

Kash felt his heart-rate rising, feeling utterly humiliated, as Lambert's loud guffaws finally dwindled to a last little chuckle.

'Forgive me, Dr Devan. I'm sure you were very devoted to Mr Trenchard. And it's understandable you're finding it hard to deal with what's happened. But I think you need to face the facts. Nobody did this to Mr Trenchard except himself.' He snapped the folder shut and put it down firmly on the table. 'This case is closed, Dr Devan. Or, perhaps, Miss Marple?'

20

When he was drifting, he couldn't really think, not properly, and he sometimes forgot who he was or what had happened to him. Mostly the blackness remained, but there would occasionally be a bright light at the end of the tunnel. The afterlife beckoning? More likely, something had happened to damage the occipital pole at the back of his brain where the 'seeing centre' sat. Generally, then, the sensation was of being no more than a speck of fragmenting effluent, flushed through an endless, and rarely illuminated, sewerage system. On and on, smaller and smaller until . . . eventually he would stop, the sense of buffeting would end, and he'd come back to himself. He could feel his body again, or bits of it. But more importantly he could think. And the first thought he had was, ah, so this must be waking up. When I'm suddenly small, a pinprick, no more, and weightless, and the currents carry me away, that must be when I'm sleeping. When I stop, then I'm awake. I'm myself again. And I can think.

I can also remember.

Funny the order it all comes back, he thought. First childhood, apparently. All sorts of strange things he didn't even know he had a memory of. Being in a pram. Then falling off a swing and banging his nose. The first time he'd ever seen blood. It was all so vivid, that at first he'd been confused, and even thought for a moment that he was still a child. But then other memories came, in a great rush, like pieces of a jigsaw being furiously fitted together by an unseen hand: school, homework, rugby, a girl with blonde plaits laughing at him, names and faces, on and on, into medical school, a woman smiling at him and taking his hand – Isabelle! – the first time he held a scalpel – his hand steady as a rock – faster and faster as he got nearer to the present, a blur of images, the Victory, Nurse Vale mopping his brow under the lights, a patient, a woman, unconscious . . . then a final furious fast-forward that left him dizzy – and the picture was complete. He was whole again.

He felt an immense sense of relief.

He wanted to breathe. He so wanted to breathe. But he couldn't feel air passing through his mouth or nose. Why not? No matter. He knew who he was. Now he needed to find out where he was and how he'd come to be there.

Don't panic, he thought. Be logical. That was what he was good at. Go back into your memories and fast-forward to the very last one, the thing that happened before ending up here. That would explain everything.

* * *

Trenchard threw his surgical scrubs to the floor, slipped the silk suit jacket from the hanger in his locker and strode from the changing rooms. All he wanted now was that glass of claret. He'd been thinking about it all day.

The storm that had been threatening all afternoon had now begun its assault on the Victory hospital. As Trenchard made his way through the empty halls, the distant squeaking of a ward trolley was drowned out by shrapnel-bursts of rain slamming the skylights above, like rice being flung at tin trays. It would be a dreary journey home tonight – but, then, Trenchard had no intention of making the journey, not yet. Isabelle would be waiting and he couldn't bear the thought of forced television and empty talk. Better his own company than that.

Besides, the claret was waiting.

Trenchard's office might have been in the basement of the outpatients block, but there was nothing dingy about it. The mahogany desk was decorated with a simple crystal decanter, a sheaf of papers awaiting Trenchard's name – and, in pride of place, a small bust of Socrates, a gift from a suitably grateful patient, next to a box of expensive cigars. He opened the box and took one out, slicing off the tip with his silver cutter – another gift – before holding a match to the end. He sucked the aromatic smoke deep into his lungs. In the background, the coffee maker gurgled – but that could wait. Instead, he opened the decanter and permitted himself a glass of the rich, light-filled claret.

On the ceiling above, the smoke detector flashed a desultory warning but made no noise. Trenchard had disabled it long ago. For some, rules should not apply.

Lounging in a cloud of rich smoke, he wondered what music would best match his mood. It had been a long day. He'd known that he should never have tried to bypass the arterial narrowings in the old fart's legs. The pipes below were no more than threads themselves. But colleagues elsewhere had pronounced the patient inoperable. And as much as he'd wanted to help the man, he also wanted to prove the upstarts wrong. The grafts had failed almost at once and he'd had to resort to some heroics to get them going. Which he had. The ache in his arms and back was a small price – and one that could be numbed with wine.

He was sliding Holst onto the turntable when he heard the door begin to open. 'Mars, the Bringer of War' was already rising out of the speakers when he turned.

The door was two thirds open, and it was dark in the corridor outside. The figure standing there was little more than a silhouette, framed in the dull office glow. Trenchard tried to adjust his eyes, but all he could see was the trench coat covering the body, the dark hair tucked down into the collar.

'Michael.'

That voice – almost unrecognizable. But then the figure drew back the hood.

'Oh,' Trenchard ventured, with just the hint of a smile, 'it's *you*.'

'Who else?'

The figure stepped into the office and, in moments, the door was locked behind her. One by one the trench coat buttons came undone. Inch by inch, the body beneath was revealed as she held Trenchard's gaze. She was just the same as he remembered from last time, every inch of her.

Trenchard ground out the last of his cigar, drained his glass and drew himself up, towering over the new arrival. With his eyes still on her, he loosened his tie. She would do the belt. It was what she was here for. There could be no other reason.

When she stepped toward him, his breathing deepened. He could see her milky flesh appearing, glowing in the lamp-light. Mastering himself, he took a step back. The woman stepped slowly past him, reached for the record player and turned up the volume. Holst roared, and the desk shook. He watched as she turned to face him. Somehow, when she was looking the other way, the trench coat had slipped open even further. A dark triangle of hair revealed itself below her waist, just where the folds of the coat still touched.

'Sit down, Michael.'

So it was to be like this. She liked the charade, pretending she was the one in control. He would let her have her way, if only for a little while. Trenchard returned to his chair and lay back. Now she was on top of him. Her finger was tracing his jaw, a bright-red nail sliding under each of his shirt but-tons, slowly, deliberately popping open each one. Her coat fell like a blanket between them – and now she was on her knees, tracing that same sharp finger around each of his nipples, down the ridge of his stomach, exploring the knot of his navel and further, further down.

Trenchard held his breath. Soon, his belt was undone. Then the buttons on the waistband. Her hand closed around him. When her lips enveloped him he lay back and closed his eyes. One hand groped for the decanter. With the glass too far away to pour, he drank straight from the crystal. With the touch of her lips every nerve in his body quivered.

This is going to be one to remember, he thought.

21

'He laughed. He literally laughed.'

Kash took a sip from his bottle of lager, briefly noting that he had been all but teetotal only months ago. The alcohol had done nothing to calm him, his pulse racing all the more as he relived the moment. Tiff and Claire sat together on the other side of the table, which had already accumulated a decent number of empties, the buzz of a Friday night crowd in the Balti ebbing and flowing around them.

'Bastards,' Tiff said, simply, taking a deep pull of her own beer.

Kash wasn't sure if she meant the police or just men in general. Now that he'd spent a bit of time with her in Claire's company, he'd got used to her generally sour feelings about the male sex. But it still made him feel uneasy. If all men were bastards, that included him. Which meant she could hardly be happy that he and Claire were together.

Not for the first time, he wondered about Tiff's feelings for Claire. They had a bond, that was clear to see. And Tiff did seem genuinely protective of Claire. But was there more to it? After his interview with DI Lambert he was wondering if he was in fact hopelessly naive about sex, about men and women and what they did together. Did everybody have a secret life, like Michael Trenchard, that no one else knew about? Was it even obvious to everybody but him that Tiff and Claire were lovers? That would at least explain why random people kept asking him 'How's it going?' with a smirk.

Well, right now, he wasn't at all sure how it was going. He'd expected sympathy if not actual outrage at DI Lambert's treatment of him, but didn't seem to be getting it from Claire.

'It was very unprofessional of him,' Claire soothed. 'No doubt about that. I mean, you can't just laugh at people who are trying to help.'

'It wasn't just that,' said Kash. 'He didn't even listen to what I was telling him.'

'About Trenchard injecting himself?'

'Yes, he just dismissed it.'

Claire and Tiff shared a look.

'Well,' Tiff began, 'you can sort of see where he's coming from. I mean, maybe Trenchard was ambidextrous.'

Kash was getting fed up with people talking about Trenchard in the past tense. 'He isn't!' he said too loudly.

Tiff sat back. 'Wow, steady, Sherlock.'

'I just mean,' Kash said more evenly, 'that it would have been more natural to inject himself with his left hand. That's all,' he added sulkily.

'Well, I'm not sure you can exactly call injecting yourself with morphine before putting a noose over your head natural, can you?' Claire countered. Beside her, Tiff tittered.

'Fine,' Kash said, knowing he should try and chill out, but finding it impossible. 'Now everybody's laughing at me.'

Claire gave Tiff an admonishing look. 'Nobody's laughing at you, Kash. We're just trying to be objective. I'm sure the police have considered all the facts. If they found evidence there was someone else involved, they'd be pursuing it. Or maybe that detective was just embarrassed you'd shown him up, because they hadn't thought of it themselves. He's probably looking into it as we speak.'

'I doubt it,' Kash grumbled.

Tiff shrugged. 'Either way, there's nothing else you can do, is there?'

'You've done your best. And I think it was very brave, actually,' Claire said.

Kash didn't think she sounded very sincere. He had meant to tell them – well, tell Claire, anyway – about the tap. Just to see what she thought. But now he was glad he hadn't. No doubt she would have dismissed it as just one of those things that happen in any busy hospital. Just as DI Lambert had dismissed his theory about Trenchard being injected by someone else. He needed something more solid. Something no one could shrug off as a coincidence or an accident.

'Come on, Doctor,' Tiff said brightly. 'I get enough gloom and doom from nine to five in my job. It's Friday night and I, for one, intend to get pissed.'

She and Claire clinked bottles, and Tiff held hers out for Kash to do the same. Reluctantly, he complied.

'Right,' said Claire. 'Let's call it an education, Kash. Where are we going to go after this?'

22

How strange. To remember what he had experienced so intensely, every sensation almost unbearably vivid, when now his body felt as if it was somewhere else, a million miles away, unreachable. Unplugged. He thought about what had happened next.

*   *   *

He was still concentrating on the mounting ecstasy, eyes closed, when he felt her hand pressed into his. At first he thought she was clinging to him, but when he opened his eyes, he saw the tiny plastic bag around which his fingers were closing. He lifted it up. A familiar smell. Amyl nitrate? And . . . something else? Something sweet.

He reached down to run his fingers through her hair. How did she know? She just did. She knew everything he wanted and more. He brought the bag to his nose and inhaled deeply. Instants later, the rush hit him. The world receded, leaving him alone with his pleasure.

One of her hands was around his buttocks. She gripped him, taking him deeper, and suddenly he was lost. Hypnotized. His world was only the pleasure of her lips, the exquisite pain of her fingernails raking his flesh. He breathed in again. At that moment, not a thing in the world could have wrenched him out of his reverie. The hospital might have burned down around him and Michael Trenchard would not have cared.

The pain, when it came, was so little different to her fingernails that, at first, he barely noticed. Just a pinprick of discomfort in the constellations of pleasure through which he sailed. The pleasure and the pain were inseparable, intermingled, echoing and amplifying each other. But then that one point started burning more fiercely than the rest. He looked down – just in time to see the 2 ml syringe dropping out of her hand, back into the small leather case she had open at his feet. But the pleasurable sensations were so overwhelming that he paid no attention.

His breathing quickened. His tension mounted. It had never felt like this before. It would not be long. He started to gasp – gasp with pleasure, gasp with anticipation; then, finally, to gasp . . . for breath.

Something had changed. This faintness he was feeling, it was not ecstasy. He could feel his heart. It was hammering, not with excitement – but with panic.

Trenchard knew at once. He'd seen the effects enough times, the way it made a body flutter then freeze. He was becoming paralyzed – not just metaphorically. The needle had been her own poisoned dart. Curare?

Suxamethonium.

Trenchard had often watched anaesthetists at work through the small round window in the door separating the anaesthetic room from the operating theatre. To take over the breathing in an emergency, the muscles had to be rapidly paralyzed, and there was something strangely exhilarating about watching someone's power being sucked from them. In his panic, he tried to remember. There must be something he could do? Suxamethonium was a powerful drug. It raced remorselessly around the bloodstream, reaching the tips of each nerve, wherever they met the body's muscles. There, where specialized connections carry nerve impulses across to the muscle, the drug caused the connections to short out, showering off small electrical impulses until they ceased to conduct at all. That, Trenchard knew with terrifying clarity, was what was happening to his body now. His connections were being fried. The messages sent from his brain to his muscles were being cancelled along the way.

He tried to take a breath. The effort was immense. Just like the patients on his operating table, he was losing all power. Without an anaesthetist to take over their breathing, the patient draws no breath. They go blue. Two minutes, and irreparable damage to the cerebral hemispheres – the thinking part of the brain – begins. Much longer, and the brainstem itself begins to die. The connections between the thinking brain and the peripheral nerves are destroyed. Finally, the brainstem gives up. The heart slows and stops. The patient is dead.

He repeated that last thought to himself, locked immobile and powerless in his personal prison. He was about to die.

With that realization came a strange kind of calm – but it was not acceptance; it was only the suxamethonium infiltrating the deepest parts of his body. Even the muscles of his middle ear were becoming weaker. The sounds of his own breath grew louder, then softer, then distorted. In that same moment his body tumbled forward, no longer able to keep itself upright. He slumped in the chair, sank to his knees, tried to reach for the desk to steady his fall – but the muscles of his arm simply refused to respond.

Her arms were around him now. Her naked breasts pressed up against him. She supported him as he sank downwards, laying him quickly and efficiently upon the neatly splayed coat. No breaths came now. His vision was fading to black, the storm of blood pounding and pulsing in his ears. He slipped from the surface and sank beneath the waves.

23

Over the next week, Kash had resolved to just carry on as normal, to stop obsessing about Mr Trenchard and concentrate on impressing his new boss, Dr Carney, which felt as if it was going to be an uphill struggle. Carney gave the distinct impression, without actually coming out and saying it, that Mr Trenchard, for all his surgical brilliance, had been too much of a showman, and had recently been focused more on polishing his image than on the current needs of the hospital – which as far as Kash could tell, meant meticulously following procedure, filling in paperwork promptly and trying not to overspend the hospital's budget. Kash, Carney seemed to feel, was guilty by association: as Mr Trenchard's favourite, he must surely be liable to the same deficencies. His message had been clear: now that Mr Trenchard was out of the way (he referred, through pursed lips, to his 'unfortunate accident'), things were going to change, and brash young whippersnappers like Dr Devan would be quickly put in their place if they didn't knuckle down. With Dr Carney's angular face, still pocked with acne scars, blade-like nose and piercing eyes, Kash couldn't help thinking of a Soviet Commisar, gleefully running the palace now that the Tsar had been deposed.

'I appreciate that you have spent much of the last six months working for Trenchard.' There it was. Just a surname on a register. No longer a person. 'It'll be odd to have now to care for him. I trust that you have the necessary . . . fortitude? That you can remain professional, whether you view him as hero and mentor, or distasteful deviant.' He smiled coldly.

It felt as if he was being tarred by association. He was a tainted product. But he'd show Carney. He'd be the doctor he always wanted to be. The doctor Michael Trenchard had tried to train him to be. Exceptional. Kash nodded. 'Yes, sir.'

* * *

When he entered the ward, he made a point of stopping at Liz Murray's bedside first and only quickly glanced over at Mr Trenchard, who was slumped sideways in his chair on the opposite side of the six-bedded bay, a couple of spaces down.

He looked at Liz's chart, then felt her calves for clots and checked her lungs. Physically she seemed to be in fine fettle, apart from the fact that she was dying. But she definitely wasn't her normal cheery self.

'Are you sure he can't see me?' she asked, pointing across the ward at Trenchard.

'If it worries you, we can get you moved to a different bed.'

'I don't mean that. Can he see? He stares and stares all day.'

Kash was about to launch into an explanation of how 'seeing' wasn't really anything to do with the eyes, it was something that happened in the brain, and Mr Trenchard's brain was no longer functioning, then decided against it.

'No, Liz, he can't see.'

'Terrible . . . terrible,' Liz muttered, shaking her head.

'Yes,' Kash said simply.

'He was a gentleman, I'll tell you that much. Came to see me himself. Took an interest, even in an old woman like me.' Kash could see tears forming in her red-rimmed eyes. 'I can't believe he's ended up here. Such a cruel thing . . . so cruel. A man like him . . .' She turned to Kash. 'Is it true then, all those things they're saying about him?'

Kash stiffened. 'What things?'

'In the papers. All those stories. Sister Vale, she came in and snatched them all up, so nobody would read what they were saying. But Mr Duffy, the one with the cough – keeps me up all night sometimes, hawking and spitting like I don't know . . .'

'What about him? What did Mr Duffy do?' Kash asked, sounding more impatient than he meant to.

'Complained, didn't he? Said if they didn't bring his paper back he'd sue. Sue! Who does he think he is? Silly old fool. He only wanted it for the racing. The horses – or was it the dogs? And *that's* a fool's game if ever there was one. Both of them. Anyway, she had to bring them back. Didn't look happy about it, but she did. Practically flung them at him. The look on her! And there it was, all over the front page!' She patted her chest, over the heart. 'It takes a bit to shock me, I can tell you, but I almost . . . well, I won't tell you what I almost did, but it made me feel sick – sick to my stomach. And then the stories . . .' She grabbed Kash's arm. 'I can't believe it. Not Mr Trenchard!'

'You shouldn't believe everything you read in the papers, Liz.'

'I don't. That's why I'm asking you.'

'Some parts of it are true,' Kash relented. 'What happened here in the hospital. But you know the gutter press; a lot of it seems to be made up.' Kash thought about the story Hilary Williams had told Ange, about Trenchard propositioning her.

'Which parts?'

'Well,' he said carefully, 'there seems to be a lot of speculation about his private life, with no evidence. "Sources close to the hospital" and all that sort of nonsense. People just making stuff up, basically.'

'Awful people,' Liz muttered. 'They shouldn't be able to get away with it.'

Kash shrugged. 'People tend to say unpleasant things when they know the person can't answer back. Sometimes just to sell papers. Sometimes to get their own back for some slight, however small.'

She looked appalled. 'Why would anyone want to get their own back on Mr Trenchard?'

'I don't know, Liz. I guess anyone who's successful has ene-mies. People who are jealous of their success. You said not everybody likes him.'

Her brows knotted. 'Did I?' She thought for a moment. 'Oh well, for someone who isn't popular, he seems to have a lot of visitors.'

Kash felt his blood beginning to boil. 'I thought we'd stopped them? The journalists, you mean? And the photog-raphers?'

Liz shook her head. 'Not those lowlifes. They've learned their lesson after Sister Vale turfed one out only a few weeks back. Grabbed him by the scruff of his neck!' She chuckled at the memory. 'No, not them. There's a young bloke, turns up with an older lady. Lovely hair she's got. Silvery. I heard them say he's her godson, but I don't believe a word of it.'

'Why not?' asked Kash.

'Well,' Liz went on, 'I can't see much without me specs, and they're still at my son's, so I can't really make out faces. But I can see some things well enough. Like when they say goodbye . . . you don't have to have the eyes of a hawk to see he's touching her up. Hands all over her bottom! Godson, my arse!' she said gleefully. 'I tell you what, if my godson ever did that to me, he'd get a lot more than a clip round the ear!'

Kash was intrigued. 'How many times have you seen them?'

'Oh I don't know – three, maybe four, and that's only the times I've been watching, mind. I doze off most afternoons.'

'You said he gets lots of visitors. Who else do you see?'

She thought for a moment. 'Girls, mainly. I shouldn't call them that, should I? Some of them are doctors. I can see the white coats. And then there are nurses. And then ones in blue uniforms. They must be cleaners, I suppose.'

No, not cleaners, Kash thought to himself.

Kash let Liz ramble on for another ten minutes, then said he had to go. He'd check on Mr Trenchard later. At the nurses' station, Sister Vale was looking at the duty roster.

'I see you were chatting up our Mrs Murray,' she said without looking up.

'She told me one or two interesting things,' Kash replied.

She put the roster to one side. 'Such as?'

'Mr Trenchard gets a lot of visitors, apparently.'

'Hardly surprising, considering his reputation.'

'Yes, but there was one she took particular notice of, or rather two. A couple. A young man and an older woman. Liz said he was "feeling her up" – in front of Mr Trenchard. Rather odd behaviour, don't you think?'

Sister Vale made a dismissive sound. 'Overactive imagination, that one. She doesn't know what she's seeing half the time, and the other half she makes it up. I wouldn't pay her too much attention.'

She seemed adamant, and Kash decided not to pursue it.

'I'm sure you're right.' But he did have another question he wanted to ask. 'There was something else, though, while I've got you.'

She raised an eyebrow.

'Hilary Williams – the anaesthetist.'

'I know who Hilary Williams is,' she said.

'Yes, of course. I was just wondering – somebody told me she was hard up for cash, after her husband died. He made a lot of bad investments or something, and left her with nothing?'

Sister Vale snorted. 'I don't know who told you that. You need to improve your sources if you want to keep up with hospital gossip. Not that it's anyone's business, and I don't know exactly how much, but I know for a fact he left her pretty well off. Well enough off that she didn't need to work again, anyway. I think the only reason she carried on here at the Victory is because Mr Trenchard begged her.'

'Oh, I see,' said Kash, who didn't see at all. The more questions he asked, the less he understood.

There was only one person who could untangle it all, he thought.

And he was the one person who wasn't talking. Who couldn't talk.

24

Kash struggled to sleep. For two hours he'd tossed and turned, his thoughts a chaos of contradictions. Could he be wrong about Mr Trenchard injecting himself? Was he clutching at straws, desperate to avoid the truth: that the man he had admired was in reality a pervert who would also abandon patients in need? Everybody seemed to want to believe the worst of Trenchard now. But were people just trying to make sense of that terrible tableaux in his office, restrospectively attributing to him a history of imagined sexual misconduct? How often in the mess had he heard people saying, 'Now that I think about it, there was always something a bit creepy about him . . .' But then there was Hilary Williams. Had she made that story up? Or was Sister Vale the one not telling the truth, loyally covering up for the man she'd worked alongside for twenty years?

It was, of course, much easier to accept that Mr Trenchard had always been a monster than that he was the victim of a malicious and cunningly executed attack that had rendered him a living corpse – with his reputation in tatters into the bargain. It would not only be easier, Kash had to admit, it would also be good for his relationship with Claire. She was never less than supportive, but he sensed that her patience would sooner or later run out. In the end, would he have to choose between the living dead and a beautiful, funny, sexy young woman?

Now *that* was definitely what they called a no-brainer, he thought wryly.

If he was going to pursue this, he realized, he'd have to do it on his own. He certainly had no intention of going to DI Lambert again, just to be humiliated. Which meant he'd have to try and figure it all out himself: firstly *how* it was made to look as if Mr Trenchard had accidentally half-killed himself; and then, *who* had done it and *why*. Kash felt ill-equipped for the task on so many levels, but in a strange way, DI Lambert's dismissal had emboldened him. It wasn't exactly part of the Hippocratic Oath, but wasn't he bound, somehow, to pursue the truth, whatever the cost?

When sleep finally came, his dreams were no less turbulent than his daytime thoughts, a roiling mass of disturbing images, ending with a long and complicated dream in which he was lying on a trolley in the ICU, unable to move, Claire leaning over him with a sad expression, as his monitor trace became flat and its alarm was triggered. Bleep. Bleep. Bleep.

He bolted upright, breathing hard, and reached out reflexively for his pager. Rolling over, he silenced it, read the number, lifted the receiver of the bedside phone, and dialled, his heart still thumping against his ribs.

At first, he expected the bark of an angry registrar. Or perhaps it was Dr Carney demanding him on ward, or Sister Vale dragging him up to ward fourteen. But he wasn't on duty – was he?

'Kash, it's Ange. You haven't forgotten, have you?'

'Forgotten?'

'Edmund Chaloner,' Ange said. 'The inquest starts in, what, three hours . . .? We were going to get breakfast?' She paused. 'I was going to *buy* you breakfast. Something to fortify us, down at the Hombre? Kash, are you listening?'

He tucked the receiver between ear and shoulder as he reached for some clothes.

'On my way.'

He wrenched the wardrobe open to snatch at his one smart suit and a shirt straight from the dry-cleaning packet. He shaved while chewing on some toothpaste. Then he was out the door.

He couldn't believe he'd forgotten. It just showed how much was going on his head that the inquest wasn't the thing keeping him awake. But the strange truth was, he realized, going to the inquest would be not so much an ordeal as a blessed relief from the hospital, haunted as it was by Mr Trenchard's restless and unquiet spirit demanding justice.

* * *

The Hombre styled itself as a Mexican breakfast bar, which seemed simply to mean green peppers in the eggs, chilli sauce in bottles, and nachos with everything. Even the nachos.

Kash never did have an appetite for any breakfast beyond caffeine. Angela would normally add cigarettes and peppermint gum. Whatever, her nachos sat untouched in a bowl to one side, her fingers trembling each time she lifted the coffee cup to her lips.

'DTs?' Kash ventured. 'You don't shake like that when you hold a scalpel. Thank God.'

She raised her head, but didn't smile. 'Courtroom quaking. The fear of what I can't control.'

Kash ordered a coffee of his own, his eyes wandering over the other customers. To the right sat a man with a thick, heavy beard, his multiple layers of clothing, split shoes and darkened complexion suggesting a life on the streets. It seemed to Kash that all-night cafés were the last sites of holy sanctuary, where a small offering to the Gods of the Gullet could be exchanged for a roof over a wanderer's head through the cold hours of the night.

'What is it with you, Kash? You don't look anxious at all . . .'

He smiled. 'It's quite nice to be in a situation I can't control for a change, to be honest.'

She shook her head. 'There speaks a man who's never been to an inquest. You remember all the years of exams? Two for A-levels, six at medical school, and always the fear of fucking it up no matter how hard you'd worked? Well, an inquest feels like going into an exam for which you can't prepare and where they're actively *trying* to fail you. The examiners don't want your grades – they want your blood . . .'

Kash took a sip of his coffee. 'How many have you been to?'

'Only one,' she admitted. 'But I've heard the stories. And for me, one was quite enough. I was a doctor in the emergency department, doing a locum weekend. Some chap came in with a headache. Said his girlfriend insisted. He'd been drinking hard all the day before, after playing a rugby match. Still smelled of booze, as a matter of fact, but he seemed well enough. All the bloods were fine. There was nothing on his neuro exam. I'd wanted a CT scan but the chap plain refused. Just didn't like the thought of all those X-rays. All he really wanted was some painkillers, he said. We laughed about it. He said he supposed he deserved a headache, after a session like that. And I agreed, Kash. "Divine retribution" I called it! Only, when he got back home and his girlfriend sent him to bed to sleep it off, it was the last thing he ever did. He was dead in bed the next morning. Turned out he had a massive extradural bleed pressing on his brain.'

'Oh, Ange . . .'

'I got it easy at the inquest, actually. I'd made really clear notes. And the family were good about it too. They even sent me a card, thanking me, if you can believe it. Grief does some funny things to you. The coroner said I wasn't to blame and that was that.'

She stopped talking. For the first time, her fingers weren't trembling as she put the coffee cup to her lips.

'The thing is, I *knew* I should have pushed him. Call it an instinct, whatever. Made him have the scan. But I just didn't. And that night the Chaloner boy came in – I had the same feeling, Kash. I *knew* he was sick. That I couldn't do it, and needed a consultant. That I *needed* Michael Trenchard. And instead I marched on anyway . . .'

Kash reached out and took her hand. 'Nonsense, Ange. It *wasn't* your fault. You tried to get him. *I* tried to get him. We couldn't. And the boy couldn't be left. You know that. You *had* to press on. It's not your fault that Mr Trenchard was off doing what Mr Trenchard was doing and . . .'

There was silence as both Kash and Ange stared into their coffee cups, reading the runes of the sediments within.

Kash was first to speak. 'What about today?'

'It could be bad,' Ange whispered. 'I can't imagine the coroner being quite as friendly to me this time around.'

'Switchboard will have logged all my calls, Ange. I can testify. We tried to call him. I even called him at home. His pager, his telephone – we did everything we could.'

Ange was up on her feet, heading for the door. 'It goes deeper than that, Kash. It's *me*. I wasn't up to the operation. If I couldn't get hold of Trenchard, I should have called another consultant in.'

Kash caught up with her and followed her out, turning up his collar as their breath fogged the air. 'Ange, there wasn't time. Edmund Chaloner would be dead if we'd waited. And you'd be beating yourself up just as much. You—'

'That's not the point. It's not the reality, but the perception. I should have been *seen* to call another consultant, and I didn't.' Together, they walked to her car. 'I'm exposed here, Kash, and you know it.'

Suddenly the inquest seemed far less like a day away from the hospital. Wherever he went, Trenchard would haunt him.

25

There, she thought, he's gone. But her work was far from done. Slipping a plastic Guedel into his mouth to depress his tongue and keep the airway clear, she reached into the small leather bag once more. She lifted out a black rubber bag and pressed the portable mask attached to it to his face. Supporting his jaw with one hand, she squeezed the bag firmly with the other. One, two, three, four, five. She smiled, watching as Trenchard's face turned from black to blue to its old ruddy hue, fresh oxygen surging back into the blood. One, two, three, four, five. One, two, three, four, five. Somewhere in there, she knew, Trenchard was surfacing, called back to the light.

She stopped, placing the bag and mask to one side. Moments later, she had a tourniquet in her hands. She rolled back his shirt sleeve, tightened it around his biceps, and ran her fingers along the veins in his left hand, flicking them to engorge them further. Again, from the bag, she produced a green butterfly needle, and deftly slipped it into the vein at the first attempt. She would leave no bruises. Trenchard was aware now. A moment later, he felt a cold flush in the vein.

A second syringe. Atracurium, thought Trenchard, understanding now what was happening to him. That would extend his paralysis.

Once again came the drive to breathe, the pounding heart, the black ocean sucking him down. But once again, her fingers clamped beneath his jaw, pressing the mask to his face. His chest rose and fell. One, two, three, four, five. One, two, three, four, five. One, two, three, four, five.

Then she stopped. With splayed fingers, she hauled his eyelids upwards, lowering her face to look deep into his eyes.

'Does it feel as if you're dying, Michael? Well, I'm not going to let you.'

What did she mean? Trenchard's body cried out for more breath, but his tormentor had returned to her case. From its bottom she produced one of the hospital oxymeters, and clipped its split-thimble clamshell over his middle finger. The LCD display lit up, a beep just about audible to him through the Holst, its tone reflecting the blood's oxygen level. The woman glanced down. 'Heart rate one-seventy, oxygen saturation ninety-six per cent. Pink and paralyzed and petrified.' She kneeled and watched as, slowly, the oxygen started to deplete. The beeps became faster, their tone lower. Nonchalantly, she returned to the mask and began manually inflating his lungs. 'Relax, Michael,' she whispered. 'I have control now.'

The oxymeter showed his blood saturation at only 76 per cent. With each squeeze of the bag she brought it back to 80, to 90, to 95. 'Good,' she said, gently stroking his forehead. 'You don't have to worry about a thing. But I wonder . . .' Here she paused before inflating the bag. On the oxymeter, the heart rate started to spike as it fought desperately to pump what little oxygen it had around his body. 'How does it feel, Michael?' she leaned closer and whispered in his ear. 'What's going through that head of yours? What's happening in there?' She again pried open one of his half-shut eyes, certain he could see her peering in. 'I'll say this fast,' she began, one hand caressing his hair, sweeping it back from his eyes. 'You must be feeling pretty faint by now.'

She toyed with the bag, watching as his oxygen levels slipped once more and his heart rate surged in response. Slowly, somehow, she found a pattern: just enough terror, just enough life left in the bastard. One, two, three.

She leaned close to his ear and whispered. 'Do you know why I've done this? Do you know why it had to be me? Think about all the things you've done in your life.'

When she drew back, she was no longer smiling. A few more breaths from the mask, and one last look at the oxymeter. The moment was right.

'I have some things for you, Michael.'

She reached into her bag and, from the bottom, pulled up a stack of magazines. These she splayed around the floor and desk above. Whether Trenchard could see or not hardly mattered. He would know exactly what kind of magazines these were.

'Control, that's what turns you on, isn't it? You controlled everything, everyone around you – but now that's gone. You'll never have control again. You can feel it, can't you?' In the background, the tone of the oxymeter was in freefall, as the blood supply to his body dropped. 'Every second, brain cells dying. Every second, your future fades. Will you ever control *your limbs again? Stand? Feed yourself? Control your bowels? I don't think so, Michael.'*

She fed him some breaths. Literally, a handful as she squeezed the bag. One, two, three. His heart rate 160. His oxygen at 44 per cent. And for the next ten minutes, she continued, holding the oxygen levels just high enough to sustain life, but low enough to damage the brain.

'Oh,' she said, finally, 'I almost forgot one thing.'

The laces were easy, and the shoes and socks quickly slipped off. The trousers and underwear, already round his ankles, were next. She had the black lacy knickers bundled up in the pocket of the overcoat. It was a bit of a struggle with a man of Trenchard's size but, with some effort, she hoisted them up. Saturation: 34 per cent. Then, with the same breezy motion, she produced her pièce de résistance: the rope. It had already been tied in a neat hangman's knot. She fed it over his lolling head, pleased with the rough abrasions it produced when she tightened it around his neck. For now, the blood could no longer return from his head to his heart. The pressure in his veins rose. The heart rate hit 190, and then fell dramatically as his face became engorged. Small blood vessels popped in his eyes. Little red dots appeared. Petechiae. She loosened the noose just a little.

She was arranging him into the best possible position when, out of the corner of her eye, she saw a flutter in his chest. At last, he was breathing of his own accord. As the oxygen levels rose in his blood, she lifted the mask from his face. The pattern of his breath wasn't good. Sometimes it stopped, only to start up again.

Cheyne Stokes ventilation. It was only to be expected. Even his brainstem – the most primitive part of the brain – was struggling to survive. She hoped she'd not overdone it, that he would still know, still be, well – in there somehow. Enough to suffer properly.

A final syringe would help keep him going, at least until the doctors got there. Four milligrams of dexamethasone, a powerful steroid. Perhaps it would stop the brain swelling too much too soon.

She surveyed the scene. The monitor was safely stashed away, as was the gauze soaked in glyceryl trinitrate and the anaesthetic halothane was sealed up. In its place, she'd left a similar bag of gauze and just the glyceryl trinitrate. His hands were cupped inside the black lacy panties he now wore. She knelt and gave him one last shot – a tiny dose of morphine, enough to constrict his pupils further. She squirted the rest on the carpet and threw the ampoule to one side.

She stood back to survey the scene. Before her, a naked man in women's underwear, surrounded by pornography. A bag of GTN-soaked gauze. A noose around his neck where he had been strangling himself for sexual pleasure. The knot jammed. A failed slipknot. Facial petechiae confirming he'd overdone it. A needle in his hand where he had been giving himself morphine. Too much morphine. The ampoule left lying at his side would confirm the dose. Too tight a noose. Too little oxygen to the brain.

How disgusting.

How pathetic.

How sad.

There had been two things that Michael Trenchard lived for: his reputation, and his ability to control those around him. In a matter of minutes, both were gone. Goodbye reputation – and farewell control.

Holst was still booming through the speakers. Leaving the scene of tragedy behind her, she lifted the needle from the record and picked up the telephone at its side.

* * *

In another basement, a line lit up on the hospital switchboard. 'Crash desk?'

There was no voice on the other end of the phone, only loud music.

'Crash desk?' she repeated.

And still there was no answer. Momentarily stunned, she looked at the extension number flashing in red lights on the switchboard; 232 was Mr Trenchard's office – but surely that had to be an error?

Lives had been lost on hesitations like this. She spun in her office chair, punched a code into the console and spoke: 'Cardiac arrest. Mr Trenchard's office, outpatients department. Cardiac arrest. Mr Trenchard's office, outpatients department. Cardiac arrest. Mr Trenchard's office, outpatients department.'

26

Kash was surprised by the coroner's court. He had expected to find some cinematic courtroom, all gavels and gowns, wigs and witness boxes, mahogany, mellow lighting and 'm'lud', but in truth the building was more like a parochial town hall. Plastic chairs had been arranged in neat rows in front of a small oblong table. To its right, only eight feet away from where Kash and Ange took their seats, sat an elderly form mistress of a woman, straight-backed and immobile above the shoulders. As the courtroom prepared, she set about organizing her papers and pens and some form of typewriter, by the look of it. Kash and Ange exchanged glances but said nothing to each other as they waited.

Anna Chaloner, Edmund's mother, sat in the front row in a plain grey suit, her hair pinned back sternly, face immobile. There was a dignified beauty to her. And it was only now that he got to wondering what she was thinking, how hard it must be to even manage routine daily rituals, let alone come here to face an inquest with no one to support her.

At precisely nine o'clock, the coroner entered. Taking his place behind the small desk, he positioned a large lever-arch file in front of him. Dressed in a slighty shabby dark blue suit, his headmasterly look perfectly matched that of the form-teacher clerk who sat nearby. When he spoke, his voice was deep and sonorous – and he only had to raise it very slightly to silence the room.

Anna Chaloner was visibly nervous now. Through the other bodies, Kash could see her fingering a small gold locket that hung around her neck, rubbing it between her fingers. Perhaps it contained a picture of her boy, or a lock of hair from when he had been a baby. Kash tried not to think about it.

The coroner opened his file and started to read.

'Case 45-417. The inquest into the death of Edmund Chaloner, aged fourteen. It is to be noted that Mr Chaloner died at the Victory Hospital, having undergone emergency surgery. It is further noted that the testimony of Professor Whitely, the pathologist acting for the Home Office in this matter, is not disputed. Post-mortem serological examination confirms that the patient was infected with the Epstein Barr Virus.'

He looked up from his notes and scanned the court room. Epstein Barr was one of the most common viruses a person could contract; almost 90 per cent of all adults would show signs of prior infection if they were to be tested. Most never knew they were ill. For some, infection seemed nothing more than a common cold. Others developed debilitating glandular fever, and perhaps chronic fatigue. But in rare cases, it could prove fatal.

'Edmund Chaloner suffered a rare, but recognized, complication of this illness,' the coroner went on, 'that of spontaneous splenic rupture. It is further accepted that such a complication carries a high attendant risk, and a significant associated mortality. None of these facts are in dispute.'

Then what are we here for? Kash wondered. This would be a simple cut and dried case. He relaxed, and glanced at Ange. Then his pulse quickened once more. There was a dead set to her eyes. She stared forward, intently. This was the look of *anticipation*. She was waiting for something to happen.

'It is an uncontested matter of record that, under normal circumstances, such a death might not be subject to a formal inquest such as this . . .'

Kash tensed. 'Ange,' he whispered, 'something isn't right here, something . . .'

Some heads were turning towards them. 'Be quiet, Kash.'

'In addition,' the coroner went on, his voice rising fractionally again, 'I am mindful of the fact that proceedings such as these may cause distress to the child's mother.' He looked to his left. 'You have my apologies. We shall do everything in our power to ensure that today's events cause as little such distress as possible. No, today's inquest is held in response to information received from one of those involved in the care of the deceased.'

Now Kash understood. He turned to Ange once more, but she would not look at him.

'For those of you unacquainted with such matters, the individual who signs a death certificate must be confident the death was not due to violence, privation, or neglect. In this instance, the certifying doctor could not provide such assurance. Under such circumstance, it is a matter of legal process that a post-mortem examination and inquest be held. To make such responses is to choose the more difficult path – a choice for which the certifying doctor should be commended. However' – and here the coroner looked up, scanning the crowd until he found Angela sitting there, her knee trembling instinctively – 'I would appreciate more factual, and less theatrical, referrals in future.'

The coroner coughed and returned, momentarily, to his notes. In the fleeting silence, Kash hissed, 'What did you do, Ange?'

'Later, Kash.'

'Not later, Ange. *You're* the one who brought this on? You could have completed that certificate yourself . . .'

1a – Direct cause of death: splenic rupture. 1b – Factors which led to that: glandular fever. 2 – Other factors contributing to but not directly causing death: none. The coroner would have accepted that, surely. And yet something Ange had done had dragged this to court. Whatever she had done, it had also dragged Anna Chaloner into this room, to live again the moments of her only son's death . . .

'You reported him missing, didn't you? Missing in action . . .'

At the front of the room, the coroner was speaking again. Ange replied in a strident whisper, 'Somebody had to.'

'Those called to give evidence will be sworn to tell the truth in its entirety. Any perceived lack of gravitas associated with this environment,' he waved a hand around the room, 'should in no measure be taken to infer any laxity of process. Witnesses will give evidence under oath. As in any court, the full weight of the law may descend upon any who might choose to tell incomplete truths.

'This case may involve discussion of the appropriateness of behaviour of the staff involved. In particular, the role of a Mr Michael Trenchard will be the subject of scrutiny. Few of us here can be unaware of the recent reports of Mr Trenchard's illness. However, I must point out that Mr Trenchard is not on trial here. Indeed, the purpose of a coroner's court is not to establish guilt or culpability, but merely the facts. Neither should any reports which one might have read in the papers be in any way considered pertinent to this case. The propriety of Mr Trenchard in the management of this patient must be viewed in isolation.' The coroner paused, seemingly for effect. 'All this said, let us begin.'

* * *

Anna Chaloner was the first to take the stand. She walked to the coroner's side with what seemed to Kash great effort, holding her head up high. As she sat down, and before she read her oath from a small laminated card, the coroner offered his further condolences. Kash thought it seemed like an empty gesture, considering what was to come.

'Mrs Chaloner,' the coroner began. 'Might we start by explaining, to the court, a little about the evening in question.'

'Edmund was my only . . .' She was about to say 'child' but changed tack suddenly and said 'son' instead. Her voice had an edge of steel to it, flinty, without a tremor. To Anna Chaloner, this was a reckoning, the final chance to speak about her son before returning to the terrible privacy of grief. 'I had a daughter once, but I was young – a young fool, you might say. So when Edmund came around, I knew I had to cling on to him with everything I had. Even when his father left us, I knew it would be OK, because that was how much I loved Edmund.

'But when he got sick . . . I'd done some training to be a nurse myself, and I just knew something wasn't right. He'd been off school, which wasn't normal, not for Edmund. Our doctor thought it was flu, so when it got worse, I just did as he'd said and gave Edmund paracetamol. It wasn't until he got the abdominal pains, though, that I took him in. He looked grey. He was sweating, icy cold. So I got him in the car and rushed him here as fast as I could . . .'

Anna described the emergency department, how a very nice doctor called Marcus had been with them at once.

Marcus, she said, had examined her son with speed and compassion, taken blood samples, put up a drip and immediately called another doctor.

'Is that other doctor in the room?' the coroner asked.

Anna Chaloner lifted a finger. 'She's there. Dr Warner. Dr Angela Warner.'

'What happened next, Mrs Chaloner?'

Angela seemed to have come straight away. She'd brought with her the other doctor, Kash Devan, and after another quick examination, they'd announced that they needed to operate at once.

'Did Dr Warner offer a diagnosis?'

'No,' Anna replied, 'but you could see in her face it was serious. I signed the form without hesitating. But that was the last I saw of Edmund . . . alive . . . as they wheeled him away towards the theatre. I gave him a kiss. You know. "See you soon." The next time I saw him . . . Well, it wasn't him. Just his body.'

It was the first time Anna Chaloner had betrayed her devastation. She paused to smear the tears on each cheek. Only when she was finished did the coroner, respecting the moment, resume.

'And Mrs Chaloner, can you tell me – do you have any concerns?'

'Plenty,' Anna replied. 'How to cook for one. What to do on a Saturday afternoon now that I'm not taking Edmund down to his football. But about his operation? No, none at all.'

'And you had heard that Dr Warner operated alone?'

'I had.'

'That Mr Trenchard had not been in attendance in his capacity as senior surgical opinion?'

Anna Chaloner nodded.

'And were you aware of the difficulties Dr Warner and Dr Devan had in contacting Mr Trenchard that night?'

'Not at the time, but . . .'

Kash tensed. Surely, she *had*. He'd been standing only yards from her when he'd been making the calls. He felt Ange, at his side, likewise freeze.

' . . . I'm quite certain everything that could have been done was done. Mr Trenchard wasn't there, but Dr Warner did everything she could. I want . . . I want to put this to bed, you see. Nothing is bringing my Edmund back, nothing at all. They tried to save my son but it was too late to save him and . . .' She looked around, found Ange in the sea of faces. 'I want you to know: it was nobody's fault.'

It was a beautiful balm, a simple homeopathy of few words but great power to soothe Angela. But there was something else in them, something that Kash found hard to fathom. This was too calm, too measured, too . . . *understanding*. A beloved fourteen-year-old boy snatched from the world, a man to blame being offered up on a platter – and she'd turned it down.

'Ange, they're calling you.' Kash nudged her firmly.

At his side, Ange was lost in a reverie of her own.

'Ange, it's your turn on the stand.'

She looked at him abruptly, as if only now coming to her senses. She straightened herself, stood, and strode to the front of the room.

After she had taken her own oath, Ange began to recount that night in the Victory. There was no drama to it, none of the flourishes of a storyteller with a point to prove, but a scalpel wielded by an expert surgeon: pure, cold, surgical steel. Never make an unnecessary cut. Only cut when you can see your target . . .

'The spleen had ruptured by the time we got in there. With the first incision, it was evident. We tried to staunch the bleeding but Edmund died there, on the operating table, and didn't respond to resuscitative measures.'

'I want to come back to the start of the events in hand. You tried reaching Mr Trenchard, but he was not to be found?'

'I had tried, and I had failed. I then instructed my colleague, Dr Kash Devan, to continue those efforts.'

'Yes, I have his statement here. We may yet hear his testimony separately, but perhaps recount for us . . .'

'Mr Trenchard did not respond to his pager. We were confident he was not in the Victory – we'd called his office and he wasn't in the operating theatres. Kash tried to locate him at St Philippa's.'

'St Philippa's?'

'The local private hospital, sir. He wasn't there. But it turns out he *had* been: earning money when on call for the NHS. But now he had gone. Nor was he at home, where he might otherwise be expected to be. In fact—'

The coroner cut in sharply, silencing Ange before she could go on.

'Let's keep to the night in hand, shall we, Dr Warner? Allow me to paint a picture. Mr Trenchard could not be found, the boy was in a life-threatening situation – and, as senior surgeon on site, you decided to carry on alone. Is that correct?'

'It is.'

'And you felt capable?'

'For most eventualities, yes.'

'For this case?'

Ange hesitated. Then, haltingly, she said, 'Probably.'

'Was probably enough?'

'It had to be. The boy was in trouble. Minutes mattered. The on-call consultant couldn't be found. There was no more time to waste trying to contact the uncontactable. So I did what I had to do. I carried on alone.'

'How did you feel about this, Dr Warner?'

Ange spat out a single word: 'Bitter.'

'Bitter and angry?'

'Bitter and . . . furious.'

'And is that why you signed the death certificate as you did, Dr Warner? Out of anger?'

Ange pitched forward, as if accusing the coroner directly. 'Yes, I felt angry. I'm in a court under oath and I don't mean to lie – not to anyone, not today. But I didn't do it because of what I felt. I did it because to have acted dishonestly would also have been to act illegally – but, more than that, it would have been *wrong* as well.'

'Dr Warner, you may retake your seat.'

Angela did not move.

'Dr Warner, have you something else you wish to say?'

'Edmund Chaloner,' Ange began, drawing herself up, filling her lungs with air, 'had a life-threatening illness. He would have died without an operation. He might have yet died with one. But his chances were not improved by the lack of availability of a senior surgeon. A man who had abandoned his NHS patients that evening in favour of private ones. A man who, some might speculate, had put his own financial interests, and his personal and sexual ones, above the life of a fourteen-year-old boy. A man who—'

The coroner rapped sharply on his desk. 'Dr Warner, might I remind you that no man – let alone a man currently incapacitated himself – is on trial in this courtroom. The purpose of an inquest, as you already know, is to establish cause of death, not to apportion blame.'

'The cause of death, in this circumstance, is directly con-nected to—'

'Dr Warner, we have heard enough. Take your seat, please.'

Kash stared directly at Ange. There was a moment in which she refused to move, a moment in which she locked her eyes on the coroner as if to say: make me. But then, across the other heads, somehow, she saw Kash as well. His eyes were pleading with her, and something inside melted away. Quietly, her head now bowed, she returned to her seat.

Meanwhile, the coroner returned to his notes, scribbled in his ledger, and looked up. 'It is my duty,' he proclaimed, 'to reach a conclusion as to the cause of Edmund Chaloner's untimely death. This is the sole purpose of this hearing. And it seems clear to me that the patient suffered a rare and life-threatening complication of a common – and usually minor – illness. It was this of which he died. The verdict as to the cause of death must therefore be one of natural causes.' The coroner paused to lower his half-moon glasses to the desk. 'However,' he went on, 'I would add a narrative verdict. There are aspects of this case which do indeed cause me alarm. In particular, the behaviour of the consultant surgeon in question would seem to leave a great deal to be desired. It is not my place to pass further comment, nor to investigate. In light of Mr Trench-ard's current condition, obtaining further testimony from Mr Trenchard himself would seem impossible. Nonetheless, I shall be referring this case to the General Medical Council, with the recommendation that the professional competence and judgement of Mr Trenchard be the subject of review. I do this whilst appreciating that such investigation may have little direct impact upon Michael Trenchard's future professional registration. I recognize, however, the importance of such transparency in maintaining the confidence of the public in our medical profession, and in warning other surgeons who might be similarly tempted, that shirking personal and professional responsibility is not considered acceptable. And so I end this inquest by saying: verdict – death by natural causes. This case is closed.'

27

They drove in silence, the regular squeak of the windscreen wipers filling the silence where conversation should have been. The crowd had dribbled rather than poured out of the courthouse, Anna Chaloner disappearing into the rain-slick streets. Kash had stared after her, wanting to say something, anything – wondering all the while why she had seemed so undisturbed at Ange's declarations, why she was not lashing out like a wounded animal – but, by the time he had formulated a sentence, she was gone, off into a waiting taxi and away. Instead, he had followed Ange.

At the lights, Angela opened the glove compartment with her left hand to rummage for her cigarettes. The lighter clunked out, and she drew against its hot orange rings. Through the smoke, Kash watched the traffic ahead.

'Pull in, Ange.'

She glanced at him briefly, anxious not to take her eyes from the rear red lights of the car ahead. 'What?'

'Come on, Ange. We need to talk.'

'We're running late. We've got to . . .'

He cut in, his voice calm and measured. 'Ange. Just pull the car over, please.'

This time she did as she was told. Beneath the railway arches there was a supermarket car park and she swung into it, through the deepening rain.

'I had to do it, Kash. He was wrong. And he'd been getting away with it for years.'

'You know, everyone keeps saying it about Michael Trenchard: that he'd been getting away with *it* for years. But if that's the case, if he'd been marching around the Victory turning everything he touched into ash, well, why didn't anybody say anything? Why the garlands and awards? Why does everyone crawl out of the woodwork now to say what a bastard he was?'

Ange fumbled for another cigarette. For this, there was no answer.

'You should have told me, before we went in there. You should have told me it was *you* who'd pushed for this. And all to . . . to do what? Expose Michael Trenchard – after the fact, when he can't stand up for himself, when he isn't there to put up a fight? That's . . . cowardice, Ange. If you really thought that about the man, you had years to . . .'

Ange studied her cigarette, watching as a finger of grey ash slowly developed. Her voice was low.

'I had to go to patient affairs the next day. You know, to do the certificate. I planned to just sign it. The mother wasn't going to cause a fuss. Sometimes they don't – they just don't want more pain. So I could have done it. Just signed it. You know how hospitals work, Kash. In there, you're a prisoner to reputation. Doing anything else wasn't going to do me any good – certainly not to my career prospects . . .' She paused. Then, through tight lips, 'I could have done it, but my hand, my heart wouldn't let me. It wasn't right, Kash. Trenchard murdered the boy. He used my hands, but he did it. And if I'd said nothing before about his behaviour, it was because I had put my own career first. If I said nothing now, it would have been worse. I couldn't do that.

'I couldn't sleep that night, Kash. I couldn't even close my eyes. The next day, I sat there in the patient affairs office with my pen in hand, about to sign the certificate. 1a – Factors leading directly to death: ruptured spleen. 1b – secondary to: Epstein Barr Virus infection. 2 – Factors contributing to death without actually causing it . . .' She paused. 'That was when I did it. I had to tell the truth. So I wrote: "DERELICTION OF DUTY BY A SENIOR SURGEON" in capital letters. And I put a ring around *neglect.*'

'So when the coroner said you'd been theatrical . . .'

'It makes it sound so tawdry, doesn't it? And perhaps I should never have done it. I saw Trenchard that same day. The bastard was all smiles, business as usual. But he knew something was up. And then I was called by a trust manager that morning . . . The woman in the office had actually given the certificate to Anna Chaloner. She'd called them back, asked them what it meant. They called it a clerical error and came after me. All hell broke loose. I'd have been up before the trust with an axe over my neck, but for some reason Anna Chaloner didn't cause a fuss.'

She didn't cause a fuss today either, Kash thought. She glided through the inquest as if it barely mattered to her. Perhaps that was just the numbness of death. Perhaps it was empty days and quiet nights, the sudden evaporation of love and hope. But she had seemed so serene. Most grieving people lashed out, wanted somebody to blame. Anna Chaloner wanted only to keep her head down, accept fate, and move on. There was something admirable in that. But perhaps there was something unnatural too.

'After that, I knew it was going to go horribly wrong. Nothing was ever going to stick to Michael Trenchard. One by one, witnesses would drop out. I'd have been left on my own.'

Kash grasped her by the shoulders, held her so that he was looking directly into her eyes. 'You're forgetting. It was *me* who made those phone calls, *me* who tried to pin him down. I'd have—'

'Oh, Kash, you're a good man, but you're *Trenchard's* man, still.'

'Ange, Mr Trenchard was good to me, but it wouldn't have—'

'It would, Kash. For everything a man like him hands outs, he exacts a price in return. If Trenchard had bent your ear, what would you have said? When the issue of your career came up? Your reference? If everything fell down around you, what then? What if you had to go back home, tail between your legs, nothing to show for everything your family did for you but letters after your name and bad debt? Would you really have done the right thing? He had control, Kash. He always did.'

Kash was silent for a moment. Then he whispered, 'I would, Ange.'

Ange's face was slick now in the storm's light. For the first time, he saw the tears that were streaming down her cheeks. 'You have to look after yourself in this life. And you would have done, just like all the others, when push came to shove.'

'I think you underestimate me, Ange.'

Ange picked herself up, drying her eyes on her sleeve. Tears gone, she seemed suddenly in control of herself once again.

'Kash, this has gone far enough.'

She reached for the ignition and started the car, but Kash put his hand on her arm.

'One more question, Ange. Only one – but I want an honest answer.'

'Don't you understand what I did today? Kash, I'm honest to a fault,' she said bitterly.

'Then answer me this. Did Mr Trenchard – did he get what he deserved?'

She shrugged his hand off, stared fixedly at the road ahead.

'You want an honest answer?'

'Yes.'

This time, when she turned to him, she was not trembling at all. Now she was as calm and still as only the very best surgeon could be.

'Yes, Kash. Yes, that bastard deserved everything he got.'

28

When Michael Trenchard first realized that he could see, he felt like crying with joy. The psychedelic lightshows of his sleeping state, interspersed with bouts of ultra-vivid recollection, had an extraordinary intensity. Nothing could compare with the simplicity of reality. But when truly thirsty, cold water would always beat champagne. And it proved beyond doubt that he really did have quite considerable brain function. And that it was improving.

And just as importantly, as far as his morale went, it meant he was reconnected with the world, even if it was, he surmised, the rather depressing world of ward fourteen. He couldn't 'look around': his eyes were fixed in one direction, or rather, two, meaning that he had unpleasant double vision. But by concentrating, he found that he could unite the images in his mind, leaving him with tunnel vision. And the first sight of peeling grey paint around a light-fitting – once he'd recognized it for what it was – was a revelation. He was a shipwrecked sailor, adrift for an eternity without hope of rescue, but now cast ashore. The atoll might be bare, but it was home. And a place to regroup, get strong, build a signal fire, await rescue and move on.

But the joy was short-lived. He watched in time-lapse as the paint seemed to peel further around the light-fitting. Was this it? This barren little island of reality? His focus was fixed, unable to see what was happening to left or right. And then – how exquisite! How exciting! – a nurse crossed his field of vision. She had a plastic apron over her green uniform and wore yellow rubber gloves. Clearly she was about engage in one of the less pleasant tasks of her day. Thickset, with a waddling gait, bleached-blonde hair framing a pale, pinched face, she was, to Trenchard, a thing of beauty. Or had once been. How sad he couldn't remember her name, if he had ever known it.

And then she was gone, and the light-fitting was back. He called out to her. Come back! Don't leave me! But no sound came. He was mute bar a whistle that seemed to come from his neck. He was just a face with no mouth. No more than just a pair of staring eyes. His heart-rate quickened, the sudden panic of one who wakes up to realize he's been buried alive and has no way of alerting the assembled funeral-goers. I'm here! I'm alive! Somebody open this damned coffin!

He tried to calm himself. A porter came through, pushing a meal trolley, trailing steam and the scent of custard and overcooked cabbage. So I can smell, if not sniff, too. And hear. He'd been aware of the ward's muffled mumblings for some time now, he realized, without the sounds resolving themselves into actual speech. But now he was beginning to decode the odd word from the static, before whole sentences started to rise to the surface.

'What's this soup? I never asked for soup.'

'You always have soup, Annie. It's tomato, your favourite.'

'Tomato soup? I don't like tomato soup.'

'Oh dear. Would you prefer the vichyssoise?' Laughter. 'Here you go.'

His heart-rate rose again. My God. Was this it? His future? Was he to sit here, soaking in banality and mundanity? At least a man of his stature deserved a room of his own. Why hadn't Isabelle . . .?

'Hello, Michael.'

He heard her before he saw her. That warm, gentle sing-song voice that had been the soundtrack to his professional life for as long as he could remember.

Sister Susan Vale.

'Time to turn you over. And then we'll get you cleaned up a bit.'

She moved into his vision, looking down at him sadly, but with a tinge of something else, like a teacher disappointed in a prize student. Her eyes found his, and she stared long and hard into them, as if seeking a response. But then she looked away. Torture! She saw him as blind or inanimate, unaware of the emotions she had stirred in him by her mere presence. A moment later, the world tilted violently as he was turned on his side and then all he could see was the green of the curtain surrounding the next-door bed.

He felt pressure. His bottom being wiped? From the smell, yes. But all the while, he could still hear her voice, firm and business-like, telling him what she was doing. Did she really think that he could hear her? Of course not; it was just the habit of a lifetime, the same soothing professional voice she used on every patient, a way of showing that you were treating them as a human being, not just another body to be cleaned and fed and medicated. In truth it was more for her own benefit than the patient's – who was more often than not in no state to appreciate it. Sister Vale, he decided with a lurch of despair, was just going through the motions.

'Going through the motions'. Ha, he'd made a joke. Even if a poor one.

'Can you help me, please, Irma?'

The world tilted again, as he was lifted by strong hands, off the bed and into his chair. Objects zoomed in and out of view as the angle was adjusted, and then everything steadied and he found he had a new viewpoint. He was now angled towards Mrs Murray. My God, was she still hanging around? She was propped up in bed staring back myopically at him, as if she was trying to remember who he was.

Then she raised a bony hand, fluttered her fingers and gave him a wave.

* * *

He must have fallen asleep. All the excitement of a busy morning on ward fourteen had worn him out. Being fed, washed, medicated, put in his chair, put back into bed, being turned. Being examined – not medically but quizzically, by *the great unwashed masses, even patients shuffling over on their zimmer-frames to peer at him as an exhibit. But he had no door to shut. He just had to wait for his little window onto the outer world – if you could call ward fourteen the outer world – close of its own accord, the light fading, the sounds dwindling to nothing, and then the other sights and sounds, those of his inner world, to take over.*

At first it was rather pleasant, just drifting in a slow-motion vortex of ever-changing shapes and colours, a tiny shiny lump in a lava-lamp.

Then the pulses of colour gradually began to take on recognizeable shapes.

Things. People.

The shapes started to group together, to organize themselves into memories.

One particular memory.

A memory that was like a door.

On one side was life, in all its sensuous glory.

On the other was this.

She was standing there, in the doorway to his office, with that seductive smile on her face, and it all came flooding back.

The pleasure.

The panic.

And finally the torment.

She gently closed the door, the smile still fixed on her face.

29

As they approached the Victory, the siren song of ambulances promised deliverance. Or death. Within, Trenchard's hunched homunculus. Kash shuddered. Did he really deserve what had happened to him? *Oni soit qui mal y pense.* Evil to him who evil thinks? Or did that apply to him, Kash, for even harbouring such a suspicion?

And was that true of Ange? The way she had said those words had shocked Kash to the core. 'Trenchard deserved what he had got.' Did that mean . . .? No, he couldn't go there.

Besides, right now she needed him to support her, to stand up for her. As he stepped out of the car, promising to see her soon, she reached out her hand and instinctively he took it. They shook formally as she held his gaze. Moments later she was gone, off to pick up on the day's work.

Kash made his way back to his flat to change. He was far too smartly dressed for ward work. As he removed his clothes, he caught sight of himself in the mirror. It had been days since he'd eaten a proper meal, and he certainly hadn't taken Mr Trenchard's advice on exercise.

'A healthy mind in a healthy body.'

He winced at the irony of Trenchard's situation now.

It was then that he noticed the bed. It was unmade – or, if not unmade, then certainly crumpled, the duvet lifted from where it usually hung over the ends of the mattress and piled up on the bed. Kash was normally fastidiously tidy – but, then, he had woken late for the inquest this morning, bolted out of the door still half-asleep, his mind full of other things. Perhaps, for once he'd neglected to put his bedding in order.

He forced it from his mind, and finished putting on fresh work clothes. But still it nagged. The bed. Something *was* wrong. He was sure he could remember it now: even in his haste to be away, he had flicked the duvet flat across the bed. He always did.

Somebody had been here while he was away – and now, suddenly down on his knees, staring into the black cavity beneath the bed, he knew why.

Michael Trenchard's holdall had been hidden here since that night. More than once, Kash had thought about how to get rid of it, perhaps throwing it off Waterloo Bridge or dragging it down to the hospital incinerator, a supplement to its usual diet of amputated limbs and medical waste. Yet every time, something had stopped him.

And then he'd forgotten about it.

He reached beneath the bed, but his hands found nothing. He lifted the mattress to peer down through the slats. The holdall had been there this morning, but now it was gone.

He whipped around, imagining that somebody might still be there. And yet, when he had come back, the door had been locked. The windows, which looked down onto the narrow gap between the hospital buildings, rickety fire escapes and boilers huffing steam, were closed and uncracked. Nothing else – not a thing – in the room was different from the way he had left it. And yet . . .

On the bedside, his pager bleeped. It was ward fourteen. He glanced at his watch. Almost 2.15. He needed to get going.

*　*　*

Kash was determined to 'see every patient every day'. A lot of patients were under his care now, and he was determined to get to know them properly, even if, in the grand scheme of things, there was nothing much he could do for them. Whenever the chance arose, he decided, he'd choose one patient, and sit with a pot of coffee – all night if needs be – to read their notes, before performing a complete general medical examination.

First in line was Mr Sinclair Creedy, one of the long-stay patients. With a neuro tray under one arm, Kash set off up the ward and found Creedy already out of bed and eagerly awaiting him. Creedy, Sister Vale had warned, was a garrulous old boy who would talk Kash's day away if he got the chance. But Kash didn't mind. In fact, he'd welcome anything to distract him from the inquest, his nagging thoughts about Mr Trenchard, the knowledge that someone had been in his room – and the appalling idea slowly dawning on him, that these things might be connected.

This examination was from earhole to anus, and every orifice in between – the full works – but Kash knew within a minute of speaking with Creedy that he was doing it for appearances and nothing else. Creedy's breath came in short wheezes, he pursed his blue lips with each expiration, and every now and then he'd bark out a rattling cough, stirring a soup of secretions around somewhere deep in the last vestiges of his lung tissue. Kash was nevertheless scrupulously thorough and professional: there might be nothing to add which could help this man – but at least he could show him and Dr Carney that he was taking his new job seriously.

The skin of Creedy's neck hung in turtle-folds. The chest boomed like a bass drum when tapped. The skin of the old man's belly stretched like parchment over the proud protuberances of his pelvis.

Kash continued, his gloved finger revealing a hard craggy prostate. Cancerous, without a doubt. 'All fine down there,' he said. There was so little point in even recording the finding. Creedy would be gone long before the prostate caught up with him.

After an obligatory five minutes' chat (football and TV, both of which were complete mysteries to Kash), he extracted himself from Creedy and moved on to Henrietta Liu, a lady so diminutive she might have been taken for a prematurely aged eight-year-old, when Sister Vale caught his eye across the ward. There was something of a summons in the way she glowered, so, making his excuses, he followed her into the office where towers of files tottered against the far wall.

'Have a seat, Kash. I'm afraid we have to talk.'

Afraid. That didn't bode well.

The seat she was offering was the battered plastic one where she variously dressed down nurses whose standards were slipping, or consoled relatives who had stalwartly listened to bad news at the bedside and crumbled the moment that visiting hours were over. But Kash did not resist. There was a certain severity in the way Sister Vale was looking at him but, in the way her eyes creased, he could still see the same woman who had rescued him on the bus that first morning, brought him here and introduced him to his new world.

'Has something happened, Sister?'

'I'm afraid so, Kash,' she said. 'You should be aware that Dr Carney had a call from the Metropolitan Police yesterday. One of their inspectors – something about a junior doctor criticizing the handling of the Trenchard "case", as if there was any case to handle, and wasting his time with ludicrous conspiracy theories.'

Kash simply stared.

Sister Vale's expression softened. 'I'm not your boss, Kash. I'm saying it as a friend – so please try and take it that way. You don't want to get on the wrong side of Dr Carney, and involving the hospital in more controversy is exactly the way to do that. Suggesting that what happened to Mr Trenchard was anything other than a case of misadventure is just going to prolong all the negative headlines the Victory has already had to endure and keep the whole dreadful story going – exactly what the tabloids want. Dr Carney is interim medical director, as you know, and determined to restore our reputation and the best way for us all to do that is to keep our focus on caring for our patients, not indulging in wild fantasies out of some sordid crime novel.'

At first, Kash wasn't sure how to respond. Sister Vale had been close to Mr Trenchard. He didn't want to upset her. Perhaps it was better not to bring up the idea that someone had done this to him. But on the other hand, he didn't want her to think he was just making up silly stories for his own amusement.

He told her about the butterfly needle being in the wrong hand. How Trenchard would never have acted as he did behind an unlocked door. About the impossibility that Trenchard had summoned his own rescue.

Her expression darkened. When she spoke, her response was icy disdain.

'That's it? Really?'

Kash was emboldened to go further.

'There's something else. That tap I found, under Mr Trench-ard's buttock. I think someone put it there, deliberately.'

'And why would someone do that?'

'To cause him pain, I suppose.'

'You suppose.' She folded her arms. 'You think I did it?'

'Of course not!'

'One of the nurses, then?'

'I've no reason—'

'Then who?' she persisted.

He sighed in exasperation. 'I don't know. I just know there are people who think he got what he deserved.'

'Who?'

He suddenly wished he hadn't spoken. 'I don't know. I can't say.'

'Can't or won't?'

Kash felt his heart-rate rising. He had to get himself under control. Whatever happened, he didn't want to lose Sister Vale as an ally.

'I'm sorry – you're right. I'm not thinking straight. Look, thank you for the advice.' He got up. 'I should get on with my ward round.'

He went back to Mrs Liu and performed a perfunctory examination, hardly hearing her mouse-like chatter as he did so. Shit. So now he was in Carney's black books. And

Sister Vale was warning him off. Out of kindness? Or was there some other motive?

He stepped outside the bedspace, pulled back the curtains which surrounded it, breathed deeply and sighed. He had to think. Think about his patients, who depended on him.

Who next? Mrs Murray. He'd save Mr Trenchard for when his nerves were steadier.

Liz Murray's platelet count, he knew, was only in the twenties now, and her haemoglobin probably half what it should have been. There were plenty of white cells, but none that worked well. It was hard to know what would get her first: a bleed or an infection. Either way, there was little he could do to stop it. Much as for Creasey, seeing her in his capacity as a doctor was pretty pointless. But seeing her in his capacity as a human being was essential: right now, he needed reminding of his humanity. He turned the corner into the next bay.

Liz Murray was looking perkier than she had for a while. Only two weeks ago she had developed a chest infection. She'd fought it off in only five days. She was, as she described herself, a tough old bird. This morning, as if she was planning on going out on the town, she had even applied some rouge to her cheeks. It gave her the appearance, Kash thought, of a faded actress making an ill-advised return to the music hall stage. He quickly berated himself for being so uncharitable. He was just in a bad mood.

'You're looking very glam, Mrs Murray.'

She beamed, showing a remarkably gleaming set of teeth, none of them her own.

'Got to keep up appearances, Dr Devan,' she winked. 'You never know who's going to be dropping by.'

'And who might that be?' Kash asked with a tired smile, trying to get into the spirit, as he pulled his stethoscope from around his neck.

'Not so many now. Just the one, actually.'

For a moment he didn't know what she was talking about.

'I'm sorry? Just the one what?'

'Visitor.'

'For you?'

She rolled her eyes. 'For Mr Trenchard.'

'Ah.' He listened to the soft but steady beating of her heart, and the faint rattle of breath in her lungs. 'That woman and her toyboy – they've gone then?'

How could he have forgotten about them?

'Oh yes – more's the pity.' She chuckled. 'I quite enjoyed watching them. It brought back memories.'

'Liz!'

'Oh, don't be such a prude, Doctor. Anyway, it's not them.'

'Who is it, then?'

'I don't know who it is, do I?' she said impatiently. 'It's dark at four in the morning. And I haven't got my glasses. I still can't find them.'

'I thought you left them behind at your son's house?'

'Did I? Oh well.'

'So you couldn't describe this person.' Kash wondered if he was pushing too hard, seeming too eager. The last thing he wanted now was for Liz Murray to complain to Sister Vale that he was interrogating her about Mr Trenchard's night-time visitors or, worse, that he'd been putting ideas into her head.

Liz screwed her eyes up. 'I told you before. Perhaps you weren't listening. She's got a blue uniform.'

Oh, her again – theatre scrubs, Kash thought.

'She talked to him for ever such a long time. Well, whispering. I couldn't hear what she was saying. But she gave him a kiss. And left him a card.'

Kash looked over to Trenchard's bed. He couldn't see anything on the bedside table.

'Are you sure?'

Liz set her jaw. 'I know what I saw.'

In the middle of the night? With just enough light for the nurses to move around without bumping into things? Without your precious glasses? *I wonder.*

'Well, it's not there now,' Kash shrugged. 'It's not Valentine's Day or anything, is it?'

'No dear,' Liz said, with a little twinkle at the corner of her eye. 'That was yesterday.'

30

He walked out of the ward as slowly and calmly as he could, then once he was out in the corridor broke into a sprint. If anyone saw him, they would just think he was heading for the emergency department or ICU.

When he got to outpatients, he stopped for a moment to steady his breathing, before approaching the desk.

'Is Nurse Barker around?' he asked as casually as he could.

The ward sister looked at him quizzically and consulted a chart.

'Only covering for a fortnight. Day off,' she said without looking up.

'Right. Yes. Thank you.'

Damn.

He left the ward, found a quiet corner on the stairs and dialled her flat. Straight to voicemail. He launched into an apology as soon as it was answered.

'Claire! It's Kash. I'm an idiot. I forgot. Valentine's. I had to go to an inquest – with Angela. It was all a bit stressful . . . but I'm still an idiot. I'm sorry, I . . .'

He spluttered to a halt.

'Hello, Kash, it's Tiff. Claire's gone out.'

'Tiff? Oh, hello.' Now he felt like even more of an idiot. 'Gone out where?'

'I'm not sure that's any of your business, Kash.' She must have known he really meant 'with who?'

'Well, I don't see any reason to . . . I mean, it's not as if we aren't . . .' Dammit, why couldn't he just say what he meant? Tiff always had a way of making him feel nervous.

'It's all right, Kash, I'm just messing with you.'

'Right.' He took a deep breath, tried to recalibrate. 'So . . .'

'Where is she?'

'Yes.'

'No idea. She left me a very nice card, though.'

Goddammit, everybody was leaving cards for each other except him.

'Right. OK. Could you tell her I called – say I was sorry, for, you know, yesterday?'

'Will do. If I see her. Bye, Kash.' She ended the call.

Kash leaned against the metal bannister, a confusion of fragmented thoughts chasing each other like random scraps of paper in the wind. Claire and cards. Angela. The Chaloner boy. Hilary Williams. Sister Vale. The police and Carney. The missing bag. Torture and taps on ward fourteen. He needed to sort them out.

Luckily he had a tried and trusted method for doing that: writing a letter to his mother. Admittedly, up until now he'd skated over a lot of what was on his mind. Just as he didn't like telling her about people dying, he normally avoided anything of a sexual nature. But right now there didn't seem to be any way round it, not if he was going to get his thoughts into any sort of order.

He silently apologized to her in advance.

In fact, just the decision to write had made him feel calmer.

He started to walk up the stairs, towards his flat, then stopped and abruptly changed direction.

There was something else he had to do first.

*   *   *

He approached the double doors leading into ward fourteen cautiously. If possible he didn't want Sister Vale to see him. Ideally he'd have liked to avoid getting into conversation with Liz Murray, too. Peering through the glass, Sister Vale's desk seemed empty. He pushed the doors open again and walked in with a purposeful stride. It was a quiet time, before supper, and he was gambling that the nursing staff would be congregating in the kitchen area, preparing the food from the trolleys. As he passed the empty nursing station, it looked as if he was right. He stopped at Sister Vale's desk. If she walked in at that moment, he could still plausibly say he'd been looking for her. After that, it would get trickier. He dropped to one knee, as if to tie his shoelace.

The waste-paper bin was now inches from his foot. He breathed in and quickly peered inside.

Well, well.

He deftly scooped up the contents and transferred them to a pocket of his white coat. Then he stood up, checked he was still not being observed, and walked out the way he had come. Perhaps I'm not so bad at this sort of thing after all, he thought.

*   *   *

He had been driven by instinct to go to the bin. And now the same instinct drove him towards the mess. The lockers behind were mainly for those doctors who didn't 'live in', and used primarily for storing white coats. As he turned the corner, his eye was instantly drawn to his own locker, its door slightly ajar. He swallowed, feeling a pulse twitching at his temple, as he walked forward.

He gently pulled the door fully open, already knowing what was inside.

He peered into the open holdall and saw the glint of a pair of handcuffs; there wasn't enough light to see what else was in there but he didn't want to expose it to find out.

How long it had been there? My God, anyone passing could have seen it. A wave of nausea washed over him and he wondered if he was going to faint. Whoever had set up

Trenchard was doing the same to him. Or was it someone different, with quite different motives? And, regardless, what was he going to do? There was only one way of disposing of it. The furnace in the basement – but what were the chances of transporting it there unobserved?

Damn. Why had he ever taken the blasted thing in the first place? He certainly wasn't going to carry it through the hospital and back to his flat now. He took a deep breath. *Think.* Making an instant decision, he grabbed the bag, hauled it out and shoved it into one of the empty lockers further down the row. He then fished in his trouser pocket for his key ring, found the small silver key for his locker, closed the door and locked it firmly.

He heard the swish of a door closing behind him and caught a glimpse of brown coat. A porter. Had he been seen? Nothing he could do about that.

Hopefully, the bag would be discovered before the person who'd taken it from his flat and put it in his locker found out he'd made the switch.

He felt a chill, and for the first time it properly hit him.

Someone had broken into his apartment. Someone who knew the bag was there. And then they'd put it in his locker, waiting for someone to find it.

But the only person who'd known it was there was Claire.

And he couldn't believe she'd pull a stunt like that just because he'd forgotten Valentine's Day.

No, there was malicious intent behind this. The perpetrator wanted Kash to be publicly shamed. Discredited. He paused, as another thought occurred to him. Perhaps they hadn't meant the bag to be found at all.

Perhaps it was a warning.

Don't go poking your nose in where it doesn't belong. Let sleeping dogs lie.

He felt his pulse quicken.

The only person who would send a warning like that was the person who had left Michael Trenchard drugged, paralyzed and with a noose round his neck.

31

The problem with being a top surgeon at a busy London hospital was that you didn't have any time to think. It wasn't just that you had to make instant life or death decisions on the operating table; that was the essence of the job. It was more that there was always paperwork to file, meetings to attend, talks to be given, and mentoring to be done. Every minute of every day was accounted for several times over, and even though Trenchard had made a point of making time to enjoy himself, to savour the fruits of all that labour, there was a kind of pressure there, too – the pressure to fill every free moment with pleasure.

What he'd never had was time to simply let his mind wander. Until now.

Now there was nothing for his mind to do but wander.

And remember.

He'd been over that last night a hundred times now, and each time a new detail revealed itself, until the whole bizarre and extraordinary picture was complete. He now knew exactly what she'd done, and how she'd done it.

The only thing that was still puzzling him was why.

The first thought that occurred to him was that she was simply mad: reducing healthy, vigorous males to a state of living death was how she got her kicks. Which showed what a great judge of character he'd been. But after a while he dismissed the idea. Yes, what she'd done was by any normal standard insane, but in itself that didn't explain anything. It was really just a way of saying that her behaviour was beyond the normal range, off the spectrum. For a man who believed in science, in facts, it was intellectually lazy. Thinking about it logically, she had gone to immense pains planning the whole thing so meticulously and had exposed herself – he used the word advisedly – to some serious risks during the execution. There were easier and safer ways, surely, to satisfy your desires, however dark and perverted they might be.

He thought about that for a while, as what he was coming to think of as the nightly neurological light-show flickered and danced in the background, without coming to any conclusions. Frustrated, he wondered if he was not approaching it from the wrong direction: perhaps it was not about her *pleasure; it was more about* his *pain. Was this punishment?*

In which case, perhaps the punishment had been designed to fit the crime.

But what terrible act had he committed to merit it? He was no angel, admittedly, but surely nothing he'd ever done could match this living hell.

Perhaps she was *just mad, after all. And he would simply have to live – if you could call this living – without ever knowing what had driven her to an act of such obscene cruelty.*

*   *   *

He was woken by the sound of footsteps in the dark. Tormented by his churning thoughts, circling round and round and going nowhere, it was a relief to be reconnected to the outer world again, if only to the bare corner of it that was ward fourteen.

The soft steps came nearer. He knew it was pathetic, but he hoped they didn't start to fade away again, as the nurse or orderly or whoever it was passed by his bed on their way to another patient. Perhaps it was Sister Vale – Susan – come to mop his brow and offer some soothing platitudes. Or Kash Devan, dutifully checking his vital signs. Judging by the feeble, greyish light, and the general lack of noise, aside from the usual grunts, snores and moans from the other inmates, it must be the middle of the night. So who else could it be? Not Isabelle, hopefully. Perhaps a random porter with nothing better to do as he sleepwalked through the night shift?

The footsteps stopped, and a figure materialized out of the darkness at the end of his bed, lit only by the distant halogens along the ward.

He felt his heart begin to race.

'You!'

She came nearer, until her face filled up his whole field of vision.

'Hello, Michael. I just thought I'd come to see how you were.'

He thought he saw her smile; perfect white teeth winking in the gloom.

'No change? Good job! I must have got it just right! You should be proud of me.'

She passed out of his vision again. Perhaps now she was sitting in the chair at the edge of the bed, the one he'd spent the day slumped in. Or perhaps she was lingering over one of his shoulders, just outside his field of vision.

What was she doing? His body strained to scream or shudder, his eyes to dart.

Suddenly, for the first time, he truly felt the terror of total paralysis.

But he could feel, now.

And what he felt now was the soft pressure of her fingers walking up his leg in imitation of the dance they used to make.

What was she doing?

He felt her fingers following the line of the catheter tube as it entered his penis.

He groaned inwardly. Was this meant as some tawdry reminder of a love life long lost? To taunt him with the fact that he would never touch or be touched like that ever again?

No. Her hands had now stopped just short of his groin and were busy beneath the bedclothes. Something else, then. But what?

And then he knew. And he screamed silently.

32

'Kash, what is it?'

They were walking in a nearby park, taking advantage of the mild, clear day. The path passed by a pond, where mallards chasing each other suggested that spring was not too far away. They meandered past a children's playground where empty swings trembled in the breeze.

He squeezed her hand. 'Nothing.'

She stopped and turned him round to face her, her hands on his shoulders.

'Come on, Kash. I know you're trying to make a fresh start, make up for Valentine's and all that – not that there's really anything to make up for – and it's very nice and I appreciate the effort – the flowers were lovely – but you're not very good at hiding your feelings, you know.'

He gave her a panicked look. 'Claire! I really do care about you.'

'I don't mean that!' She smiled reassuringly. 'I know you do. And I care about you too. Which is why when there's something on your mind, you need to tell me what it is. No secrets, right? No saying everything's fine when it isn't. If we're . . . serious, we have to tell each other everything.'

She led him to a bench overlooking the pond.

'Look, I know you're making a huge effort not to talk about Trenchard and all of that. You don't want – I don't know – a storm cloud hanging over our relationship, casting its shadow over the good things, the nice things. And yes, I would very much like us to be able to go out for a drink, or a meal, or to the cinema, and spend a few hours just having fun and not thinking about what happened. But that's not going to be possible if the whole time you're just bottling it all up inside. So why don't you let it out, now, and then maybe we can move on with our lives?'

He took both her hands in his and looked deeply into her eyes. 'You're right, as usual. I *have* been thinking. But they've been some pretty dark thoughts. I've even scared myself, wondering if I'm not going a bit mad.'

She smiled. 'I'm a trained healthcare professional. Let me be the judge of that, OK?'

'OK. You're sure?'

She rolled her eyes. 'Just tell me, Kash.'

'Right. I've made a list.'

'Of . . .?'

'Suspicious things. Clues. The line in the wrong hand. His unlocked office door. The call to switchboard and the crash desk. The kit left in his open locker. And if someone drugged Mr Trenchard, then put the noose and the women's underwear on him, and left the other stuff lying around where it would be found, it had to be someone who knew him, who he trusted. Possibly someone he'd been having a . . . sexual relationship with.'

'Go on?'

'But also someone with medical training. Who could get hold of the right drugs and knew how to administer them; who knew how to knock him sideways without actually killing him.'

'And you suspect . . . ?'

'Well, that's the next bit: who could hate him enough to do it? And why? There's . . .' He hesitated; he'd never said this out loud until now, and it scared him a little. 'Anna Chaloner. Her son died and she knew Trenchard should have been there. Grief can make you do all sorts of things.

'Then there's the woman who came to visit Mr Trenchard with a younger man, and Liz said they were fondling each other in front of him.'

'Liz Murray? The one you've mentioned without the glasses? Is she really a completely reliable witness? A myopic nonagenarian?'

'Well, she seemed pretty certain. Then there's this.' He put his hand inside his coat and came out with a Valentine's card with a huge heart on the front and an arrow through it. The card had been torn in pieces and carefully taped back together with Sellotape. 'Look inside.'

Claire took the card and looked.

'The writing's a bit smudged, and it took me a while to fit the edges properly so you can actually read it.'

'*Violets are blue, Roses are red, So how does it feel, Now you wish you were dead?* Jesus. Where did you find this?'

'In the bin under Sister Vale's desk. Liz saw someone put it next to Mr Trenchard's bed, I think, so Sister Vale may have taken one look and got rid of it. Unless it was her who put it there, and then destroyed it.'

'Have you asked her?'

Kash looked sheepish. 'She's not too pleased with me at the moment. Not after Dr Carney got wind of my visit to DI Lambert.'

'Ah, I see.'

'Then there's the person who took the holdall from my apartment and put it in my locker.'

'You think that's the same person who . . . assaulted him, and left the card?'

'It would make sense. And maybe also put a bit of plastic under Mr Trenchard to cause a bedsore.'

Claire blew out her cheeks. 'It's a lot to put together, Kash. I mean, I'll admit, taken on their own, each of those things is a bit strange.'

He gave her a look.

'OK, more than strange. *Disturbing.* But do they really all fit together? Do you really think Anna Chaloner's behind it all? It's hard to imagine. And if it was her, who was the woman with her toyboy?'

'I don't know, I don't know,' Kash said, shaking his head. 'I've only just started trying to figure it all out. Angela, of course, was left in the lurch and thinks she has blood on her hands because of him. Hilary Williams, by all accounts, was pretty pissed off at being propositioned. But enough to do, well, that? Anyone in theatres that night must have been furious. They all knew. Sister Vale . . . Oh, I don't know. I need to do some more digging.'

Claire slipped her hands out of his. 'Don't take this the wrong way, Kash, but the holdall – you don't think you could have put it in your locker yourself, and then forgotten about it? You have been under a lot of pressure. I mean, you managed to forget Valentine's Day . . .' She saw his face crumple. 'I'm joking! Come on, Kash, I just don't like the idea of someone breaking into your apartment and . . . threatening you. Also, how would they have known you had it? The only other person who knew was me.'

'I know. I haven't worked that bit out yet.'

'You haven't worked much of it out yet, really, have you? I mean, let's put aside all the strange goings-on after the event, for a moment, and just look at what happened. I know you think he couldn't have injected himself, but it's all a bit speculative, isn't it? And it is just possible that he took the risk with leaving the door unlocked, and that he did manage to dial 333 just before collapsing. In which case, if people are gloating now, or even making his life unpleasant, they are just seizing an opportunity. Bullies, not attempted murderers.'

'You're right,' Kash agreed. 'But I thought of something else when I was administering some antibiotics . . .'

33

He'd been on call when Rose had been brought in. According to the nursing home, she'd been a bit shaky and confused. He did the usual tests: white count 17.8. Mostly neutrophils. Urine dipstix positive for white cells, blood, protein and nitrates. She had a urinary tract infection.

'I'll just put a drip up, so that we can give you some antibiotics.'

'Will it hurt?'

'Only a little, I promise.'

'Can I have some local anaesthetic?'

'I wouldn't usually. It doesn't hurt that much.'

'I'd rather, you know.'

He'd sighed, and glanced at his watch. There really wasn't any need. But then again . . . He'd smiled. 'As it's you . . .'

She'd smiled in return. 'You're a love.'

He'd gathered the bits and pieces together in a cardboard tray.

He'd affixed a green needle to a 1 ml syringe, cracked the 2 ml ampoule of 1 per cent lignocaine, and drew up half. Discarding the larger green needle, he'd affixed a thin orange needle and placed the assembly on the tray.

Easily carried, it would fit in a pocket: green intravenous cannula, alcohol swab – to prevent infection around the cannula – plus tape to fix the cannula when the patient moved.

Like the tape holding Trenchard's butterfly needle in place in his vein when he was found. But why would he have taped it in, if he was only going to inject once and pull it out?

He'd returned to her trolley and pulled the tourniquet tight, allowing the veins to rise. Selecting a large blue worm of a vein running on the medial aspect of the wrist, he'd injected a small bleb of local anaesthetic. The skin whitened. Now the cannula. In through the white patch. No problems.

'All done.'

The old lady had looked round, and smiled. 'I didn't feel a thing.'

'All part of the service.'

As Kash had walked to the wards, he'd thought about it some more. An orange needle was so small that you didn't even feel the scratch. Especially not if you were in the throes of passion. And you'd only need to tape a butterfly in place if you were going to move him later. Or removing clothing – or putting it on – might dislodge it.

'So you see? It all makes sense, Claire. Or at least a big part of it does.'

She looked thoughtful. 'So what are you going to do now? Go back to DI Lambert?'

Kash shook his head. 'And get laughed at again? No, thanks. Besides, Dr Carney would have my guts for garters. No, the next time I see DI Lambert, I want to have the whole thing worked out. I want to give it to him all tied up with a pretty bow so he can't ignore it.'

Claire touched his cheek. 'Oh, Kash. But I'd still rather you dropped it. It would be better for the both of us, I think.'

*   *   *

Ah, there it is. Kash always left his bumbag in the ward office. Now, had he put new batteries in his pentorch? Claire had made him worry that his memory was going. Clicking it round his waist, he unzipped it and started to rummage. *Oxford Handbook* . . . biros . . . tourniquet . . .

Shit! What the hell was that?

He pulled his right hand from his pocket. Embedded obliquely in the pad of one of his fingers was a green needle. He pulled it out. *Damn!* A dirty, used green needle. Up to its hub through the material of his tourniquet, preventing it from lying flat. How the hell had that happened? He quickly dropped it into a sharps bin. Running his finger under the cold tap, he squeezed it to express some blood. It swirled like crimson ink down the plughole. What was a needle like that doing in his bag? He never ever put used needles in there. Never.

He went out to the store room and found a gauze swab, then hunted out Sister Vale in her office.

'Just got to pop along to occupational health for a mo. I've had a needle-stick.'

Sister Vale looked concerned. 'Are you OK?'

'Nothing to worry about. I won't be a minute. Could we do our round at two?'

'That's fine, Kash. I'm on a long day. I'll bleep if we need you.'

Kash headed out. It wasn't that it hurt, although in fact it did. The needle had gone in very deep. No: it was what the needle might be carrying.

Just what he didn't need.

And almost as worrying: who had put it in there, if it wasn't him?

* * *

Occupational health ran an open doors policy for staff. Kash walked in without knocking.

The receptionist was on her mobile phone. 'Hang on, love.' She glanced up, spotting Kash compressing his finger with gauze.

'Needle-stick?'

Kash heard accusation in her tone. How could a doctor be so careless? There was no point in trying to explain.

'Sorry. Yes. Is Doc Wilson available?'

'Name and DOB?'

Kash gave her the details.

'Take a seat.'

She buzzed through, then picked up her phone. 'Sorry, darlin'. Carry on. No . . . he did *what*?'

Kash waited, trying not to listen and failing miserably, until Dr Wilson appeared with a rumbling cough. Wilson had run the occupational health department for as long as anyone could remember. People joked that she didn't look a day over seventy, when everyone knew she was at least ten years younger than that. She wore two nicotine patches, billboard badges of honour for long service to smoking.

She beckoned Kash through and waved him to a seat. She already had his folder out on the table.

'So. Needle-stick. Bad luck, young man. Happens to the best. High or low risk?'

'Well, I'm not altogether sure. A used green needle, and a bloody one at that. But no idea whose blood.'

'What was it? Sharps bin too full?'

'Yes.' Kash couldn't be bothered to explain.

Dr Wilson leafed through his file. 'Hep B titres were OK when you came. I'll give you a booster, anyway. That just leaves the HIV.'

She paused. 'Have you ever been tested?'

'No.'

'No risk factors?'

'No.'

'Sure?'

'Quite sure, thanks. I think that I'd know.'

She looked him in the eye. 'Sometimes people come to see me because they think that they might've been at risk for other reasons. That wouldn't apply to you, would it?'

Kash tried to remain polite. 'No, Dr Wilson. As I say, no risk factors.'

She tried again. Jovial this time.

'One of the great pleasures of this job, you know. I've been here so long now that everyone knows me. When people care about each other, they often come and let me know. Tip me off, as it were. You know the sort of thing. Drink problems. Depression. That sort of stuff.'

Kash smiled wryly to himself. He needn't have burdened Claire, after all. He could have just come to occupational health and poured out his heart to Dr Wilson.

She waited just a second or two more, giving him a last chance. Then she picked up her pen, and started writing.

'OK, then. We'll send the Hep B, C and HIV for the record. A dry needle is low risk, but post-exposure prophylaxis makes sense. So it's twenty-eight days PEP for you.' She scrawled a prescription, before continuing. 'Barrier contraception. Safe sex.'

He tried to sound nonchalant. 'Of course.' How was he going to explain *that* to Claire? And would she believe that the 'risk' was really from a needle?

Kash walked to the pharmacy, handed in his prescription, and waited at the hatch.

After a minute or two, the young pharmacist appeared, and presented him with a plain white paper bag.

'Enjoy,' he said.

Ten minutes later, Kash's troubles had been placed in perspective, as he started Mr Trenchard's routine daily examination – on his own. Sister Vale was nowhere to be seen. The charts were uncannily steady. Trenchard's temperature was always stuck at about 36°C, but he knew that a slightly low temperature wasn't uncommon in those with severe brain injury. The skin was warm, and very slightly sweaty. Heart-rate a bit higher than usual, at about 98 bpm.

He found it hard not to talk to Mr Trenchard as if his former boss could hear and understand him. He felt slightly foolish, remembering how he had spent hours as a boy talking to a pet goldfish as it circled mindlessly in its bowl. But it just didn't seem right to treat him like a cadaver. At first he just followed standard procedure, describing what he was going to do: 'I'm just having a look at your charts, Mr Trenchard, then I'm going to . . .' But soon, without really meaning to, he found himself talking more earnestly.

'I just want you to know, Mr Trenchard, that I don't believe you did this to yourself. I don't believe it was an accident. I think that someone . . .'

He paused.

That was a bit odd. He looked at the chart again. No. The temperature was normal. And he'd done some routine bloods only yesterday and they had been fine, without sign of infection.

Then why the heart-rate?

He continued his examination methodically until reaching the abdomen. Normally, every abdomen should be examined with the patient lying flat, and with the doctor standing to the right-hand side. But Trenchard could scarcely hop back into bed, so seated would have to do. Kash laid his palm on the abdomen's four quadrants, expecting them to be soft, non-tender, without reflex response to pressure. But they weren't. Well, the upper quadrants were. But from a line just above the umbilicus, and extending all the way to the pubis, the abdomen was solid. Firm. He percussed it. Dull.

A full bladder. A very full bladder indeed.

But Trenchard had a urinary catheter in, which had been changed only two weeks ago. It couldn't be blocked now, could it?

Kash followed the catheter towards the bag attachment, to find that it had been clamped. It was sometimes done when changing the bag system. But this one had urine in it already.

He looked at the chart. Someone had filled in the urine volumes for the day already. A cursory look, and the assumption would be made that another nurse had done the observations. Yet this catheter had to have been blocked for hours. He slid the clamp to one side and, sure enough, urine flooded the bag. Kash walked briskly to the sluice and returned with a measuring jug to decant into. Overall, Trenchard's bladder had been distended with nearly three litres of urine, inflating until the pressure within it must have almost caused it to split, while blocking the drainage from his kidneys. Hence the signs of distress: the raised heart-rate and the sweatiness. Of course, that didn't mean that Trenchard was meaningfully aware. Responses like this were reflex, automatic.

Kash shuddered. But if he *had* been aware, he'd have been in agony.

He quickly looked round for Sister Vale. She was now back at her desk, but caught his look of alarm and hurried over.

'There wasn't a problem with the catheter when he was hoisted back into bed before the evening handover, I'm sure of it.' She looked down at Trenchard, slack-jawed, expressionless, and then gently wiped a line of drool from his chin.

'His bladder?'

'Still intact, I think. But three litres – that's a lot.' He didn't put into words what he was thinking: that much urine could only have been produced in such a short time with the help of a powerful diuretic, something like furosemide.

'Oh, Michael.'

She looked back at Kash and he held her gaze. *Now, do you believe me?*

34

Together, Kash and Sister Vale finished Mr Trenchard's examination and did a thorough check to make sure he hadn't been interfered with in any other way. Neither of them referred to the clamped catheter or what it implied.

Which was just as well. When Dr Carney bleeped him, Kash doubted if he'd called for a friendly chat.

'My office, please,' Carney said before putting the phone down.

Kash hurried downstairs, not sure what to be worried about most: the business of the holdall, the needle-stick, or the continued assaults on Mr Trenchard. Soon after Dr Carney had waved him into a chair opposite his desk, he found out.

The holdall.

Dr Carney, Kash had discovered, was in almost every way Mr Trenchard's polar opposite. His shapeless grey suit, shiny at the elbows, accentuated his bony frame, as if proudly proclaiming that appearances didn't matter. He talked about people as if they were numbers: for him patients were simply statistics and hospital staff an unfortunate drain on financial resources. Kash had never heard him talk about lives – saved or improved – but only of outcomes, positive or negative, as if everything the doctors and nurses, anaesthetists, radiologists and all the rest did to improve the lives of the people in their care was just an enormous mathematical equation he was trying to solve. In a nutshell, he wasn't trying to make a difference; he was trying to balance the books. And he was happy to make it clear that as far as he was concerned, that job had been made a lot easier by the fact that Mr Trenchard was now languishing in a bed on ward fourteen instead of gallivanting about the hospital as if he owned the place, disregarding procedure for the sheer joy of it.

There was another reason, of course, that Jack Carney might be pleased to see the back of Mr Trenchard: he was now the most senior clinician in the hospital and not just Kash's boss but everyone else's, too. And if a man as uninspiring as Jack Carney had once seemed an unlikely candidate for the job, his limitations – in the light of Trenchard's spectacular fall from grace – now suddenly seemed like virtues to many on the hospital board. He might be short of creativity and have the charm of an undertaker's accountant, but at this critical moment in the life of the Victory, safe and boring worked just fine. The chances of Carney being caught *in flagrante* were as slim as the man himself.

Dr Carney finished putting the papers on his desk into neat piles, then settled his glasses on his hawk-like nose and looked up.

'Have you anything you wish to discuss with me, Dr Devan?'

Kash was momentarily taken aback. He was expecting some sort of dressing down, not an invitation to open his heart. Wasn't that what occupational health was for?

'I'm not sure I understand, Dr Carney.'

Carney looked disappointed. 'I thought it was only fair to give you the opportunity of unburdening yourself, before I present you with my . . . findings.'

Findings? What had Kash done now?

'You're going to have to help me, I'm afraid,' Kash said tentatively. 'I'm really not following.'

'A holdall,' Carney said simply, a smile hovering around the edges of his thin-lipped scowl.

Kash went cold.

'A holdall was discovered in an otherwise empty locker behind the doctors' mess.'

Kash focused on keeping his voice steady. 'Right. But what exactly has that got to do with me?'

'You were seen taking the holdall out of your own locker. So I assume it must be yours.'

'Ah, that's the thing,' said Kash, thinking quickly. 'I'd just come down to put my white coat in my locker when I saw it was open – I must have forgotten to lock it – and there was a holdall inside. I assumed someone had put it in my locker by mistake, so I took it out and just put it in the nearest one that was free. I suppose I should have handed it in, but I was in a hurry. Sorry.'

Dr Carney looked at him over the top of his glasses, his expression unreadable. Kash felt a drop of sweat forming on his brow.

'At least it was found. I mean, so whoever it belongs to can reclaim it,' Kash added.

'No one has reclaimed it,' said Dr Carney.

'Oh,' said Kash.

Dr Carney fixed him with a beady gaze. 'Did you look inside it before you put it in the other locker?'

'No!' said Kash, too quickly.

'So you have no idea what was inside it?'

'Obviously not,' Kash replied. He tried to put some steel in his voice, reasoning that it was best to seem annoyed rather than defensive. 'What *was* inside it?'

As soon as he'd asked the question, he realized he didn't want to hear the answer.

'Some items of what I would describe as sadomasochistic paraphernalia.' Carney pursed his lips as if he'd just swallowed something unpleasant and looked at Kash. 'So these items aren't yours?'

'Of course not!' said Kash with convincing indignation. 'I've told you. The holdall doesn't belong to me. Someone else put it in my locker.'

Dr Carney continued to look at him steadily, clearly unconvinced.

'You're sure about that?'

'I think I'd know if I had a holdall full of . . . that kind of stuff. And don't you imagine if I did, I would keep it securely locked away?' He folded his arms and returned Dr Carney's stare.

Carney made a little grunting noise. 'Yes, well, that does seem logical. Assuming that the owner does not come forward to reclaim it, then, we can probably never be certain of their identity.' He sounded disappointed. 'Although I have my suspicions, obviously.'

Kash started to rise. 'Is that all?'

'Not quite.' He waited until Kash was seated again. 'It must be hard not to be influenced by a man like Mr Trenchard. He was undoubtedly very charismatic. Very *persuasive*.'

And still alive, thought Kash, annoyed at Carney's use of the past tense.

'I only hope his influence wasn't . . . corrupting?'

Meaning what, exactly? Was Carney suggesting Kash was somehow involved in all the S&M stuff? That he and Mr Trenchard . . . Kash didn't need to feign his indignation now.

'I hope you don't mean what I think you mean, Dr Carney.'

Dr Carney threw his hands up, palms towards Kash. 'I'm not implying anything, Dr Devan. My job – one of my jobs – is to restore this hospital's reputation, a reputation that at this moment in time is, thanks to your former mentor, somewhere down in the gutter. I want to make sure that the kind of distasteful practices that he engaged in within the walls of this hospital have no place in it from now on. Do I make myself clear?'

'Crystal,' Kash said and this time he got up without waiting to see if Carney was finished with him. 'If you'll excuse me,' he added curtly, 'I have a ward round to make.'

Out in the corridor he leaned back against the wall and took several deep breaths. *Bastard*, he thought. He's really enjoying it, finally being able to be superior to a surgeon he isn't fit to ... Kash stopped and thought. Could it be more than that?

He made a mental note to add Dr Jack Carney to the list of suspects.

35

The pain had been indescribable. He had truly wanted to die. But he knew that wasn't what she wanted. She wanted him to live. To suffer. To suffer more, if that was possible. No doubt she had some new torture prepared for him when she next appeared. The thought of it filled him with terror. Such terror that he – a man who had never prayed before in his life – found himself on the verge of praying for death.

The experience was humiliating. To pray to a God you didn't believe in for a relief he couldn't grant. But fear and humiliation were soon superseded by an even stronger emotion – shame. Shame at having given in so readily. Yes, he was paralyzed and utterly helpless. Yes, he was completely in her power. But was he completely powerless himself? Was there nothing he could do? Well, he could still think. He had always prided himself on his superior intellect, and when you put that together with his unrivalled knowledge of human physiology, surely he could yet be master of his own destiny.

The idea that a brain did not have some capacity for repair was, he knew, simply wrong. True enough, you couldn't grow new brain tissue and heal it as you might skin. But you could reprogram the circuits that remained. Make new connections. Strengthen existing ones. And create new internal software.

Some parts of the brains of songbirds grew in the spring. Scans of London taxi drivers showed marked increase in the size of some brain parts as they learned the city's routes. Patients with severe brain injury sometimes learned to talk again even when the relevant control centres had been utterly destroyed: other parts of the brain simply got re-tasked. Of course, such 'plasticity', as it was known, was much greater in the young. But it was all Trenchard had to pin his hopes on. He could yet improve. Regain some sort of control. And then . . . well, one step at a time. He decided that every morning – and then several times each day – he would do a 'body scan'. Sensation first: what could he feel in his toes? Feet? Ankles, and so on? Could he amplify those sensations? And then movement: imagine it, will it to happen and watch – where he could see – to look for even the slightest flicker. Nothing yet, of course. But it would come with time. It had to. And one thing Michael Trenchard had was time.

His thoughts were interrupted by the appearance of Sister Vale.

Up close, and through the night-slime which coated his eyeballs, she did not look as beautiful as he remembered. And she had certainly been beautiful, in the early days. Unable to look away as she bent over him, he could see the familiar trio of moles marking her neck.

Trenchard could feel his body being moved as she changed his gown, but could not feel her touch. Parts of his body had normal sensation, but in others it was either distorted or absent. Altogether, his body felt incomplete and misshapen, with huge bites taken out of its side where he could feel not a thing, both legs hacked away below the knees, and half of his face lifeless and inert.

Sister Vale stepped back until she was finally in Trenchard's full view. He tried to force a smile, her lack of response confirming that he had failed to move the smallest muscle. You looked good once. And still could, with a tad of effort. If only you scraped that lank hair back from your brow. Applied a little make-up. Ate a little less. If you cared, *like you used to care.*

'Funny how things turn out, Michael. You, the great Michael Trenchard, in my *power. Me in control. But I'm here for you now. This is my ward, and you're my patient. Nothing that happens here will happen without my sanction – of that you can be quite sure.'*

Inwardly, Trenchard tensed. What did she mean by that? Not without her sanction . . .

She paused. 'Wait! I almost forgot! You still seem to have some thrush in the groin. I'll put some antifungal cream on that for you, Michael.'

She was back moments later, dropping back between his legs, rising intermittently to look at him with an expression which could have been pity and could have been contempt.

Not so long ago, if she had touched him like that, his breathing would have been ragged, the veins on his neck engorged, his face puce. But none of those things had happened. He could, however, feel his heart pounding, and his fists balled up in anger. Tight. Ready to strike. But, of course, that wasn't possible.

He moved his internal focus towards them and, in the corner of his vision, saw something.

What?

Surely not.

In his mind, he balled his fists again, and there it was. The index finger of his left hand, lying on the arm rest where Sister Vale had left it, had twitched.

He desperately wanted to incline his head so that he could see it better – but even this pathetic movement was beyond him. All he could do, now, was concentrate . . . and hope. He worked himself up again: deliberately, methodically, thinking about her touching him and his inability to respond, letting the anger and frustration build. And then . . . FIST! And there – there it was. Hardly anything, just the tiniest flexing at his knuckle. But it had been movement.

He felt that familiar surge of power that came with success. And this was just the start.

He rested for only a second, then tried to flex his finger again, test the reliability of the action, what kind of strength he might have had left – but in that same moment Sister Vale got back to her feet, brushing his hand and knocking it sideways as she stood. Inwardly, Trenchard cursed. The finger he had flexed might have remained on the arm rest – but, by moving only a couple of inches, she had pushed it outside his field of vision.

'Damn you' he screamed. 'DAMN YOU!'

His mind was a frenzy. He sent what wild messages he could, not knowing if he was making the finger flex or if it remained rigidly still. Then, struck by another epiphany, he stopped.

Sister Vale was looking at him oddly. Had she noticed? No, he thought. She couldn't possibly have seen. Which was actually a relief. After all, did he really want her to know what he could do?

36

Kash had been emboldened by his interview with Dr Carney. At least he didn't have to worry about the holdall and its dreadful contents any more. And he was damned if he was going to let a bean-counter like Carney intimidate him, nor whoever had reported him. Still, his heart was beating a little faster than normal when he gently pushed open the door to Mr Trenchard's office. His eyes went straight to the place where Trenchard had been lying, half expecting to see a wilted bunch of flowers, like the ones you see at the sites of traffic accidents. But no, the room seemed pretty much as he last remembered it. Most importantly, nothing on Mr Trenchard's desk seemed to have been moved. He stepped round and looked at the three framed pictures arranged in a loose triptych. Trenchard in mortar board and gown, flanked by beaming parents. A frightening-looking brown dog (Kash was no good with breeds). And then, the last one, a severe but attractive woman with silver-blonde hair, looking into the camera as if she rather disapproved of the whole business of photography.

Isabelle Trenchard.

He picked the photograph up and put it into the pocket of his white coat.

* * *

A few minutes later he was pulling the curtains around Liz Murray's bed.

'What you doing that for? I've already had an examination today. And you did it, too. You're not going senile, are you?'

'No, Liz. I haven't forgotten. I just thought we could have a little privacy.'

'Ooh!' Her eyes twinkled in a way Kash found slightly disturbing.

'Nothing like that,' he assured her. 'I just wanted to show you something.'

'Ooh, Doctor,' she said again.

'Come on, Liz. We're not in a *Carry On* film. This is serious.'

She assumed a sober expression. 'Is it something to do with Mr Trenchard?'

'Yes, it is. At least, I think so.'

He took out the photograph and handed it over. She held it at arm's length, squinting at it.

'Who's this, then?'

'I was rather hoping you'd tell me.'

'But I've never seen her before.'

'Haven't you?'

'Oh, wait a minute. That lovely hair.' She ran a bony finger through her own thinning frizz. 'You might not believe it, but I used to have beautiful hair myself. When I was a girl I sat in front of the mirror for hours and hours just brushing it.

Almost down to my waist, it was. I could have made a rope out of it, like Rumpelstiltskin.'

'Rapunzel.'

'That's the one. Our flat was on the ground floor, though. No point. I had plenty of suitors back then, too.'

'Liz . . .'

She squinted some more, turning the frame this way and that.

'I couldn't swear to it, mind. But it could be her.'

'Who?'

'That woman who came to see Mr Trenchard – with her godson or whoever he was. I'm not daft, you know.'

'I know you're not,' Kash said, stooping to kiss her lightly on her forehead.

* * *

The house was on a wide, tree-lined street in Belsize Park, and looked very grand. As the cab pulled up, Kash saw a white Range Rover parked next to a gardener's van in the drive. He paid the driver and got out. She must have been watching out of a window, because the door opened before he had a chance to ring the bell.

'You must be Dr Devan.' She opened the door wider and ushered him in.

'Thank you.'

She led him wordlessly through the hall and past the kitchen to a large, sunny living room with French windows overlooking a spacious garden. Kash saw a wide lawn, borders teeming with shrubs and what looked like a bronze statue of a woman in the lee of a wall.

'Please.' She indicated an overstuffed leather armchair and settled herself on the cream sofa opposite. 'Can I get you a cup of tea? Or coffee?'

'No, thank you.'

She was older than the woman in the picture, the hair, pulled back in a tight ponytail, less silver than grey, but still striking, her sculpted cheekbones and wide blue eyes giving her an unnerving, slightly doll-like look.

'So, I know you worked with my husband. We spoke briefly on the phone once, didn't we? He thought very highly of you as I remember.'

Kash swallowed, not knowing what to say. What could you say to a woman whose husband had been found drugged up to the eyeballs, wearing women's underwear, and who now sat slumped with drooling saliva?

'Good. I mean, thank you.'

She gave him a brief half-smile. 'Look, it's very nice of you to come. It's not as if his colleagues are queuing round the block to pay tribute, or even be polite. For the most part they've wisely decided to pass over his misfortunes in silence. Well, I don't mind. Easier for everyone. So if you feel you need to say some nice things about my husband, you really don't.'

She absently fingered the pearls at her throat, and Kash couldn't help noticing how well she'd managed to keep her figure.

'I understand, Mrs Trenchard,' Kash said eventually. 'It's a difficult time for everyone. And yes, I admired – admire – your husband very much. I'm helping to look after him at the hospital, but if there's anything I can do . . .'

She raised an eyebrow, with another half-smile. 'I don't think there's anything anyone can do, is there, really?'

You could have put him in a private hospital, couldn't you? Kash thought. But maybe he was being unfair; perhaps she thought the care her husband would receive from people who had known him and worked with him would be better.

However, Kash couldn't help the feeling that, far from being distressed by his presence, Isabelle Trenchard was actually enjoying his discomfort. It made him feel less self-conscious about what he was going to say next.

'There was something I wanted to ask you, actually.'

She looked intrigued. 'Yes?'

'Have you been to visit your husband?'

Her eyes went cold. 'Why do you ask?'

'It's just . . . it's just that a woman did come to see him – with a young man. And their behaviour was . . . rather odd.'

She continued to look at him with those cold blue eyes, and he was sure she was on the point of angrily demanding to know what he was talking about, before asking him to leave.

But then, to his amazement, she laughed.

'Oh dear, so we were spotted, were we? We did try to be discreet.'

'So it *was* you. And the man? May I ask who he was?'

'It's none of your business,' she said mildly. 'But since you ask, he's my boyfriend.'

Kash swallowed. 'So you were . . . taunting him. Your husband, I mean.'

She shrugged. 'I suppose you could call it that. It's not as if he didn't deserve it,' she added.

Kash didn't know what to say. 'Because . . .?'

'My husband, Dr Devan, liked to say he lived life to the full. I'd prefer to say he took whatever he wanted. *Whoever* he wanted. If you think our little performance was somewhat in bad taste, then I suggest you imagine living with him for thirty-odd years. Believe me, I have had to suffer far worse humiliations.'

Kash was reeling. He could understand her being bitter if Mr Trenchard had been unfaithful, but to torture a man like that, on the smallest chance that he was in any way aware . . . didn't she feel any pity at all? Could he really have done anything to deserve that?

'What about the thing that happened to him? Weren't you shocked?'

She shrugged again. 'It was certainly a surprise. I really didn't suspect that he tended that way. But actually there was more than a touch of poetic justice to it, don't you think?'

Kash felt dizzy. Listening to Isabelle Trenchard sitting there, cool as a cucumber, talking about her husband as if he was a character in a play, was more than he could stomach. But he knew that if he walked out now, she was unlikely to invite him back for another chat. He needed to find out all he could while he had the opportunity.

'Who, then? Who were these women?'

She shook her head. 'I'm sorry, Dr Devan. I'm not going to make you a list. I don't have the time. Ask any of the nurses. Many of the doctors. But if you're really curious about my husband's murky past, I can give you one tip.'

Kash leaned forward in the chair.

'Talk to Susan Vale,' she said, smiling coldly. 'Ask her about the baby.'

37

As Trenchard grew used to the daily routine, he began to fear
something else almost as much as the prospect of another
night-time visit. Boredom. The sight of nurses and porters,
coming and going, the chatter of the other patients, muffled by
the constant background hum of soft jazz, nursing observations in ceaseless cycles, the ironically named dressing changes
where nothing changed, or the rehanging of a plastic container
of feed (a grow-bag for a vegetable, as he heard someone whisper one evening) – all these things had once been sources of
wonder, evidence that through sight and sound he was still
connected to the world outside his brain. But repetition had
rendered them meaningless. He was trapped in a Groundhog
Day – where nothing different ever happened. He found himself dreaming of the same banal routine, the line between
sleeping and waking becoming so blurred that he could not
always tell which was which. His determination to make his
body come back to life, piece by tiny piece, was in danger of
fading away, snuffed out by a vast cloud of tedium that sapped
his strength and drained his will.

The day after the finger-twitching had happened he had
tried, over and over, to replicate the movement. But every time
the same thing had happened: his finger remained rigid on the

arm of the chair in which he was trapped, refusing to flicker no matter how hard he strained. Soon he got to thinking that the first tiny tremor he'd seen had itself been a dream, his subconscious taunting him with false hopes of escape. Giving up, his mind had wandered disconsolately back to the night of his downfall. He relived his lust, his disbelief, his fear and then his anger at what was being done to him. His fury festered and, once again, he felt his anger boil over, his fist clenched.

And suddenly, there it was again, in the corner of his eye: the same finger miraculously twitching. The trick, he now realized, was to harness the power of emotional memory to cause his finger to move; just willing it consciously was not enough. He'd heard that of patients with Parkinson's disease: they might struggle to walk at all, but could sometimes stride out in time to music. Sometimes, it seemed, you just had to find another switch when the first was broken. Once he'd understood how the process worked, he could learn how to control it. The challenge was exhilarating. He had spent a life understanding and mastering complex skills. This would be no different.

It was amazing, however, how quickly a body that could not move could still tire. On the first day, it took mere minutes before exhaustion overwhelmed him and, in that time, he had found no real success at all. But, as the days passed, and if he allowed sufficient periods of rest between his efforts, his endurance increased. As he was able to focus for longer periods, he began to be rewarded with success. But this was an inexact science. Sometimes the messages he sent out reached his finger; sometimes they fizzled into nothingness, losing themselves in a tangle of dead ends and blind alleys. At first frustrated, he eventually discovered that when he was thinking about moving it most intensely, and stoking his rage, the finger steadfastly refused to move; but if he was half thinking about something else and only half about his finger and what had been done to him, it was more likely to start twitching. There was, he decided, a Goldilocks zone – just enough concentration, not too little and not too much – in which his brain and his body could come together once again, however fleetingly.

But while he honed his skills, there were other things to consider, as well. Perhaps she had not acted alone. Was it paranoid delusion, or could she have joined forces with others equally bent on his destruction? It would certainly have been a remarkable feat to have done it all on her own. It was therefore best to assume the worst; that there were others. And even if there weren't, prematurely revealing his secret could still prove fatal. Suppose Sister Vale buried the finding or alerted others, being part of The Coven? Or perhaps she'd alert that shit Jack Carney. A team of neurologists would appear, new tests would be ordered, porters would be scurrying hither and thither, and soon the whole of the Victory would know: Michael Trenchard wasn't brain-dead at all; he was conscious and capable, however feebly, of communicating. Soon she would hear – they would hear – and understand the danger. Then she would come for him, to make sure he took her identity with him to the grave.

He had to be careful. He needed to choose a person he could trust. Someone who couldn't have been involved but who would also appreciate the dangers.

Of course!

Kash!

Had it been his imagination, or had Kash been there, after the bitch's last visit, when he'd been writhing in unimaginable agony? The intensity of the pain had made it impossible to concentrate on anything else, but he was sure he'd heard Kash's voice, telling him he knew it hadn't been an accident. There were dangers, of course. Did he not know her well? Might he not tell her, or someone else who would? No. Not Kash. If anyone could be discreet, it would be him.

So where was he?

It felt like weeks since he had seen him. Had he been warned off? He found it hard to keep track of time. Kash would only have six months on the ward. How many had passed already? If Kash moved on to a new hospital, it was over, the chance gone.

He felt a rising tide of panic.

38

Nights on call went one of two ways. Occasionally, it was possible to retreat to bed in the small hours, to be woken every hour or so with a bleep to offer telephone advice or make the odd foray to a bedside. More often, a junior doctor was a pinball, flicked randomly between wards and the emergency department. Tonight had been one of *those* nights. The medics were down on numbers, so Kash was hauled in to help and the emergency department was receiving a steady stream from the streets, a smorgasbord of acronyms: BIBs (brought in by ambulance), DIBs (difficulty in breathing), CAPs (community acquired pneumonias), ODs (overdoses, both accidental and deliberate), LOCs (loss of consciousness) and the odd East Ham (one stop short of Barking). On top of that, all the wards still had IVs to give, drug charts to rewrite, and patients to review.

By dawn, the red-rimmed skyline matched Kash's eyes. But today was a Sunday; he wasn't facing another thirty-six hours of continuous labour. But he did have work to do, and he wasn't looking forward to it.

A thin drizzle was falling over London as he set out. The Victory hunched behind him, squatting and squalid and grey behind a rippling veil of rain. The skies above were steeped in pale grey clouds, the traffic crawling like crayfish onwards through pools of oily rainwater. Kash paused at the first bus stop outside the Victory. Few shoppers were venturing out on a day like this, and the bus, when it arrived, was almost empty. He settled into a seat on the upper deck, watching through the fogged-up windows as the city rolled indistinctly by.

*   *   *

The ground floor flat on Albany Street looked surprisingly dingy from the outside. Somehow he'd imagined that Sister Vale's home would reflect her own qualities: neat, tasteful, well-preserved. Instead, there was an air of neglect about the peeling paint and chipped stucco.

He knocked nervously at the front door, wondering if he'd actually come to the wrong address, but when the door eventually opened, it was her standing there, looking pained, as if he'd caught her in an embarrassing situation. 'Kash, what on earth are you doing here? Has something happened?'

'I think it has, Sister. I think you know it has.'

She stood there for a moment, as if weighing something in her mind. 'You'd better come in.'

He squeezed past her into the narrow hallway, his raincoat dripping onto the threadbare carpet. She was wearing a shapeless grey pullover and sweatpants, and her feet were bare.

Inside the flat, she took his coat and hung it up on the door, then cleared some books and magazines from a sofa so he could sit, while she went into the kitchen to make tea.

Soon they were sitting at opposite ends, steaming mugs in their hands. She tucked her feet up under her.

'So, tell me.'

'You know about the catheter,' he began. 'You can't believe that was some sort of accident. And I found a card, a Valentine's card. Liz Murray says she saw someone leaving it for Mr Trenchard.'

A look of alarm passed across her face, but he ploughed on.

'I think perhaps you tore it up. I looked in your wastebin – I'm sorry. I don't think I need to tell you what the message was. Somebody's working on the assumption that he is in some way aware – able to feel mental and physical distress at some level or other. Somebody who has access to ward fourteen. Whether you believe what happened to him was an accident or not, somebody's definitely going after him now.'

Sister Vale stared into her tea, saying nothing, but breathing harder than before.

'I went to see his wife, Isabelle.'

Her breathing quickened once more.

'He had visitors. A woman and a younger man. They were flaunting themselves in front of him. I had a hunch it might be her, so I confronted her about it. She basically admitted it, said that he'd cheated on her and she was just getting a bit of her own back. A pretty macabre way of doing it, but she seemed to think he deserved it.'

Sister Vale nodded slowly.

Kash went on. 'Whoever put him in this condition – and yes, I still think that is what happened – must have hated him with a passion – still hates him. But they'd also need medical training, I think. That makes Isabelle Trenchard unlikely. She's not been a nurse for decades, so far as I know.'

'It sounds like you've been making a list of suspects.'

He had. And there were several names on it, but three at the top. Four, if you counted Dr Carney. But he didn't want to reveal that now.

'I wouldn't go that far. I'm just trying to find out more. Mrs Trenchard implied he'd been involved with lots of women.' He looked at her. 'Did you know that? I mean, you worked together for so long. You knew him as well as anyone.'

She paused before answering. 'Sometimes you can work closely with someone for years without really knowing them.'

'I suppose that's true,' Kash agreed. 'If it's a purely professional relationship,' he added.

'What do you mean?' Her grip on her mug tightened.

'I don't mean to nosey.'

'Yes you fucking do,' she said, suddenly animated, and launching from the sofa.

He had a horrible feeling she was going to throw her tea over him. Instead she paused, and slammed it onto the little coffee table.

'I think you should go. Michael Trenchard is dead. Maybe not legally, but in any way that matters. There's nothing you can do for him. Why don't you think about the living? Think about yourself.'

'What do you mean?'

'You're already in Carney's bad books for going to see the police. If he hears about your little trip to see Isabelle – not to mention coming here – he'll have you slung out of the Victory before you know what day it is.'

'Is that a threat? If it is, it's a weak one. He couldn't . . .'

She snorted. 'Couldn't he? Look what he did to Angela Warner. After the stunt she pulled at the Chaloner boy's inquest, he decided she was either trying to bring the Victory into even greater disrepute or was suffering from a stress disorder. Officially it's the latter, but either way, she won't work at the Victory again. If you carry on the way you're doing, you'll be next.'

Kash was momentarily lost for words. He'd been purposefully avoiding Angela, ever since he began to think she might be the one. Either her, or with someone else. She had the motive, the opportunity, the medical skills . . .

'It doesn't matter about me,' he said, pulling himself together. 'Mr Trenchard deserves the truth – even if he'll never know it. I'm going to find out what happened – who did this to him, and why – and the hell with Carney.'

She stood with her arms folded, looking at him intently.

'That's your choice, Kash. But I'd hate to see you waste your life, throw away such a promising career, for the sake of a man like Michael Trenchard.'

He'd never heard that tone in her voice before. Real bitterness – and pain. She came and sat back on the sofa again.

He paused.

'Tell me about the baby.'

Sister Vale jerked back as if struck, her jaw slack, eyes bewildered, before recovering. Her head dropped. 'So you know. How?' Her head shook slowly. 'I guess it doesn't matter.' She shrugged. 'Since you're so determined, let me tell you a story, before you go. And then you must do as you will. Just don't expect me to help you.' She took a deep breath. 'Hard to believe, but I was young once, like you. Full of dreams, a bit naive. I was a trainee nurse. And I fell in love with a handsome doctor, just like in a romantic novel. We were going to get married and live happily ever after. But then I got pregnant. I was so happy, even though it wasn't what we'd planned. But he wasn't quite so happy. Said I had to . . . get rid of it. Those were his exact words, actually. We'd have children when the time was right, when he'd made it, when he was a surgeon with all those letters after his name. Then he could provide for me properly and we could bring the children up the way we planned.'

She looked away for a moment. When she turned back to Kash, there were tears in her eyes.

'So I did. I *got rid of it*. My daughter. I loved him that much. There'll be more, I told myself.' She wiped her eyes on her sleeve. 'But there weren't. God punished me for throwing away his most precious gift. I couldn't have any more after that.'

'And . . . the doctor?' Kash knew she was talking about Trenchard, but couldn't bring himself to say his name out loud.

She looked at him then with such bitterness it was like a physical force. 'Oh, he met someone else. Someone better. A bit . . . *fancier*. Turned out to be the perfect wife, in fact. No children, but I'd worked out by then he didn't really want them.'

'My God.' He didn't know what to say. 'But then why . . .?'

'Why did I work with the man for the next thirty years?'

'Yes. How could you bear it?'

'Oh, it's not so hard, when you have a plan. You just need patience.'

A terrible realization crept over him. 'What do you mean?'

'I've probably said more than I ought. You should go. Keep in mind what I said about wasting your life, though, Kash. And if you do decide to sacrifice it all for the sake of that man, at least now you know the sort of man he was.'

39

On the bus ride back to the Victory, Kash thought about the young Susan Vale, her heart broken, her life in ruins. Had Trenchard really done that to her? He could see how losing a baby, and then finding out it was for nothing – love, marriage, motherhood, all gone in an instant – could make you do almost anything. The wonder was that she had not gone mad. Or did you have to be mad to spend the next thirty years working alongside the man who'd done all this to you? And then, when the time was right, or the opportunity presented itself, or for some reason you simply couldn't bear it any more, to deliberately turn him into a living corpse, so you could spend the last years gloating at his bedside – did she really do that?

Part of Kash refused to believe it. The Sister Vale he had come to know was dedicated, conscientious, someone who had devoted her life to caring for people. Could she really have coldly and deliberately consigned another human being – even one as despicable as Mr Trenchard had been painted – to a living death?

But she'd as good as admitted it, hadn't she?

Kash closed his eyes and tried to think. Had Hilary Williams made up a story about Trenchard propositioning her? Had Sister Vale made up this story about her pregnancy? Perhaps she had lost a baby, and Trenchard had then left her for Isabelle, and over the years, as Trenchard had grown more successful, she'd woven a fantasy about how it was all his fault.

But then if she had done it, why tell Kash the whole story? It only seemed to prove her guilt.

Did she want to spend the rest of her life behind bars?

Perhaps she did.

Perhaps that would be *her* punishment.

Kash shook himself. It was all too much. He simply didn't know what to believe any more. Isabelle Trenchard, Hilary Williams, Angela, Mrs Chaloner, and now Susan Vale: they all had reasons to hate Michael Trenchard. But how much did you have to hate someone to do what had been done to him?

* * *

Back at his flat, Kash took to his bed. He was dog tired after a busy night and, in the end, just had to give in to leaden limbs and lids. His eyes felt as if they'd been sand-blasted.

* * *

He awoke – predictably, dammit – shortly after midnight. Eight hours sleep, and his body was telling him it was dawn.

There was nothing for it. Toast, telly, and try again in a couple of hours.

Chin in one cupped hand, Kash licked the marmite from his fingers, pausing at the end of the one where the needle had penetrated. Whether it had been a warning, or simply designed to discredit him – given that someone seemed to have been whispering to Doc Wilson – he was unsure. But that dark forces had been behind it was clear. And someone – perhaps the same someone – had broken into his apartment, taken the holdall and deliberately put it in his locker, hadn't they? If it was Trenchard's attacker, they were capable of anything. The finger was reddened and sore – the signs of an early infection spreading. If it was worse in the morning, he might have to seek some antibiotics. Maybe that had been their intention? If so, he wasn't just risking his career by pursuing the truth, as Sister Vale had suggested; he was risking his life.

In which case he had two choices: give up, walk away, and leave Trenchard to his fate; or fearlessly unmask the perpetrator.

He looked at his hand again. The muscle at the base of the thumb didn't seem to like the infection. It was twitching intermittently, the tip of his thumb jerking involuntarily. He smiled. Oddly, the sensation wasn't that unpleasant.

It was then that the thought occurred to him. Was it possible? God! What an idiot! Why had he not thought of it before?

Moments later, he had exited the flat and was hurrying towards the stairs as fast as he could.

* * *

By the time he arrived, the background drone of the radio had been silenced, and the dim glow of the bedside lights was all that kept the darkness at bay.

'Mr Trenchard? Mr Trenchard?' Kash murmured in his ear as loudly as he dared. 'Can you hear me?' He kneeled down and took Trenchard's right hand in his own. Kash worked his way through Mr Trenchard's fingers, feeling each one to see if he could detect a spark of life. What if he were essentially 'locked in'? Conscious but unable to move anything but the smallest muscles – the eyes, or a finger? He remembered his old registrar, Doug Fairweather, telling him of such cases – yet neither he nor anyone else had checked on Trenchard for weeks. Months. It was a longshot, but . . .

'Mr Trenchard? If you can hear me, I want you to try and move your index finger. Can you do that?'

He waited. Kash tried to imagine Trenchard willing his finger to move. Seconds passed. Kash could feel his own pulse, beating against his chest.

Then it happened. The faintest twitch. Kash wouldn't have detected it if Trenchard's hand had not been in his own. He tried to steady his breathing.

'That's brilliant. Can you do it again, Mr Trenchard?'

There was a pause, and then Trenchard's finger jolted once more. Once, twice, three times, it twitched like an epileptic in the grip of a seizure; and then, all its life force spent, it fell limp into Kash Devan's palm.

'Yes, Mr Trenchard! Yes!'

Kash cradled the finger as if it was the most precious thing on Earth: this one element connecting the world outside to the world in there, to whatever was left of Michael Trenchard. He peered into the eyes that, until now, had seemed so dull, knowing now that there was a consciousness on the other side looking back.

*   *   *

There were footsteps out on the ward. One of the night-shift nurses doing a cursory round, or perhaps a patient heading to the toilet. Kash held his breath, knowing that his presence here at such an hour would take some explaining. If Carney found out . . . Well. It wasn't worth thinking about. But the footsteps passed, and all was still once more.

Even so, the longer he waited, the greater the risk of discovery. He laid Trenchard's hand gently back on top of the bedclothes and leaned forward, whispering. 'Mr Trenchard, I know that you can hear me and understand. I'm sorry that I didn't think to check before. I also think that someone did this to you. So I need to think what to do now. To keep you safe. But to let you communicate.' He glanced about. 'I'll think of something.' And with that, he left.

* * *

Back in his flat, Kash paced the kitchen.

What to do now? It was all very well that Trenchard could obey a simple command. But who should he tell? How could Trenchard communicate? Who could help?

* * *

On ward fourteen, Trenchard could not sleep. Had he been able, he'd have been jumping for joy.

Yes! Kash, my boy. You came good.

40

'Bloody hell, Kash, I thought you were supposed to be the quiet one!'

Doug Fairweather seemed virtually unchanged from the slightly chubby registrar ('I'm just the wrong height for my weight') who Kash remembered from his first year on the wards as a medical student. He was a solitary and book-ish sort, who had happily confessed to a greater love for Dungeons and Dragons, heavy metal and computers than for more traditional social congress. The thick-rimmed black glasses and wispy facial hair were the same, too, and even the black T-shirt with a pattern of grinning skulls looked vaguely familiar. Doug had been a great teacher and, in Kash, had recognized a similarly solitary creature. They had spent some time drinking in pubs – real ales and diet colas, respectively – at the time. They'd stayed in touch as Kash progressed to qualifying as a doctor, and Doug burrowed ever deeper into the world of neuroscience. He had spent a year doing neurorehabilitation, so had likely met more Trenchards than Kash had had pints of lager. Not that this was too great a number, truth be told.

* * *

It had been a few days before Doug and Kash had been able to meet, but now they were sitting in a café far enough away from the Victory for Kash to be confident that they wouldn't be overheard by any of his colleagues.

Shaking his head at the tale Kash had just laid out before him, Doug picked up his mug and took a gulp of his coffee.

'Believe me, Doug, I didn't want any of this to happen.'

Doug wiped his mouth with the back of his hand. 'So let me get this straight. Your Mr Trenchard, the one who got caught with his pants down – lacy knickers up, whatever – and a noose round his neck, you reckon somebody injected him with some sort of muscle relaxant, dressed him up like a Christmas turkey, called the crash desk and scarpered. And now you think he's not brain-dead at all, just locked-in. So if I can help him to communicate, then he can reveal the identity of the person who did it – *but* it's all got to be done in secret, in some dungeon in the bowels of the Victory. Because that ghoul, the one we're trying to unmask, may well be stalking the corridors of the hospital as we speak, with a syringe of something nasty clutched in their hand, ready to do the same thing to you.' He leaned back. 'Is that about the size of it?'

'I wouldn't have put it quite that way,' Kash began. 'But yes. Basically.'

Doug grinned. 'You are a fucking dark horse, Kash, and no mistake. I didn't know you had it in you. Next thing you'll be telling me you've been taking our Lord's name in vain.'

'Once or twice,' Kash admitted.

'And drinking? Please don't tell me you've been drinking.'

'A little. For my nerves. Strictly medicinal.'

Doug nodded sagely. 'I would say a bit of self-medication would be essential in a caper like this. I need a general anaesthetic just listening to you.'

'So will you help me? I know it sounds mad.'

'Neurologists don't use the word "mad", Kash. Just a chemical imbalance somewhere or other. Anyway, "mad" doesn't quite do it. "Bonkers" perhaps? Or maybe "totally fucking insane"?'

Kash pushed his mug across the table. 'So you're not interested?'

'Are you kidding?' Doug grinned. 'I'm bored shitless with my research, and no one knows where I am half the time, or even cares. I rather fancy myself as Holmes to your Watson, to tell you the truth, and it'll be a welcome break from spreadsheets. It'll only take me a couple of days to move the kit over, if you can find a room. So count me in!'

41

It was a little after eleven, and the evening round was over for the nurses. Kash knew that the current crop of agency staff were soon to be propped up asleep in their office, and were very unlikely to reappear without a call alarm being activated. And that wasn't going to happen in *this* bay. Liz was totally stable and slept like a log. Anyway, her vision was too blurred to see anything, and no one even believed her when she talked of visitors at night. Meanwhile, Kash had earlier reported Trenchard to have a tracheostomy and chest partially colonised with resistant pseudomonas. As a result, Trenchard was now in the far corner of the ward, and was — under Kash's instructions — to remain sitting in his wheelchair at night while his chest improved. With a curtain partially pulled across, his absence would hopefully not be noticed.

Kash leaned close and whispered, 'Are you ready, Mr Trenchard?'

Kash focused on Trenchard's hand, but no movement was discernible.

Kash knew he'd have to be quick. The ward was empty but a nurse could appear at any moment. As they passed through the curtains, Trenchard saw the rest of the ward in stark relief. Liz Murray was snoring gently in an adjacent bed, and the one directly opposite was empty; it must have been the only one in the entire NHS. But then winter had turned to spring, and bed pressures were always less as the weather warmed.

They passed swiftly through the nearby door and into the back corridor, past an admin suite and, alongside that, the relatives' room, mostly used for breaking bad – but hardly unexpected – news. Through they went, and on towards the service elevator – the 'Dead Drop' used by porters to ferry bodies from ward fourteen to the hospital mortuary three storeys below.

Rattling its chains like Marley's ghost, the lift groaned towards the basement. Doug was waiting for them as the doors opened, now dressed soberly in a dark grey suit and checked shirt.

Kash smiled nervously. 'Mr Trenchard, this is Doug.'

Doug nodded briefly at Trenchard, and together they pushed the wheelchair into the gloom along the corridor, flanked by locked doors on each side, until, finally, they reached a corner where a spill of yellow light pooled like urine. Doug led them into a room deep with clutter, the hulks of old machines nestling under tarpaulin sheets.

Hospital basement corridors were generally used for storage – of beds, wheelchairs, and equipment unused or obsolete that could nevertheless be cannibalized for parts whenever things went wrong – which they invariably did – in the hospital above. But there was a corner that Kash had cleared to use as a workshop, and it was here that Doug had set up the interface. This was specialist equipment not available in most hospitals, and certainly not in the Victory. Smuggling it in, piece by piece, had been a logistical challenge, to say the least.

Trenchard could see the green glow of the monitor, a knot of cables leading to a simple ball and joystick set up on a coffee table ahead. Doug gestured to a spot in front and Kash wheeled Trenchard alongside.

Doug kneeled down and lifted Trenchard's hand. He turned to Kash.

'And you are sure?'

'The EEG was consistent with oxygen starvation – severe diffuse hypoxic cerebral injury . . . But then we found this.' He turned to Trenchard. 'Can you show him?'

They both looked – and Trenchard's finger danced.

Doug nodded to himself. 'When they made the diagnosis it was likely correct. But things change. The human brain, it's an incredible thing. It can find a way. Give a man a few months, some flickers of his old self can sometimes – just sometimes – start to emerge. If he's in there, we can get him out.'

Lifting each of Trenchard's limbs, Doug moved them passively through all ranges of movement.

'He's paralyzed, but that doesn't mean the body's just a shell. There are still involuntary movements. Mr Trenchard, I'm just going to rub hard on your sternum. Sorry if it's a bit uncomfortable . . .'

Doug pressed his knuckles over Trenchard's breastbone and rubbed hard. Instinctively, Trenchard's arms flexed and his legs extended, like a newborn chick kicking from its shell. Kash knew those were just so-called decorticate responses; they didn't mean there was any actual voluntary brain activity going on. Nor did the reflexes Doug revealed when, placing his own fingers over the tendons in each of Trenchard's limbs, he tapped them with a patellar hammer and watched them leap forward.

Doug went around the body, going through the motions one after another. Trenchard's big toes curled upwards when he stroked the outer margin of his soles firmly. He exhibited the palmo-mental reflex, pouting when Doug ran his fingers across his palm – a primitive reflex seen in babies. Next, he stroked Trenchard's cheek and Trenchard involuntarily turned a fraction towards the stimulus. Another primitive reflex; the body's way of helping a baby first find the breast.

'OK,' he concluded. 'The damage is diffuse. The motor cortex is impaired. So are his frontal lobes, judging from those release reflexes.' He raised an eyebrow to Kash in secret signal. If he was sexually disinhibited before, he was likely to be a whole lot worse now.

Doug reached into one of the drawers at the computer desk and came back holding a pen torch between his fingers. 'It's just this finger, is it? You've seen no movement anywhere else?'

Kash shook his head. 'Not a thing.'

Doug nodded. 'Sorry for the bright light, Mr Trenchard. Here it comes . . .'

Doug flashed the light into each eye in turn, observing the responses. The pupils were of irregular shape, of slightly different size, and responded sluggishly to direct light. The opposite pupil was, in each case, unresponsive.

Then, when Doug was just about to hide the pen torch again, he stopped.

Kash had noticed it first. It took Doug a second to catch up.

Trenchard's pupil was flicking repeatedly a fraction of a millimetre to the left, in time with a rhythmic jerking of the tip of his left thumb.

Doug stepped back. 'All right! He's in there. All of him. Mr Trenchard, if you can hear me . . .'

The finger jumped erratically to the tugs of an invisible puppetmaster. And above, the right eye glanced rightwards in synchrony.

'The eye.' Kash whispered. 'That's new. I didn't know about that. It's happening, isn't it? He really is waking up.'

'Oh, yes,' said Doug. 'Not "waking up" – that may have happened a long time ago. But it's probably only quite recently that he's found the capacity to control movement at all, and show that he is.' He looked nervously at Kash. 'Are you sure you don't want to get the rehab teams onto this? There's Ronan Astin in speech and language – I trained with him – or stroke unit or our rehab unit . . . I mean, has he even been seen by a neurologist since . . .'

Kash put a hand on his arm. 'Look, Doug, if this is freaking you out, if you want to back away, I totally understand. And I wouldn't blame you one bit. But this has to stay a secret for the moment – just until he can tell us who did this to him. Then we go straight to Carney, straight to the police, and Mr Trenchard gets everything he needs.'

Doug looked down at Trenchard and bit his lip. 'I don't know . . .'

'And you'll be the hero of the hour. The Dragon down here in the Dungeons.'

Doug turned back to Kash. 'You're a manipulative little fucker, you know that?'

Kash smiled, then checked his watch. 'If we're going to do it, Doug, we need to be quick. The longer we wait, the greater the chance his absence will be noticed.'

'I know, I know. Time is of the essence.' Doug straightened himself. 'Let's get started.'

He crouched at the computer terminal and started tapping at the keys, loading a programme up from the hard drive.

'BCI,' Doug said. 'Brain computer interface. It's in its infancy, but it's the best we've got. One day there'll not only be computers on every hospital ward, but computers you can jack straight into your head. We'll just be thinking thoughts and there they'll be, up on the screen. Thirty years' time, and a man like Mr Trenchard here might be writing and delivering lectures and – well, I'm getting ahead of myself. This one's more rudimentary. If I'd known about his eye . . .'

Doug stooped down so that he could look into the milky film of Michael Trenchard's eyes for a moment, then turned to Kash.

'We'll fit a sensor thimble over his finger. To start with we're just measuring what he can do. Can he make it move on command? Does he have the ability to control the scale of the movement with precision? Its direction? If we get it right, there's a chance he'll learn to put his own lights on and off, activate an alarm . . . even type on a computer screen. It can be painstaking, but he could have a conversation.'

'How long is it going to take?' asked Kash.

'A piece of string. It takes as long as it takes. Sometimes just days. But I've seen stroke victims spend six months learning to do this stuff – and that's with therapy day in and day out. How much time do we have?'

'Tonight? Shorter the better. We are relying on the patients all being stable long-stayers and the fact that most of the night team are bank nurses who tend to kip for most of their shifts. Longer term? Not six months, that's for sure,' Kash said. 'I don't know how long we'll be able to keep all this under wraps. There's a limit to the number of times he can vanish from a ward without someone noticing. Just do it as fast as you can.'

Doug nodded, stepping away from Mr Trenchard. He lowered his voice. 'He was a brilliant surgeon, wasn't he?'

'Surgeon? The best,' said Kash. 'Person? The jury is still out on that. But I'm not the judge.'

'A mind like that . . . well, maybe it could survive what happened. Maybe it is still lurking in there somewhere. But . . .' Doug paused, his eyes flicking between Kash and Trenchard. 'A brilliant mind, used to being challenged, used to being stimulated – imagine what it must be like to be locked up in there. Like a prisoner in solitary confinement – in a strait-jacket. He can't even scratch his nose. And gagged.' He glanced at the tracheostomy tube in Trenchard's neck. 'He can't even scream and be heard.'

Kash looked at him. 'What are you trying to say, Doug?'

'I'm just . . . what if the man who's in there, raging to get out – what if he isn't the man you think he is any more? What if he's lost his mind?'

42

Liz Murray was dancing.

A floor of black and white squares receded into the distance as her silver-shod feet whirled over it. Her partner was her husband Ken, even though he looked exactly like Fred Astaire. He gazed into her eyes as a warm breeze gently ruffled her pale-blue chiffon gown. Above was a midnight sky awash with stars, which meant the ballroom had no roof, which was odd. Also odd was the hospital cleaner in her blue uniform, who was making slow circles over the floor with her floor polisher, as if the pair of them were doing a waltz. Liz and Fred, who was also Ken whirled gracefully past, and Liz filled her lungs with the warm evening air, scented with honeysuckle. The ballroom seemed to have no end, and Liz began to feel slightly dizzy as they whirled on and on, faster and faster. At least there's no one else to bump into, she thought. Then, out of the corner of her eye, she saw them: another couple. As they moved closer, she saw it was Mr Trenchard. He was wearing a saffron evening gown, cut very low, revealing the noose around his neck, the end of which flapped behind him in the breeze. His partner, her slim frame sheathed in an elegant evening suit, was a woman with silver-blonde hair tied back in a simple bun. 'He's such an oaf,' she laughed as they went past. Her hand, Liz saw, had slipped from his waist to rest on his buttock.

'Would you like a bedpan?' Fred asked, his eyes sparkling as if he were offering champagne.

'No, thank you, darling,' she said, and woke up.

Sister Vale was standing at her bedside. 'You were making some funny old noises,' she said in a conspiratorial whisper. 'I thought perhaps you needed the loo.'

'No, thank you, dear,' Liz said, recovering herself. 'I'm quite all right.'

She reached for her new glasses as Sister Vale disappeared back to her office. Even in the gloom of the night-time ward, things were so much clearer with them on. She'd actually forgotten how things really looked, bright and sharp and not blurry at all. Funny how you could get used to things.

She looked over at Mr Trenchard. Had he got used to it, too? Probably not. The staff all said that he wasn't aware anyway. What was the point, really, in carrying on in such a state? If there really was nothing going on in there, why not just put him out of his misery now, poor dear, and have done with it?

* * *

On the other side of the ward, Michael Trenchard was actually having quite a pleasant time. He was playing the piano, his fingers, which seemed to him extraordinarily long and dextrous, flying over the keys as he hummed along. Really, he'd never played better in his life. He looked over, and an audience of about a dozen women, all dressed in black as if for a funeral, sat listening, their overly made-up faces impassive. He started to feel anxious. He realized that the only sound he could hear was that of his humming, which was actually becoming more of a gurgle. The piano itself was resolutely silent, however firmly he hit the keys. He played faster, stabbing the keys with increasing force, but still no sound came. He heard a cough from the direction of the seated women. He was beginning to sweat, beads of moisture forming on his brow. His bow-tie began to feel very tight. He looked over again and one of the women was looking at her watch, her eyes hidden behind dark glasses. His bow-tie was getting tighter. He desperately wanted to loosen it but he dared not take his hands away from the piano, otherwise . . .

He felt, rather than saw, her enter the hall. She walked slowly towards the seats, just visible out of the corner of his eye, then past, until she was standing by the piano, a dark shadow looming in his peripheral vision. He couldn't turn. He couldn't look. He forced his fingers to play faster, pressing down on the keys with all his strength, willing them to make a sound. He heard the scrape of chairs being pushed back as the other women began to get up and leave.

'But the performance isn't finished!' he wanted to say.

He saw her arm reach over. She was wearing pale green gloves. With one hand, she gently took hold of the piano lid between her finger and thumb.

He wanted to scream. 'Come back! Don't go!' But all he could hear was the clack of heels on the wooden floor, and the frenzied pumping of his heart.

In one swift movement, with a sound like thunder, she slammed the piano lid on his fingers.

* * *

When his breathing had slowed sufficiently for his mind to know where it was, he realized he was awake. His hands felt somewhere far away, the dream agony gone.

Across the ward, Liz Murray was peering at him through her new glasses.

'What the hell do you want, you asinine old bitch!'

* * *

Don't worry, thought Liz. I'm going to keep a proper eye on you now. Any more hanky panky and I'll make sure someone knows about it.

43

The next time Kash had a day off, it coincided with Claire's, a rare occurrence. Seeing each other had been hard – especially since Claire was also inexplicably unavailable so often. She had taken to 'going out with a friend', without ever actually saying where and with whom. She wasn't having an affair, of that he was certain. Her affection, when they met, was genuine, and she had promised to 'introduce him' at some point.

For all those reasons, he was desperate to see her, part of him wanting to ban all talk of Mr Trenchard when they did, so that they could pretend for a few hours that they were a normal couple – the sort of people who went to movies or visited art galleries and museums, who went shopping and watched TV together. But he'd told Claire, of course, and the other part of him wanted to do nothing else but talk about it: trying to figure out why progress was so slow, and whether Doug had been right all along when he'd wondered whether Mr Trenchard was conscious, but so psychologically impaired by his experiences that whatever communications did finally emerge would be worse than useless, just the incoherent ravings of a lunatic.

What if he identified his attacker, but it was all a fantasy? That there was none?

In the end, reluctantly and with a heavy heart, he decided that spending time with Claire in these circumstances would be counterproductive, at least as far as their relationship was concerned, and besides, there was someone else he needed to talk to more urgently. Ever since Sister Vale had told him about Angela Warner being suspended, he'd been feeling guilty. Guilty that he'd been so consumed with Mr Trenchard that her being suspended had passed him by. His doubts, his suspicions – call them what you will – shouldn't have stopped him behaving like a friend. Innocent until proven guilty. He needed to make amends, if he could.

The approach to Angela Warner's flat was cut off by road-works, so Kash crossed the expanse of Vauxhall Park, listening to the underground trains rumbling underneath, and slipped through a neighbour's untended garden to reach her front door. By the time he got there, his shoes were scuffed and his trousers torn where he had scrambled over one of the fences, making him feel even less prepared than when he'd set out.

When Ange answered the door, he almost didn't recognize her. In a stained pullover and torn jeans, with her hair down and half-covering her face, instead of tucked into a surgical cap or tied back in a neat ponytail, it was hard to imagine her as the cool-cutting surgeon. Her face was puffy, her eyes red-rimmed.

'Hello, Kash. I wondered when you were going to turn up. Just checking to see if I'm still alive? Well, now you know.'

'Can I come in?'

Ange gave a bitter laugh. 'I suppose I might just have a window for you in my busy schedule.'

She led him down a narrow unlit hall and up the stairs to her flat.

'There's coffee, if you don't mind it stewed.'

'Sure.'

The walls were decorated with photographs and prints depicting her student travels, and the year she had spent with Médecins Sans Frontières in rural Mozambique. The living room was stripped back, with pride of place given to a record player. Predictably, the little portable TV was covered in the dust of disuse. Nearby, a pile of medical journals slumped. On a sofa was a blanket, slick of newspapers and magazines spilling to the floor.

Ange handed Kash a mug of coffee and opened the doors to a little balcony, just big enough for two chairs, and let the spring evening air in. There they sat, overlooking the tumble-down gardens underneath.

'Sorry about the mess,' she said. 'If you'd come yesterday, you really would have been shocked. I went on the ciggies big time. Not any more, though. "A healthy mind in a healthy body", isn't that what he used to say?' She laughed again.

Kash was silent. He'd smelled the lingering, acrid aroma when he'd first walked in, not to mention the sour reek of booze on her breath.

'Look, Ange, I'm so sorry about not coming before. There's been so much going on – I didn't even know Carney had suspended you.'

Ange waved a hand dismissively. 'Don't worry about it, Kash. It's my own fault. We can't have the Victory's *reputation* being tarnished, can we?' She almost spat out the word. 'I mean, it's one thing when your top surgeon puts a noose round his own neck on the premises to get his jollies, but you can't have the staff complaining when somebody dies on the operating table because the sick bastard can't be bothered to turn up, can you?'

Kash had briefly wondered whether Ange's anger towards Trenchard would blow over, if she regretted her outburst at the coroner's court and that maybe it had just been her way of dealing with Edmund Chaloner's death and her part in it. She'd needed a scapegoat to deflect the guilt away from herself, and Trenchard fitted the bill. Unconsciously, he'd been hoping she would admit as much, allowing him to lay to rest the notion that she was guilty of, or complicit in, leaving Trenchard like this. She'd been Kash's trusted colleague, standing shoulder to shoulder in the operating theatre, and, he hoped, his friend. He didn't want to believe that she was a . . . what was the word? Not *murderer*, because Mr Trenchard wasn't dead. There wasn't a word to describe it, but *assailant* certainly didn't do it justice, because what had been done to him was even crueller than murder.

'What are you going to do?' he asked.

She shrugged. 'Well, I won't be coming back to the Victory, that's for sure. And *my* reputation has been tarnished now – that bastard Carney's seen to that. I'm not sure what other hospital would take me. There isn't a GMC case yet. And I've stalled on seeing the College.'

'Oh, Ange.'

She gave him a withering look. 'Don't worry about me, Kash. I'll be all right. Not like Anna Chaloner. I went to see her, you know. Not that there was anything else I could do. Just to show her I hadn't simply forgotten about her son and moved on, I suppose. She's quite impressive, actually. Anyway, as for me, there are always places that need doctors. There's no shortage of refugee camps about the place that could do with another pair of hands. Good for the soul, too. Maybe if I take a few months working day and night in some bombed-out hellhole, I'll be able to stop thinking about Edmund Chaloner.'

'It won't come to that, Ange,' he said, realizing at once how feeble his words sounded. 'We need you here.'

She swept her hair out of her eyes and regarded him coolly. 'Dr Carney doesn't seem to think so.'

He sighed, thinking about his last conversation with Carney. 'Well, the way things are going, I might be joining you in that refugee camp before too long.'

She sat up straighter. 'Why do you say that?'

'I guess I've been tarnishing the Victory's reputation a bit myself. I went to the police – you remember that detective inspector? Lambert? I told him I didn't think Mr Trenchard could have injected himself. He sent me away with a flea in my ear and then called Carney to complain I was making trouble. That's certainly the way Carney saw it, anyway. He more or less said if I didn't leave the Trenchard thing alone, I'd be out.'

'And have you left the Trenchard thing alone?'

Kash hesitated. He was desperate to believe Ange hadn't had anything to do with it. And looking at her now, a sad, forlorn figure, all the stuffing knocked out of her, it seemed inconceivable that she could have planned and executed a crime of such chilling audacity and calculated sadism.

'I haven't changed my view. I still think there's something . . . not right about the whole thing.' He was choosing his words carefully.

She nodded to herself. 'And you're on ward fourteen now. So it must be hard to put him out of your mind. What's it like?'

'How do you mean?'

'Seeing him, every day, like that.'

'Hard, to be honest. Considering what he was like before.'
He shrugged. 'I expect I should be more detached.'

'And what about his condition?'

Kash wasn't sure what she meant. 'What about it?'

'Any change? Any . . . deterioration?'

'Not really. Just what you'd expect. In fact . . . '

'What?'

'Oh, nothing. Really.'

'No, Kash. Go on. What?'

Oh, shit. Come on. She can't be guilty. Just look at her.

He sighed. 'OK. He . . . I think he might be showing signs of awareness. It's possible the brain damage wasn't as extensive as everybody assumed. He could be just locked in.'

Ange didn't say anything. For a while she just stared at the floor, seemingly lost in thought.

'I mean, I could be wrong. It's easy to imagine these things.'

*   *   *

Finally, she stood, a forced smile on her face. 'Oh, well. I'm sure you're right. Look, Kash, thanks for coming to see me. I know it must feel a bit awkward. I just need to get my act together, tidy up a bit, get focused.'

Kash followed suit and stood.

'All right, Ange,' he said, moving towards the door. 'But if there's anything you need, anything at all.'

'Oh, don't worry about me, Kash,' she said brightly, bending down to scoop an armful of magazines from the floor. She looked up and their eyes met. 'You just look after yourself.'

44

Michael Trenchard wanted to scream.

The hours since the first session with the young neurologist had seemed to stretch into eternity, leading him to wonder eventually if it had not all been a dream. But at last, in the ward's dead hours, Kash came for him, and once again sneaked him out of the ward and into the disused office that had become the focus of all his hopes, where Doug was waiting. He was very patient, this young man. He never showed his frustration or his disappointment, but always remained calm and encouraging.

Try again. You can do it. Don't worry if it doesn't happen all at once. One step at a time.

It made him feel like a child in a remedial class.

When his finger had first been placed in the thimble-like sensor rigged up to a computer screen, his pent-up frustration quickly expressed itself in a frenzy of movement he could barely control. They had tried a device to detect his eye movement, but he could control that even less well, and they had, for now, abandoned that to focus solely on the finger.

He needed to calm down, find that sweet spot between fury and detachment and concentrate on typing one letter at a time as he watched the cursor flashing across the screen. He would type a T (yes!) and then follow it with a U and a V *without being able to stop himself. But he found it impossible to coordinate his movement to erase his mistakes, so that by the time Doug had understood what was happening, a whole string of new letters had appeared, no more meaningful than if the whole operation had been performed by a chimpanzee.*

'It's all right, Mr Trenchard,' Kash had said. 'Try not to get over-excited. Let's go back to the beginning.'

He could have throttled him.

He remembered the first 'locked-in' patient he'd cared for. He was a guitarist. His fiancée bought him a day at a spa as a present. Head back in the grips of some porcelain sink having his hair washed, he'd torn an artery to his brainstem. And that was that. He'd thought, why not pull the plug? Who'd want a life like that? But the man's family, they wanted to cling on. So cling on they did. Two days later, he could communicate with eye movements. Once to the left – Yes. Twice to the left – No. He asked him if he wanted to be kept alive. No, he said. But by then, it was out of his hands. He'd lasted three years before a chest infection got him.

Christ.

He tried to focus again. Start from the beginning, like the good doctor said. But then he began to get confused, lost track of what he was trying to do. Exhaustion. It seemed to come more quickly each time. Instead of getting stronger with practice, he was getting weaker. His finger either moved when he didn't mean it to, or stayed reslolutely still. He worried that soon he wouldn't be able to move it at all.

Damn it all to hell!

And that damned bitch with it.

Doug had looked at him sympathetically, laid a consoling hand on his shoulder and said, 'It's OK, Mr Trenchard, we'll leave it there. There's always another night. I'm afraid it's sometimes one step forward, two steps back with this kind of learning. The brain can be a tricky thing to rewire.'

Trenchard cursed inwardly. The brain can be a tricky thing! Three years of neurology and that's the best you can come up with?

'If only that eye of yours had a little more control,' Doug continued. 'Tapping a finger can only get us so far.' He stood, disconnecting cables. The computer screen went black and, with it, all of Trenchard's hopes for the night.

'Yes, we'll have a proper conversation one of these nights, Mr Trenchard. You know, it would be fascinating to learn how a medical man like yourself experiences these things. Is it better to know what's happening to your own mind, your own body, or is ignorance truly bliss?' He paused in thought. 'Come on. Let's get you back to your bed before the shift change.'

Jesus Christ, man, Trenchard thought, this is life or death, not a fucking PhD experiment. And I'll skip the fascinating conversation for the moment, if you don't mind. I just need to tell you who fucking did this to me.

The way back to ward fourteen was tried and tested. The freight elevators unmanned, the palliative care offices barren and silent after dark. Trenchard's head lolled as Doug pushed him through the double doors.

'Well?' *Kash whispered. It was amazing how they still spoke about him sometimes as if he wasn't there, old habits dying hard.*

'He's worn out with it. He's making basic mistakes. He needs rest.'

Rest! Trenchard raged. All I have is rest! What I need is time. More time to get it right. Give me a whole night and I'll write you a fucking novel.

Kash leaned in close. 'It's only a matter of time, Mr Trenchard. We're not giving up.'

'Same time tomorrow night?'

Kash nodded. 'If I'm tied up with ward work, you're on your own. But the moment he communicates anything coherent, anything at all . . .' *He turned to Trenchard once more.* 'You just get some rest. I'm not sure how you do that in your situation, but I'm betting you've got something figured out. Then tomorrow night I have a feeling we'll be in business.'

Kash slipped away. If he'd looked back, he would have seen Trenchard's finger twitching frantically.

45

'And how are you today, Liz?' Sister Vale asked as she helped Liz into a sitting position and plumped up her pillows. 'Finding life a bit more interesting now that you've finally got your glasses?'

'It would be nice to get out of bed and out of the ward a bit more often,' Liz sniffed.

'I'll get Vince to come and take you for a spin in your wheelchair,' Sister Vale said.

'Not him. The other one.'

'There are more than two porters in the hospital, Liz.'

'The one with a nice smile.'

Sister Vale shook her head. 'You don't ask for much, do you, Liz?'

'You don't ask, you don't get, dear. Where are my glasses, now that you mention it?'

'You've not been lying on them, again, have you?' Sister Vale chided.

Liz pushed herself up straighter in the bed. 'That wasn't me, dear. No, I put them right here.' She tapped the bedside table, barren bar a plastic water jug and a half-empty glass. 'I waited long enough for them, so I'm careful what I do with them.'

'Well, they're not there now,' Sister Vale said. 'I'll ask if any of the nurses have seen them.'

'I reckon someone came and took them in the night,' Liz said darkly.

Sister Vale tutted. 'And who would that someone be?'

Liz leaned forward conspiratorially. 'The same person that comes and visits Mr Trenchard in the wee small hours.'

'Oh, not that again, Liz. I told you, it's just your imagination.'

Liz harrumphed. 'Anyone would think I was half mental, the way you talk. I'm not daft, you know. I know what I see with my own eyes.'

Sister Vale folded her arms. 'Well, what exactly is it you've been seeing, then, Liz?'

*   *   *

Dear Mum, Kash began.

The first thing I want to say is, Don't Worry! It is a bit stressful, I'll admit, sneaking Mr Trenchard out of the ward. A nurse or a porter or someone is bound to see us eventually, and if Sister Vale or Dr Carney finds out, well, we might need to call Uncle Terrance. Only joking! But, seriously, Doug sometimes gets a bit too involved in it all, all the brain – computer interface stuff, which I suppose isn't surprising given that this is his field – but sometimes he seems to forget what we're doing this for, and how little time we've got to do it. Anyway, the good news is that I think we'll only need one more night. Mr Trenchard just needs to give us a name. And I think he's getting the hang of the system. Then we can go to Dr Carney and tell him Mr Trenchard's not in a persistent vegetative state; he's locked in. And we can move him somewhere where he'll get proper therapy. (Doug can't wait!) And DI Lambert will have to listen to me – or, rather, he'll have to listen to Mr Trenchard. If Mr Trenchard reports an assault, Lambert can't not investigate it, can he?

I'm sorry, Mum, I'm rambling. I also wanted to let you know that the antibiotics seem to have worked – or maybe I never needed them in the first place. No symptoms from the needle-stick, anyhow, so it probably was an accident. And that business with the holdall? A cleaner could have come in and moved it, I suppose. Maybe they thought they'd nab it and then lost their nerve when they looked inside? Anyway, it doesn't matter – it'll all be over soon.

And then Claire and I – well, I may have some plans . . .

46

When Trenchard heard the footsteps, he thought it must be Kash, coming to take him for his next session. Strange: it felt like the same night. Had he missed a whole day? The sense of time was the hardest to keep hold of, imprisoned as he was in the vault of his own skull, where minutes or hours had no meaning. But it was not morning, he was sure of that, because the ward was still bathed in nocturnal gloom. Perhaps Kash had come back to give him a pep talk, to tell him to keep his pecker up or some such blather. He meant well, but by God the drivel he sometimes came out with.

The footsteps came to a halt. He could make him out now; a silent, shadowy form to the right in his tunnel of vision. Come, on, Kash, cat got your tongue? He suddenly felt guilty for having mocked him. Had Kash read his mind, and was now sulking? Don't be absurd! If mind-reading was possible, then all his problems would be over. No need for this excruciating business with his finger.

'Is it true? Are you really in there, Michael?'

He went cold.

Not Kash. Not the man who had come to save him.

Her.

He tried desperately to see more. Damn these eyes that only looked in one direction! Damn these muscles that wouldn't turn him to see! He couldn't tell how close she was, not until he felt the warmth of her breath on his neck.

He smelled her distinctive perfume, the scent that had once quickened his heart with excitement, with anticipation, but which now did so with dread.

* * *

Come on, Kash! Where are you? He vainly thrashed at the bonds that kept him paralyzed.

Still she didn't move. After a few moments he grew calmer. All right then, she's come back to torment me one more time. What's it going to be? Another card? The three-way tap? That catheter trick was a nasty one. Do your worst. Because I'll survive it. She didn't want to kill him, that much was abundantly clear. In which case, he'd live to fight another day. Just twenty-four more hours and then, with luck, he'd have his revenge. He'd give Kash the name. And then she'd be the one in a padded cell. For the rest of her life.

Mute, unable to move, he felt strangely powerful.

He was the one in control, now.

Come on, you bitch, get on with it!

Suddenly she was right in front of him. She smiled.

'You can hear me, can't you? Oh, I'd so hoped for it. But there are so many variables in medicine. You know that better than most. Will they get to you in time? How well would your particular brain cope without oxygen? Did I give you too little for too long? And the noose? What's the stamina of a man? Is he a fighter or does he give in? I'd hoped for so much and expected so little. But to find that you really were aware all that time, that you understood what was happening . . . Oh!' She beamed. 'You do know what it must have been like.'

And now, at last, he remembered. Not just who, but why.

She passed from Trenchard's sight for a moment, and then he felt her breath, curling into the cavities of his ear.

'I imagined you could, when we had our little chats, of course. I so wanted you to know what was going on. But I never really believed it. It was all a question of balance, you see. I tried so hard to get it right. Too much' – she closed her hand '– and you were gone. Too little' – she shrugged '– and you might have recovered to spill the beans. And therein lies the problem. We can't have that, I'm afraid.' She trailed a finger down his cheek. 'No, that would spoil everything.'

Moments later, she drew back and he could see her again. 'I know all about your twitchy finger, Michael. Just itching to tell all. So I'm afraid, as the saying goes, this is going to hurt a little bit.' She waited a moment, then added, 'Actually, more than a little bit. I know it can't be hidden. But it'll be some random nutter with a general axe to grind. The letter to the newspaper has already been sent.'

She stooped, producing a thick piece of towel. 'This might get a little noisy, and we don't want to wake the neighbours, do we?'

She stooped again, this time rising with a small bench vice. Again, she held it in his field of view. 'Not top of the range, I'm afraid. But then, I'm only planning to use it once.' She turned, and he could hear her gently rotating the handle to attach it to the low bedside table.

'And finally . . .' With a flourish, she produced a pair of pliers and then . . . another pair? No, these were in surgical steel. They were . . . My God, thought Trenchard. NO! NO! NO!

Trenchard felt his arm being lifted, and the dull pressure of the vice being tightened around the distal joint of his little finger. Then something pressed around the next joint down, before he felt the towel being wrapped around it.

'Here we go.'

The snap was less a noise than a physical sensation. A moment later, the surge of pain followed it, chased rapidly by the wave of nausea. He felt the sweat blister across his face like smallpox, rivulets immediately spilling from his cheeks and across his upper lip, and into his mouth.

He heard the squeak of the vice, and then some repositioning.

'OK, same finger, next joint.'

Again, the pain lanced through the whole hand, engulfing his arm.

She leaned in. 'That was loud! Just as well I brought the towel!'

And so she continued, methodically working her way across every joint, every bone, in every finger. For Trenchard, the entire universe was now nothing but raging, flaming pain.

'And finally—' She raised a new tool. Bone nibblers. More than pliers, they were designed to cut through bone. 'Let's just make sure that troublesome index finger can't make a nuisance of itself.' This time she raised the hand in front of his face, opening the jaws of the instrument around the last joint of the index finger. Closing the jaws, she gritted her teeth, and squeezed. She started to rock the instrument from side to side. Blood trickled from around the blades, an indentation appearing before, quite suddenly, the jaws closed and the finger tip tilted to one side. She stopped, seized it and, twisting and pulling, finally separated the last attachments of skin.

'Now that really should do it!' She held the hand before his face. The fingers were livid in blue and black, sticking out at crazy angles, almost unrecognizable as part of a human hand.

She stepped back to admire her handiwork.

'I hope you understand, Michael. I really don't want you to die. I imagine that's what you'd like me to do, right now. But I'm not going to. Not while you can still go on suffering. Not while you can know what it was like. That's the important thing.'

She leaned over him to study his face. It was inert, a mask, showing nothing of the agony she knew he must be feeling within.

* * *

In the corner of his vision he saw the ripple of the curtains as she passed through, back onto ward fourteen. The receding footfall told him she was walking away. They would find him here in the morning, with his ruined hands. They would get a surgeon or two. But no one would think to give him pain relief. After all, he wasn't conscious, was he? She knew that, of course. The agony would be unbearable. But, worse, much worse than that, he'd never be able to tell anyone.

He'd never be able to say her name.

She'd won. The insane bitch had won.

Unless . . . in the midst of his agony, a tiny flame of hope flickered.

And then, as unconsciousness was about to smother his thoughts, he heard a shrill voice crying out into the darkness.

47

It wasn't unusual for Liz to wake in the middle of the night. That came with old age. But this was more than her routine nocturnal restlessness. Something had definitely woken her up. Something or someone. She licked her lips and looked down past her toes. There was movement – there, in the corner where Mr Trenchard slept. A figure was stealing out from between the curtains.

Imagination, my eye! she thought to herself. She reached for her glasses on her bedside table, then remembered they were gone. She screwed her eyes tightly shut, then stretched them, wide and owl-like. She couldn't be certain, but it looked like a woman. A woman in a nurse's uniform. Just one of the night nurses, then, gone to check on him? Whenever Liz found herself despairing at the thought of her own end, she remembered Michael Trenchard and reminded herself that, even now, with her body giving up on itself, she had cause to feel good about life. There was always somebody who had it worse than you . . .

Then a thought struck her: nurses didn't usually move that fast or with such purpose. Nurses did not look back anxiously over their shoulders.

Nurses did not wear black leather gloves. They were black leather? Whatever.

Her blood boiled. This was a hospital, damn them! Couldn't they leave the man alone for once?

She propped herself slightly onto one elbow and called out, but when the figure just kept on walking, she realized she'd only made a croak. She swallowed and tried again – louder this time, so loud she was certain she would wake every soul on the ward. Right now, she didn't care. They could always go back to sleep. But whatever had happened to Mr Trenchard could not wait.

'You!' she cried. 'Yes, *you*! I see you! Leave that man alone. He's helpless! You ought to be ashamed!'

The woman dressed like a nurse took no notice; if anything, she quickened her pace.

Liz wanted to leap out of bed to stop her, but knew that she'd just end up a pathetic heap on the floor. What could she do? The woman was about to disappear through the doors into the back corridor. She tried one last desperate ploy.

'I know who you are!' she bluffed.

The figure stopped and wheeled around.

Liz's breath caught in her throat.

The woman darted back, past the alcove where Mr Trenchard lay, past the empty beds between, moving swiftly to Liz's bed space. Now Liz saw her fully, her face white in the stark shadows of the ward at night.

Liz's eyes darted around, but there was no other movement on ward fourteen. The nurses must have been dozing in the ward office. Nothing but snores from the surrounding beds.

'What have you done to him?' she breathed, her voice reduced to a rasp.

Liz's hand reached out across the bedside table where her glasses ought to be. Somewhere near was the alarm button – where she could call for help. Now where *was* it?

A strong hand suddenly seized hers, while another lifted the buzzer and dropped it over the far side of the locker, out of reach. The woman shook her head. 'Why couldn't you have minded your own business?' she asked softly. Liz thought she heard genuine compassion in her voice. For a moment she was confused. Perhaps this *was* a nurse. It was true, she did get confused sometimes, even though she wouldn't admit it.

But then she looked at the eyes and all she saw was danger.

'I'll tell them. I've seen your face, you know. *I've seen your face!*'

'I know,' the figure whispered.

The hand moved so fast that Liz could scarcely see it, the open palm clamping over her mouth like a vice. With her dentures out, her gums were forced together and her lips rode over one another, forming a soft wet seal. She spluttered and tried to shout. Nothing came out but a muted moaning. She tried to breathe in, but the hand had now sealed her mouth completely, the index finger lying horizontally across her upper lip, pushing up against her nostrils which flared and snorted noisily with each attempted breath.

Liz's eyes were drawn upwards, looking at the face of the woman who was killing her. Yes, *killing her*. That was what she was doing. All this effort by so many people to keep her alive, and now someone in a nurse's uniform was efficiently choking the last wisps of life out of her.

Liz turned her head, following the woman's gaze. She was staring, not at Liz, but at her own right hand. From somewhere she had drawn a small plastic syringe.

Liz snorted once more. It was a loud wet snort, the sort that the carthorses used to produce as they were making their way back to the brewery past their house in the morning, back when Liz was a little girl without a care in the world. She reached round with her right hand, to try and defend herself somehow – but the woman quickly leaned her body sideways across her, pinning her arm against her torso. Her head flopped back onto the pillows.

Liz struggled harder, trying to shake her head from side to side. Finally, she could do nothing but lie still. This was expert restraint, all done in a cool, unhurried manner. The word that came to mind was *professional*. Confident. Almost calming. As if the visitor were trying to make sure that no one got upset.

Liz watched as the woman's fingers deftly flicked the plastic sheath from the end of the thin orange needle. Her eyes widened. She attempted each movement in sequence. Head? Pinned. Right arm? Trapped. Torso? She tried to turn to one side, but her body was being held rigid, as immobile as poor Mr Trenchard.

Liz could feel the sheets being swept back from her left thigh.

As the woman sank the needle in, they both stopped breathing. The woman depressed the plunger, then pulled the needle out again.

Time seemed to stop.

There was a silence. They both waited.

Almost at once, Liz felt an intense local burning in her leg. The muscle seemed to be getting cramp.

She could feel the weight of the woman across her. Could feel her hot breath against her chest. The woman's breath was slow and even. In the midst of her panic, Liz, the connoisseur of nursing care, felt a flicker of admiration for a job expertly done.

Liz tried to roll again. She was still pinned. She tried to move her head. The woman pressed harder. The leg was feeling odd. It was twitching. It was as if a thousand ants were biting at her beneath her skin, or a thousand fish-hooks tugging her flesh in different directions.

Then she saw her chance. The woman thought her work was done. She had loosened her grip on Liz's arm – but Liz wasn't quite finished. She had one more last gasp in her yet. Shifting around, she grabbed the woman's forearm, sinking her nails in as deep as she could. But despite putting every last ounce of her strength into it, her grip was feeble, and weakening. She clawed back with her hand, raking the woman's flesh – but the woman hardly even flinched.

She was waiting, Liz realized. Waiting patiently for the end.

Liz tried again to move. Her whole body was heavy. It wouldn't shift at her command. Her breaths had taken on a strange quality. They sounded as if she was underwater, as if she was eight years old again and swimming in the canal that ran by their house.

These breaths were coming faster now, each smaller than the last. Weaker. A bouncing ball, where each successive bounce was lower and lower, shorter and shorter.

Her father had bought her a ball once. An old cricket ball, its red leather worn and split along one seam, and its surface scuffed and roughened. But still, no one else had a red cricket ball. Not Rose. Not Alice. None of them. And you could still bounce it. In her mind's eye, she was standing at one end of the street, hurling the ball hard onto the road towards Rose. Rose was laughing, clapping her hands in anticipation. Then Liz turned to her father. He was smiling. She looked back. The ball was bounding away, arcing onwards in a series of parabolas, each lower than the last, a stone skipping on the surface of a pond. Finally, all of its energy spent, the ball dribbled to a halt, next to a cart-track cut that ended on the street corner.

Liz looked for her father. He seemed to have gone.

She looked at the visitor who, staring down at her, gently let go and rose from the bed.

So, it was over. The canal and the cricket ball. Her sisters. Her life, laundry, and loves. The big and the small. All of it was meaningless now. And she would never get to tell what she knew. It was all so sad. It was all such a waste. It was all so . . .

On ward fourteen, another heart ceased to beat.

48

The body was discovered at dawn. The light that streamed in through the open windows found Liz Murray cold and alone, her eyes wide open and mouth gaping as if someone had just told her a particularly juicy piece of gossip.

It was not unusual for a patient to die in the night, of course, especially not on ward fourteen. Sister Vale stood at the end of the bed while one of the first shift nurses drew the curtain around. They would need a doctor to certify the death, but that was just the paperwork; Liz Murray had passed some time in the night, with nobody at her side to hold her hand and tell her that everything was going to be all right. Still, thought Sister Vale, we all go out of this world the way we came in: on our own, don't we? Dying in one's sleep was common enough, and for people like Liz whose body was slowly giving in to the cancer that filled her frail, birdlike body, it was easy to think of it as the kindest way. At least she hadn't suffered. Sister Vale drifted to the head of the bed, where Liz's face lay white and wrinkled, and brushed her hair out of her unseeing eyes.

That was when the clatter of footsteps and the screaming began.

Sister Vale stumbled back, through the curtain that hid Liz from the ward, and saw that one of the nurses – Molly, new to the hospital and not long out of school uniform too – had reached Mr Trenchard's bed, ready to turn him in his chair to start his day.

Sister Vale marched over. One of the more experienced nurses already had an arm around Molly, ushering her away from the bedside. Wrapped in his bloody sheets, Trenchard sat slumped sideways in his wheelchair. If this was a film, it wasn't hospital drama. It was horror.

The first call wasn't to Kash. It was to the police. And then Carney.

* * *

Kash wandered up the corridor with a lightness in his step, already anticipating what the day ahead would bring. Just one more day to get through, and then all this would be over, he felt sure of it.

As he approached the doors to the ward, he was surprised to see two police officers barring his entry. Frowning, he flashed his ID badge. 'Kash Devan. I'm the doctor on the ward.' They nodded and let him past.

Most of the curtains were drawn around the beds on ward fourteen but, at the far end, by the entrance to the back stairwell, a second police cordon had been established. A young WPC was standing at the foot of Michael Trenchard's bed, taking notes from Sister Vale, while Dr Carney hovered gloomily at the opening where Mr Trenchard lay. There were others at the bedside; as he approached, Kash could see them as silhouettes against the half-drawn curtain.

Carney looked over his shoulder as Kash approached.

'There's nothing you can do here, Dr Devan. I told those idiots not to let anyone else onto the ward. This situation is *not* to go beyond ward fourteen. We do not want to be on the front pages again tomorrow. And you will need to give a statement to account for your movements last night.' He shook his head, and turned towards Trenchard.

Sister Vale detached herself from the police officer and started remonstrating with Dr Carney, but Kash barely heard.

He gathered himself and walked to the foot of Mr Trenchard's bed.

'My God . . .'

The hand was mutilated almost beyond recognition. Distorted, it lay swollen, blue and red, like a jigsaw wrongly forced together. He stepped forward.

'Don't touch it,' Dr Carney insisted. 'Forensics.'

Kash stepped back unsteadily, as if at sea. They'd come for Trenchard again, in the night. But this time it wasn't to torture him. It was to stop him communicating.

So they knew.

They'd somehow learned that Trenchard was aware, could name names, could *tell*. But *how* did they know? He'd told . . .?

And now Trenchard couldn't communicate. Not anymore.
It had all been for nothing.

He turned to Carney, 'What happened?'

Carney looked away, saying nothing.

Then Kash heard a familiar voice. 'Dr Devan. Just the man
I need to talk to.'

Kash looked up. It was DI Lambert, approaching with an
expression of distaste more fitting of someone who'd just
realized that they'd stepped in dog's excrement. Kash felt
like grabbing him by the shoulders and shaking him. *You
see! You see what they've done to him?* But he had enough
sense to stay quiet.

'I wonder, Dr Devan,' Lambert said, turning to look at him,
'*why* break the fingers of a man who can't use them anyway?'

Kash said nothing.

'Devan?' It was Carney.

Kash remained gazing down at the ruin of Trenchard's
hands. The index finger no longer looked like a piece of
human flesh.

'You can step aside, Devan. There's another patient needs
your attention. Needs certifying. When you're done, give your
name to the policeman at the door. They want statements
from everyone. We'll take things from there.'

Kash angled himself so that Mr Trenchard might see him,
flashing an expression of resolve and determination which he
did not feel.

Susan Vale came to his side. 'Best be out of here, Kash . . .'

'Do *you* know what happened, Sister?'

He hadn't meant to sound aggressive, accusatory, but her outraged look made it clear that this was how his tone had been interpreted. Slowly, he backed away.

'Do *you*?'

Faces blinked at him from the curtain rails along the ward, other patients trying to catch a glimpse of the drama that had unfolded only feet away as they slept. Henrietta Liu called to him as he passed but, lost for words, he could only reply with a sad, despairing smile and a vacuous promise that everything was all right. But everything was not all right.

He hadn't been careful enough. Who had he told? Doug knew, of course. He'd told Claire. Ange. Others? He'd been an idiot to have told anyone at all. And who had *they* told?

As he reached the end of the ward, he could see more police through the glass in the office window. The blinds were down but, through the cracks, he could see DI Lambert and a constable, evidently taking a statement.

Kash walked on, leaden of legs and light of head, suffocated and dissociated from the real world. An ancient deep sea diver. Then he remembered what Dr Carney had said. Sister Vale was at the workstation, organizing Trenchard's transfer to theatres where they would assess the state of his hands, while Carney and Lambert discussed the practicalities of having forensic experts sweep the scene.

'Carney said another patient died in the night?'

She spoke without looking at him. 'Liz Murray.'

* * *

Oh, God. So Liz had finally gone. At times, she'd felt like his one true friend, the only one he could trust and who could bring cheer to his day. It was selfish, he knew. But wasn't all grief selfish in the end?

He tried to sound professional, to keep the tremor from his voice. 'I'm sorry. I guess it had to happen at some point. I'll get on and certify her. Have you called the son?'

'Says he's busy.' She returned to the telephone.

* * *

Kash walked down the ward, slipped behind the curtains which surrounded Liz's bed, and drew up a chair. Drawing it close, he sat and took her hand, stroking the cool flesh with his thumb. A tear swelled from his eye and burst down a cheek.

Her face was pallid and the wrist stiff. She had been dead for some time.

'I'm so sorry, Liz.' The tears came freely now. 'Thanks for being my friend.'

He lifted the hand towards his face, noticing that the fingernails were rimmed in brown.

Odd. She was so fastidious about her appearances, even here.

He wiped his eyes and looked more closely.

Dried blood. He manipulated the index finger of her right hand and saw, on the nail's underside, the skin that had been left behind. With heart racing, he checked each one of the fingers. He'd attended Whiteley's forensic pathology lectures, of course. They'd been given with the local coroner. Half an hour of boring lab tests and legalities, followed by half an hour of gory photographs and great stories. To get a fine dessert, you had to eat your cabbage first. But that all said, you only needed to have watched a detective drama on TV to know what this meant. Liz Murray had put up a fight before she died; she had clawed and grappled with something, with *someone* – some *people?* – before her heart gave up the fight.

* * *

He ran his hands around her neck, but found no bruising there. He touched her lips, cold and blue. They must have pushed a pillow over her face. But why? She must have seen what they did to Mr Trenchard. He gently smoothed a stray hair from Liz's brow, stepped back, then closed the curtains. He would certify – but he would refer to the coroner, saying he couldn't be certain of the cause of death. The coroner might be pissed off, given that Liz was in her nineties and terminally ill, but they'd have no choice if Kash wouldn't certify.

Right to the end, you were trying to tell us, he thought. Whose was the last face you saw, Liz?

Which brought him back to his first question: who knew? Who knew that Mr Trenchard was conscious? That he was capable of communicating?

Doug? Absurd. The man wouldn't harm a fly, and in any case, what possible motive could he have? But he *might* have told someone, of course. He'd ask.

Had Sister Vale seen what they were doing one night? Possibly, but was she really capable of this horror? She had a motive, though.

Then there was Ange. He'd tried to backtrack, but she must have understood the implications of what he was saying. And she had motive and means and, being off work, plenty of opportunity. Not her, though: he couldn't believe it was her. Surely? But then .... But then .... perhaps Ange had also told someone else ...

He swallowed hard as the thought coalesced, the image becoming clearer.

He knew where to look.

Trenchard's attacker would think they were safe now.

They were not.

49

Leaving the chaos and misery of the Victory hospital was a relief, but Kash had to wait until early evening before he finally saw Anna Chaloner. He had tried calling her flat in the morning and then again after lunch. The ward work was soon over, and once he'd given his statement, he'd had hours free to sit in his flat over mugs of coffee, thinking about what he knew – and what he could only guess.

The Higgsville Tower loomed high above the other blocks in that triangle of council developments between Chalk Farm and the sprawl of Kentish Town. A monument to post-war reconstruction, it now seemed drab and ordinary when compared with the garlanded terraces around it. Here, as in so much of London, the poor could look down on the rich.

Kash found a vantage spot in a local café, where the waitress – a Romanian girl with jet black hair – had a sharp tongue for the layabouts who came in search of the all-day breakfast. All day eating it, that was. He ordered a slice of Victoria Sponge and a large mug of black coffee, and his brow furrowed. Some things had started to make sense, perhaps. But now something else did not. The Victory was not Anna Chaloner's local hospital. Why would she have driven a sick child all the way to South London, to the Victory? Did she somehow know the hospital? Or someone who worked there?

* * *

Fortified with cake and caffeine, he was approaching the Higgsville Tower when, by chance, Anna Chaloner appeared from the other direction. She was laden with bags, the week's shopping done on the way home from work. As she entered the access code and opened the door, Kash picked up her bags. 'Allow me.'

She looked round at him, her brow furrowing. 'You're . . . the doctor, aren't you? Dr Devan?'

'I am,' he replied. 'I was there that night. With Edmund.'

'I remember. You were the one who came to tell me. And you were sat in the court, too. But what are you . . .?'

'Mrs Chaloner, I know this is highly irregular. But . . . can I talk to you?'

The lobby of Higgsville Tower was barren. It smelt of the hospital sluice and carpark stairwell, of urine and bleach and bodily fluids.

'I'm afraid I'm on the seventeenth floor.'

'I won't take up much of your time.'

Anna Chaloner weighed this up. Then she smiled weakly. 'Then perhaps you could help me with my shopping?'

* * *

The lifts could only take them to the fifteenth storey and, after that, it was a dismal trek up the concrete stairs to reach the seventeenth. They didn't speak, standing in silence in the coffin confines of the elevator before Kash followed her breathlessly up the steps. As Anna fumbled to slot the key in the lock, Kash looked out of the window, down across the rooftops of Kentish Town, all the way to Camden Lock. Night was hardening, the temperature falling, a spatter of stars crystallizing above the city, and just beginning to glitter.

Anna opened the door and, stepping through, flicked on a fluorescent light. The hallway appeared stark and uninviting – but then Kash saw, as the bulb flickered and hummed, the school portraits that covered the wall, the swimming certificates and testaments to success at Grades 1, 2 and 3 clarinet. He was looking at a *life*. Moments later, the lights stopped strobing and Anna went into the flat. Kash followed after her, wiping his feet on the mat as he did so.

'Oh, I wouldn't worry,' said Anna, gesturing to Kash to deposit the shopping on the floor by the telephone stand. 'Edmund never did that. The place was always full of mud. It was as much as I could manage to get him to take off his football boots before he came in.'

Kash smiled back. 'That's boys for you.'

'Yes. But girls aren't much easier. With boys, you can see the mud and the emotions.' She suddenly appeared distant, before her smile once more flicked on and she ushered him down the short entrance hall. A kitchen lay ahead of him, with the open door revealing a sink full of foam, and a single plate and set of cutlery draining on the sideboard.

'Please.' She gestured to the doorway on the right, which led into a small sitting room. 'A drink?'

'It's been coffee all day,' Kash smiled. 'So . . . a tea?'

'White no sugar?'

He smiled. 'Please.'

*   *   *

Kash sat on the short blue sofa beneath the window at the end of the room, and looked around. In the background, he could hear a kettle being filled.

Facing him was a large armchair in fake red velvet, with a hand-embroidered cloth lying over its back. Above it was a small picture of the Madonna and Child. To the left of the chair, a sidelight sat on a large African drum. A small corner shelving unit stood adjacent to it, and was stacked with a clutter of smaller ornaments.

He looked to his right.

A television set was positioned so as to face the armchair. Beyond this, and set in the right-hand wall, was a small faux fireplace with a glazed tile surround and a wooden mantelpiece set above it. On the mantelpiece sat a carved wooden rhinoceros and a framed photograph. It must have been taken fifteen or more years ago, Kash thought. In it, Mrs Chaloner stood holding a child, who was probably a little more than a year old. Edmund, presumably. A man stood to Anna's other side, a guitar case at his feet.

From the kitchen came the clink of crockery. Kash stood and walked over to the shelves. He was beginning to browse the books when he heard footsteps and, shoving his hands in his pockets as he turned, he saw Anna carrying two steaming, mismatched cups in her hands.

'Thanks, Mrs Chaloner.'

'Please. Call me Anna.'

Kash nodded. 'Thanks.' He'd try, but it somehow felt wrong to be so informal and relaxed. He walked back to the sofa, and sat himself down. They both sipped their drinks.

'Doctor, if you don't mind me asking, I mean to say, it's good of you to come over, but . . . I hadn't expected it. It's not necessary.' She stalled, and sipped her tea before raising her eyes. 'So what brings you here? If it's to talk about Edmund and what happened, I'd really rather not.'

He raised a hand. 'It's Kash, by the way. And not directly. I'm sorry. I'll try not to be too long, and to make this as easy as possible.'

She sipped her tea again. 'So . . .?'

'Anna, there's been some trouble at the hospital. You know, of course, about what happened to Michael Trenchard . . .'

Anna remained impassive.

He paused. 'And then . . . there's Angela Warner.'

'Oh . . .'

Kash saw how her eyes darted away, as if unwilling to look directly at him.

'It isn't a crime, Mrs Chaloner. Ange is a good person, as well as a wonderful doctor I'm . . . glad she found you. If everyone had a friend like Ange, well, the world would be a better place.'

She nodded, bringing the cup to her lips. 'She's been a comfort to me.'

Kash waited a moment before he spoke, until he felt she was ready. 'She did tell me that she'd come.' He paused again. 'When did you last hear from Ange, Mrs Chaloner?'

'I'm not sure I . . . I don't understand, Doctor. A day ago? Two? I'm afraid I'm not sure what you're . . .'

Her hand had started to tremble and now it jerked upwards, slopping scalding tea from the rim of her cup and over her left hand. Cursing, Anna Chaloner got to her feet – and Kash did the same. 'Cold tap,' he said. 'Come on, Mrs Chaloner. Doctor's orders.'

Together they moved to the kitchen, a cramped space with oven and sink and only a sliver of counter in between. A little table nestled below the window, and beside it a door led out onto the balcony where all of Anna Chaloner's laundry was hanging out to dry. Edmund's dirty football boots, still smeared with dried mud from his very last game, sat on a bed of newspaper underneath the radiator.

As Anna ran her hand under the cold tap, Kash continued, 'What I don't understand – and do forgive me, Anna – is why Ange? You must have family, people you turned to after what happened. Wasn't Ange . . . a reminder? You looked so shocked to see me today. It must have been even more raw to see Ange, to get to know her, to . . . '

Almost instantly Kash knew he had overstepped the mark. He saw a look – half sorrow, half spike of sudden anger – flicker across Anna's face. But Anna Chaloner had been through worse and, whatever it was, she quickly bottled it up.

'Angela Warner did her best to save my boy,' she said in a firm voice. 'So did you. I've met a number of good souls from the Victory hospital. I don't think they're all like Michael Trenchard.' She fixed him with a pointed stare. 'As for family? My parents died some time ago. I have an aunt in Penzance, and a sister in Rye. We haven't spoken in years, though I'm grateful she sent a card.' This last she said with some bitterness that, by the look on her face, she quickly regretted.

'I know how it is, Mrs Chaloner. My extended family, they're on the other side of the world. I'm sorry there's nobody here you can . . . '

Anna kneeled, ferreted in the tiny fridge-freezer, and returned with a packet of frozen peas with which she started icing her hand. 'I didn't say there was *nobody*. That's where my story gets a little complicated, I'm afraid.' She paused and sighed, her shoulders dropping a little, resigned to telling her tale. 'Edmund wasn't my only child. I have a daughter, you see, much older. A grown woman, if you could believe! And . . . well, there had been some distance between us, you might say. But we'd started to see a little of each other in the past year and, with Edmund gone, I wanted to . . . reach out, I wanted us to, well, be family. And life is too short to waste another second.'

'I can understand that, Mrs Chaloner.'

'I'm not a religious person, Kash, but there are some things I do believe in. And first and foremost is that, when one thing is taken from us, another thing is given. One door closes and another opens, as they say. The world turns like that. It's helped me through some dark, dark nights – knowing that if only I didn't give up, something good would come to me.' A mysterious smile played in the corners of her lips. 'And something has.' Suddenly she straightened; the smile was gone and she stood upright, as if brought to attention. 'I'm going to make more tea. Care for another cup?'

'Yes,' said Kash, 'Thank you.'

He watched as she returned to the sink to top up the kettle and thought: I mustn't push too hard. He had not come here to accuse her. He had to remind himself of that. He had come to *discover*, to know if he was right. Anything else would have been a step too far. He only had to *know*. After that he would decide how to protect Mr Trenchard. He could reveal to the Victory that the man was still there, locked inside the tomb of his body – and perhaps there was still a way that Doug, or some others on his rehab team, could puzzle out the entrance code to his mind. The technology was advancing every year. Perhaps there was a way he could still take the stand, still testify as to what had happened that awful night . . .

Anna Chaloner had found new teacups, and was setting them down on saucers she had unearthed from the back of the cupboard. As he waited, Kash looked around some more. Through the balcony doors, night had settled, the street lights glowing white and orange across Kentish Town, mapping the streets all the way to Euston and beyond.

His eyes panned down. On the table top was a bowl of fruit – six apples and two over-ripe bananas – and by its side was a small pile of letters, bills in brown paper envelopes and a single envelope in white, with delicate cursive handwriting on the front.

He caught sight of the photograph propped up behind the letters, against the side of the fruit bowl itself. In the picture a lone face beamed out, her head cocked to one side as she gazed, lovingly, at whoever was taking the picture.

Kash's eyes moved on while his brain processed what he had just seen.

He looked at the photograph again.

All of his world had boiled down to that single photograph, a little thing, six inches by four, but a window, he saw now, into another world; a window into the truth of what had really happened that last night of Michael Trenchard's former life.

This was not what he had come for. Not what he had expected, and Kash desperately wanted it to be untrue – but there was the evidence, staring up at him from the table top.

With a pounding heart, he turned.

50

'Mr Trenchard, this is Chloe. She's come to take some pictures . . .'

Pictures, thought Trenchard. What fucking good are pictures? Use your fucking brain, Vale! Kash did!

He was only dimly aware of Sister Vale parting the curtains that surrounded his bed as a police photographer entered. Briefly, she crossed his field of view, a visitor from another world. And that was what she was now, her and all the rest. He was marooned on a barren planet and the thin sliver of hope he'd had, that tiny thread connecting his lonely world to Earth, was gone. Gone in a fury of shattered bones.

The photographer appeared to be crouched at his side, each flash of light accompanied by a shutter click and followed by a high-pitched electronic whine. Nearby, Susan Vale was talking. For Michael Trenchard, all was confusion and despair.

His internal voice was screaming now. After everything, you had control. GONE! Gone with . . . with the snap of a finger. Gone like the hope that any of this might ever change . . .

Gone, the voice cackled shrilly, LIKE YOUR MIND.

And then there was another sound. It started soft and distant at the back of his brain, but grew in intensity until it was the only thing he could hear, eclipsing Vale and this policewoman *and everything outside, even pushing the awful, pulsing pain in his shattered hands into the background.*

It was not a sound which he'd ever heard before. Certainly not a sound he had ever made.

It was the sound of a man crying.

He wondered who it was.

51

Kash stared at the photograph propped against the fruit bowl. Anna Chaloner was still talking behind him, rattling a spoon as she made more tea. 'The work helps me forget,' she was saying. 'But the occasional visitor to talk to about Edmund helps too, sometimes. Because that means Edmund, well, it means Edmund isn't forgotten. Not just another statistic. A real . . .'

By the time she turned around, Kash had lifted the envelope. The slightest touch of his hand revealed so much more of the photograph. His eyes locked on to the face staring out of the picture. He knew those sad, dark eyes. He knew the way that chestnut hair turned so richly red when it was caught by the sun – just as it had in the photograph. He knew the tan lines and the single mole at the corner of her eye. Damn it, he even knew the grassland and the steep incline behind it. Primrose Hill.

He knew because he had taken this photograph himself. He had pointed the camera, he was the one who had told her to say 'cheese' . . .

Behind him, Anna had fallen suddenly silent. Kash looked up to see her staring at him.

'Anna, why do you have this picture?'

Her face had fallen. She put the teacup she had been offering down and extended her hand instead, as if to demand Kash hand the photograph over.

'I thought you came here to check up on me? To see if I was all right, how I was coping. I thought you'd come to make amends for what that bastard, that surgeon, did – or, rather, what he didn't do, on the night my Edmund died. Not to go snooping in my private correspondence . . .'

Kash held the photograph up, as if to put the girl beaming happily on a sunny day up alongside Anna Chaloner herself. What a fool he'd been! Their eyes were the same. The colour of their skin. Even the way their hair turned to flame in the golden light . . .

'You said, before, that Edmund wasn't your only child.'

Anna Chaloner softened. 'He was the only one I raised – but I was a foolish girl once and, like lots of foolish young girls, I made a mistake.' She caught the way he was looking at her, as if he'd made an assumption. 'No, not in getting pregnant. Lots of girls get pregnant. No, my mistake was in listening to my mother. In giving up instead of flouting the convention, telling them all to jump off the top of a tall building, and getting on with the business of being a mother myself. Giving my Charlotte up for adoption was the most painful thing I'd ever done. There hasn't been a day gone by, even with all that's happened since, that I haven't thought about it. What might have been, if only I'd had the support, if only I'd had my head screwed on. If only I'd been stronger. Why, I needn't be living here in this shithole at all. It could have been me and my Charlotte and my Edmund in a nice little house, two up and two down, the three of us together. A family.'

Anna Chaloner reached out and plucked the photograph from Kash's fingers.

'She's been a great comfort to me, ever since—'

'Her name isn't Charlotte, Mrs Chaloner. Well, is it?'

'She'll always be Charlotte to me.'

Kash breathed. 'Her name is Claire. Claire Barker.'

Anna was lost, staring into the picture. 'She said she wouldn't mind if I called her Charlotte. When it was just the two of us, meeting for a coffee or a stroll or . . .'

'Which is why you took Edmund all the way to the Victory. Where she worked.'

'We'd started meeting for some months before. I wanted her to know . . . that I trusted her. Her hospital. Of course, she never knew her half-brother. Had never met him.'

She looked up. 'But his loss has been our gain. She's given me such strength. Oh, Angela helped where she could – but it was Charlotte, my Charlotte, who *really* helped.'

'How did she help, Mrs Chaloner?'

'More than you can possibly—'

'Tell me,' Kash said gently, though he wanted to scream the words out. *TELL ME!*

'Doctor, Kash . . . I'm not sure I . . .'

'It's simple enough, Anna.' His voice was still quiet, but there was steely determination in it, too. 'How did she help? What did you have her do?'

'Me?' she gasped.

'It's what you wanted, isn't it? Like all the rest of them. Oh, they all have their reasons. The moments he scorned them or made them look like fools or just abandoned them. It's different with you, though, isn't it? How blind have I been? There's a simple maxim they teach you in medical school, Anna. They call it Occam's Razor. The simplest diagnosis is almost always the correct one. Don't go looking for exotic maladies, don't go looking for rare disorders that might get published, if it's really just a common cold. Look at what's in front of you. Diagnose what you see. And that's what I should have been doing. Damn it, that's what Mr Trenchard would have done . . .' He stopped, running his hand through his hair. 'Well,' he said, 'nobody could blame you. Your boy might still be here, if only Trenchard had cared. And at the inquest, where you might have said it all, where Ange had kicked open the door and practically begged you to do it, you didn't say a word. This was why, wasn't it, Anna? Because you'd already found a way, hadn't you, to settle that score?'

'I don't know what you're talking about . . .'

'Oh, I think you do.'

Anna's face contorted. 'I'll have you struck off,' she spat. 'A doctor, forcing his way into a grieving mother's house, accusing her—'

'Where were you that night, Anna? The night Michael Trenchard—'

She looked at him pityingly. 'Even if I'd wanted to – and, God damn him, I *did* want to – how do you think it might have worked? I'm a secretary. I turn up and I answer the phone and I take messages and, if someone in the office is feeling particularly lazy, I take dictation.'

'You weren't always a secretary, though, were you?' Kash said.

She looked at him incredulously. 'That was all a long time ago. I make the tea and I make the fucking coffee. All I had was Edmund! What kind of life is that – living here, day in, day out, every day the fucking same – without him? So yes, Kash, yes: I was once a nurse. And yes, I wanted the man dead. I wanted somebody to pay for what happened to my boy. What does that make me? I'll tell you, Kash. *Normal.* That's what it makes me. *Sane.* Anyone in their right mind would have the same thoughts. But did I put thought into action? *Could* I have? No, Kash. I wouldn't know how. Me? A sixty-words-per-minute assassin? You've watched too many films. Now . . .'

She paused, but only to gather her breath; she had been flailing so wildly that she was already spent, backed up against the kitchen units and holding onto the counter as if she might crumble at any moment.

'Now . . . get out of my house! Get out and never come back.'

Kash was already up and out of the kitchen door. Anna Chaloner was right behind him – as if, in her fury, she might thrust him bodily out of the flat. He looked back once, and over her shoulder he caught sight of Claire's picture, still lying on the table.

The door slammed shut behind him.

He leaned against the wall, breathing hard. He'd come, assuming that Anna was the cuprit all along. That Ange had told her that Trenchard could communicate. That she'd gone back to break his fingers. Or perhaps asked Ange to? But now this?

Claire. Anna Chaloner's daughter.

What could it mean?

To do what had been done to Mr Trenchard required two things: motive and expertise.

Well, motive was clear enough; Anna Chaloner hadn't tried to deny it.

But expertise? Maybe she was right. It was a long time ago that she'd last exercised those skills. The practice of medicine, or of nursing, wasn't like riding a bike. You got rusty. And then you forgot.

Maybe she had needed a helper.

A helper with all the necessary skills there at her fingertips, kept sharp with daily practice. He thought of the face in the picture, staring back at him with those beautiful dark eyes.

Not Anna Chaloner and Angela Warner, after all. Anna Chaloner and *Claire*.

Motive and expertise. Mother and long-lost daughter. Sister to a slaughtered brother. Or maybe just the sister, the daughter, on her own . . .? Claire had known about Trenchard's abandonment of Edmund, as he'd told her. She knew about the locker and the bag. About Kash's own suspicions. And then about Trenchard being conscious, and soon to communicate.

Kash stumbled from the flat and out into the council block courtyard just as the rain began to fall in sheets of grey all across London. He glanced back to see Anna Chaloner watching him from the balcony. Then she stepped back inside, pulled the curtain across the windows and was gone.

He splashed on hurridly towards the main road, brow furrowed and gaze fixed only a metre ahead. The Valentine's card. The plastic tap. The clamp across Mr Trenchard's catheter. He should have seen it all along.

He sprinted for the nearest bus stop, waving his arm wildly to flag down the first taxi he saw.

'Denmark Hill,' he gasped as he tumbled into the back seat.

52

The windscreen wipers thumped a drumbeat warning and, by the time Kash ducked out of the cab and onto the kerb, the pounding rain made it hard to see anything clearly. The taxi pulled away through the overflowing gutter with a splash, soaking him to the knees, but Kash barely noticed. Already he was looking up. The newsagent was locking the corrugated steel shutter for the night, but there were lights on in the windows of the flat above. Kash saw a shadow move across the window blinds: a woman in stark relief, clasping a wine glass in one hand.

Someone was home.

Kash rushed to the door and hammered once, twice, three times with his fist. It had been a night much like this, he remembered, when Mr Trenchard had been found, the rain thrashing viciously at the rooftops of the Victory hospital.

When there was no answer he tried the buzzer, then knocked again, each time louder than the last, then stepped back into the rain, looked up at the window and, with his hands cupped to his mouth, shouted her name. At first the shadow in the window remained exactly where it was. The only response came from the newsagent who had finished locking up. He took one look at Kash, muttered, 'Bleedin' drunks . . .'

'Claire!' Kash thundered.

For a moment Kash stood dumbly, the rain streaming into his eyes, and stared at the door. A moment later, he threw himself bodily at it.

Knocking down a door was not like it was in the movies. It did not explode inwards in a shower of splinters, nor fly off cleanly at the hinges, spilling Kash into the shadowy stairwell. He had to hurl himself at it three times before he heard something give. Then he wrenched at the handle, hammered his shoulder into the wood again, and finally heard a crunch as the lock gave way. Only then did he step inside.

The stairwell was narrow and neglected. Paint flaked off the walls, the naked dangling lightbulb hung dead overhead, and the carpet under Kash's feet was threadbare in patches, revealing weathered floorboards underneath.

He kicked through the takeaway menus scattered beneath the letterbox and leaped up the stairs three at a time.

He was about to hammer on the door at the top of the stairs, when something stopped him. He took a breath to steady himself and reached for the door handle. It was unlocked. He turned the handle softly, and pushed the door open.

As soon as he stepped inside he knew it was Claire he'd seen at the window, not Tiff. He could smell her perfume, ripe with honey and elderflower, floating in the air. He stopped in the hallway before venturing through. He could hear her humming, low and off-key, and he wondered, briefly, if perhaps she wasn't alone.

Then he remembered what he had come here to do and walked directly into the living room.

Claire was in the kitchenette, stirring the bubbling pan of pasta sauce which sat on the hob. She was wearing her white dressing gown – evidently preparing for a cosy night in. She had a pair of headphones on and was swaying gently to the music, holding a glass of shiraz in one hand, oblivious to all the mayhem.

For a second she did not see him, and he just stood there, frozen in the moment, watching her, a million crazy thoughts tumbling through his brain. Perhaps if he didn't move, things would stay the way they had been; he could have his old Claire, the one he had fallen in love with. Time would stand still.

Then catching sight of him out of the corner of her eye, she started, spilling her glass of wine over the stove. She yanked the headphones off, her eyes wide.

'Kash! What the hell are you . . .'

Kash was shaking. He took one more step into the room.

For a moment he couldn't speak.

'How in hell did you get in here, Kash? Christ, you frightened the life out of me. And . . .' She looked at him properly. 'Look at the state of you . . . has something happened, Kash? Is it . . . Mr Trenchard?'

Kash ran a hand through his hair, squeezing rainwater out of his eyes.

'Claire,' he breathed. 'I trusted you . . .'

The silence that followed frightened him. It was then that he knew he was right, all of it was right. Claire had been the one, the one to trap Mr Trenchard, and all along, all the time since, he'd been helping her torture him more. It was her name that Trenchard had been so desperate to say.

Claire.

'Trusted me?'

She sounded incredulous, bewildered. My God, he thought, she was good, a chill running through him that was nothing to do with being soaked to the skin; almost completely believable. *Almost.* But then she would have had to be, wouldn't she, to fool Mr Trenchard into letting his guard down? He dreaded to think how far she'd been willing to go in the role, how *realistic* her performance must have been.

The woman he loved.

A sadistic homicidal psychopath.

'Kash, you're going to have to help me out. I don't understand.' She was looking concerned now.

Kash held her gaze. Then, slowly, 'You're Anna Chaloner's daughter.'

Claire flinched as if she'd been struck a physical blow. Her face changed. And for the first time Kash thought: maybe she isn't such a good actress after all. A real actress would have fronted it out, said he was being preposterous, screamed at him for breaking down her door and making bizarre accusations – but instead her expression had become rigid and her eyes were welling up and the wine glass she was still holding was shaking, spilling its last bright red drops over the snowy fluff of her dressing gown.

'Why didn't you tell me?'

'How did you find out?'

'I went to see Anna Chaloner. I thought it had to be her. I'd let slip to Ange that Trenchard was conscious, that he might be able to communicate. Then I remembered Ange had been in contact with Anna Chaloner. What if she'd told her about Trenchard? And then I remembered from the inquest, Anna Chaloner had trained as a nurse. Who had a better motive? He killed her son. It all fitted.' He shook his head. 'And then I saw the photograph. Of you.'

'You had no right, Kash . . . no right.'

'How long have you known? That Anna Chaloner was your real mother?'

Claire opened her mouth to reply, but no words came out. Tears were flowing down her cheeks.

'You've known for a while, haven't you, Claire? You told me the clock was ticking, you wanted to find out who your mother was before it was too late. And you did. Or perhaps you'd already found out by then. You did your digging and you found her, didn't you? Or maybe she found you. Maybe she found you and you met her once or twice and . . . then found out you had a brother too. A younger half-brother called Edmund. How many times did you meet him, Claire? Did you get to know him? Did you—'

'I never met him, Kash. I didn't meet him at all.'

'No,' said Kash, and realized that it was true. 'You never did. You were denied the chance to ever know the only brother you had. And . . . how convenient, she must have thought. A nurse in the very same hospital where her little boy died. Where he *needn't* have died, if only that selfish, heartless bastard Michael Trenchard had been doing the job he was paid to do, if he'd been there that night as duty demanded – instead of running private clinics and seeing a mistress or a girlfriend, or whatever he was doing. So whose idea was it, Claire? Hers, or yours?'

'Kash, you're wrong. Whatever it is you think I did, you're—'

But he wasn't listening, the pieces of the puzzle clicking together in his mind. 'You had the motive. You had the means – the brains, the knowledge, the access to the drugs. You had the opportunity. It would be easy enough. You could have just killed him. But that wasn't good enough, was it? Michael Trenchard had killed your brother – the brother you never knew you had until it was too late. A man like that shouldn't just *die*. A man like that ought to be punished. So you concocted a plan to destroy his reputation and make the rest of his life a living hell. Well, it wasn't hard to destroy his reputation, was it? Plenty of people were more than happy to come out of the woodwork and tell stories about him.' He laughed bitterly. 'Some of them were even true. Then planting the gear from some Soho sex store in his locker, where it was sure to be found. The rest of it, though, what you did to *him*, that was more difficult. Much too difficult for Anna Chaloner to have done on her own. You on the other hand – a nurse with access to every nook and cranny of the Victory – maybe *you* could pull it off. And what you weren't sure of, you could easily brush up on from a textbook.' He laughed hollowly. 'I know how smart you are. And you did a great job, Claire . . . except for one thing. He started to make a recovery. Not much, but enough to communicate. You knew – because I told you. And that is one thing that you couldn't allow to happen.'

Claire had heard enough. She threw her glass to the floor where it shattered into a dozen pieces, and launched from the kitchen counter, bringing her hand back sharply to strike him once, twice, three times across the face.

Kash reeled backwards, just stopping himself from falling by grabbing the open cupboard door. Looking into her furious eyes, he had a feeling of curious detachment: so this was it – what she had done to Mr Trenchard she would do to him now, anything to cover up her crime, anything to protect her long lost mother.

But instead she remained still, her hands at her side, shaking. She was breathing hard, her nostrils flaring.

After a while the fire in her eyes burned down, leaving only cold ashes. 'You can leave now, Kash. If you're here in thirty seconds, by God, I'll call the police.'

'The police!' Kash half laughed. He could taste the iron tang of blood where he had bitten his tongue. 'So you can tell them how you stole the drugs? How you stole into Mr Trenchard's office that night and made out you'd come to seduce him? How you left him there on the floor – and how even that wasn't enough? The catheter, Claire. His fingers . . .'

Kash was trembling at the very thought of it. Claire. *His* Claire. Suddenly he wasn't angry any more. His sense of outrage and betrayal had disappeared. There was just a vast, all-encompassing sadness, a black cloud slowly engulfing him.

'Get out!'

Kash turned away but, before he reached the door, he came to a stop and said softly, 'Aren't you even going to deny it, Claire?'

'Deny it? What is there even to deny? I've been *helping* you, Kash. The man I thought I loved. The man I thought loved me. The man who now looks me in the eye and tells me I'm a murderer – or worse! I've been . . . I told you, long ago, how much I wanted to find my mother. My true mother. What it felt like, growing up and not knowing where I was from, who I was. When Anna found me, well, it was . . . it was like finding a missing piece of me. I felt complete for the first time in my life. All the more when I learned that I had a brother. A half-brother. But then that was taken from me. But did we get together and try to destroy Michael Trenchard? Are we getting together on a Saturday night to gloat over it?' She shook her head sadly. 'All I wanted from Anna, one day, was a mother. And she wanted a daughter. So we met. An awkward coffee in a café. I sent her a letter. A picture. She sent me one. Told me about her life. And that's it. No plots. No conspiracy. No murder . . .'

For a moment he wavered. He wanted so much to believe her. 'What about Liz Murray, Claire? Let me see your arms, Claire.'

* * *

She gave him a look of incomprehension, then slowly pulled up the sleeves of her dressing-gown and held out her arms. Her skin was pale, flawless apart from a splash of freckles. No marks, no scratches. She was sobbing now.

'Oh, Claire. But it wasn't Anna, and it wasn't Ange. If it wasn't Doug, or you . . .? No one else knew. That Trenchard was about to tell. No one . . .'

She closed her eyes for a moment. Her hands were clenched tightly, her knuckles showing white. She looked up. 'There is someone . . .'

'What?'

Realization hit him. 'You told somebody . . .'

'I'm sorry, Kash,' she said, putting a hand to her mouth. 'I just didn't think.'

'Who?' Kash demanded. 'Claire, who did you tell?'

Claire pushed past and snatched her coat from a hook on the wall. 'Oh my God, Kash,' she almost shouted, 'we've got to go. We've got to go *now*. It might already be too late . . .'

53

Trenchard was just drifting off when he distantly heard some-one arrive. 'I've come to change his dressings. Yes, I know, such a bore! But it's four times a day, I'm afraid, until we're certain infection hasn't set in. Why don't you take a break, go and get yourself a cuppa?'

Trenchard had been put in a private sideroom 'for his own protection', a police officer officially standing guard outside. His view was limited, but the window blind was up just enough for him to see her. She was dressed in a nurse's uniform, and played the part well. The police guard was resisting, determined to stand sentry according to his orders, but she gently brushed her fingers against his forearm.

'I won't be long.'

'Bring me one too, would you love? I could *murder* a coffee. White, one sugar?'

Murder. She'd said that word with relish. So, he thought, *finally we get to it. What is it has spooked you, girl? Why not continue the torture? Somebody's close, aren't they? Somebody's close to finding you out. What you did last night, not to me, to poor old Liz Murray, oh I heard all about that. Wouldn't it be ironic if that's the one you go down for; some silly, interfering old biddy who couldn't keep her nose out.*

He heard the door to the left open, followed her ballerina footsteps. Her petite frame had been one of the things that first drew him to her, its surprising strength and vigour the features that made him come back. But his feelings had changed, lust traded for terror. And now? What did he feel now? Resigned. At peace. Almost. For one question still remained.

'Michael, it's time. I wish you could have lasted a little longer, Michael.' He heard her soft chuckle. 'Not what a man ever wants to hear. But in the same way, it was about my pleasure, not yours. I wanted to be able to awaken every day of a long lifetime with joy, knowing that you were suffering. So a matter of months has been nowhere near enough. We could have gone on, of course, if you hadn't got some movement back in that finger. And if that damned Kash hadn't interfered.

'You see, nobody saw me. Not once. I was the invisible woman. Nurse's uniform, head down and busy, and you become just another worker bee. Poor Claire helped with that – not that she knows it, of course. Her uniforms aren't exactly my size, but you can't have everything. So I've flitted in and out of this hospital as if it's my very own and not once have I been stopped.

'And then that naughty finger of yours almost put a spanner in the works. Until I sorted it out for you. I really thought I did a pretty thorough job there. You might even say too thorough. But it's never enough, is it? Even after all that, there was something nagging at me, I just didn't know what. But it's your eye, *isn't it? I saw a little twitch. Look! There it goes again. If it's not one thing, it's another! The truth is, I just can't trust you, Michael, which is why, I'm afraid, the fun is finally going to have to stop.'*

She made it easy for him to see, standing directly ahead of him as she held a pen torch between her teeth and flicked the side of the syringe theatrically with the nail of an index finger.

Still, there was one more thing he needed from her. But would she give it to him?

He willed her to listen to his own internal voice, strong and confident, as in his old life, the one she had taken, booming out into the silence of the little room.

'What did I do? What did I do to deserve all this?'

He heard the rustle of fabric as she kneeled closer. He saw the syringe in her hand.

By pure force of will, she seemed to have understood. Perhaps there was such a thing as telepathy.

'I hoped you'd work it out for yourself, Michael. I thought that would be . . . a project for you. Something to take up your time. But I wouldn't want you to go without knowing, so in case you haven't already twigged, let me tell you . . .'

54

Their feet pounded the clay tiles of the floor as they tore down the Victory's main corridor, then up the stairs to ward fourteen.

Kash was the first to hurtle through the doors, past the office and onwards, Claire followed just behind. The ward was dark, the only illumination coming from the dim emergency lights that ran along the ceiling, and the lone bed-lamp of a patient.

He swivelled on the ball of his left foot, swinging into the bay where the side rooms were. Of the four doors here, only one was ajar and only one spilled out light. His worst fears were confirmed by the sight that greeted him: the police guard was gone. Kash kicked through the door – and there was Mr Trenchard, his sallow features once flaccid, now gaunt, almost skeletal, his head lolling to one side, a mucoid slick of drool spilling from the right-hand corner of his mouth and down his chin. Over his left shoulder, the wall-mounted anglepoise lamp was on, casting his right side into even deeper shadow. The dribble glinted like wet seaweed in moonlight.

He was not alone.

The nurse bending over him was frighteningly familiar. Kash would have recognized that beguilingly petite frame, the jet-black hair whose dye he had seen staining the bathroom sink in Claire's flat. He could even see the row of piercings in her left ear, where the lamplight made the dangling silver glitter. She was wearing a Victory uniform, but she did not belong to the Victory. She turned, and only then did Kash see the syringe gripped tightly in her hand.

'Tiff,' he said, breathlessly. 'My God, Tiff . . .'

Claire shouldered her way in beside him. 'Tiff – Tiffany – for God's sake put it down. Tiff, please . . .'

Tiff's face was blank, drained of all expression. 'I don't think so,' she whispered. 'Claire, it's better you weren't here. Kash, stay or go, I don't care – but it's better that Claire isn't a witness. I don't want her name being dragged through the—'

Kash leaped forward, clasping Tiff's wrist and forcing her back.

At first caught by surprise, she fell back against the bedside locker which smashed into the wall behind it, but then she seemed to bounce back with a ferocity that caught Kash off guard. He could feel the power in her tiny frame as she pummelled him back, wrenched her hand free, still holding tightly to the syringe with which she had come to end Michael Trenchard's life.

Kash staggered, managed somehow to stop himself falling as the tip of the syringe caught his forearm. A single bead of blood swelled up and trickled through the hairs of his arm.

For a moment he panicked – but then saw that the syringe was still full. Tiff had not had time to depress the plunger.

He found himself between Tiff and the bed. They stood facing one another, breathing hard and fast. Claire was somewhere behind. 'Get him out of here, Claire,' he gasped. 'Get him somewhere. Push the bed. I'll hold her off.'

'Don't you dare fucking move him, Claire,' Tiff warned. 'He deserved everything and he deserves this. Get out of my way, Kash. I'll kill you too, if I have to. But I swear to God, Michael Trenchard is going to die and you're not going to stop it.'

Kash kept his eyes on Tiff, bracing himself for the moment she would thrust herself forward, drive him bodily out of the way and sink the syringe deep into Mr Trenchard's chest.

'Come on, Claire,' he urged. But Claire was not moving, doing nothing to disentangle Trenchard from his feeding tube and hustle him out of the room. He dared not look back but he could feel her standing there, rooted to the spot. 'Claire?'

She was trembling. She looked straight past him, into the black pools of Tiff's eyes.

'Maybe we should let her do it,' she said quietly.

'Claire?' he said.

'Well, why not? It's all gone on too long. It's time it was over.'

Kash knew she must be thinking of her mother. Thinking of Anna Chaloner and the child she had been forced to give up for adoption, and another piece of the jigsaw suddenly slotted into place.

How could he have been so stupid?

Trenchard was Edmund's father. Susan Vale wasn't the only pretty young nurse Trenchard had seduced and then abandoned when she got pregnant. I'm not going to make you a list, Isabelle had said. That was why Anna Chaloner had been so bitter. It was Edmund's own father who had let him die. Did Claire know that?

'But Claire,' he said, 'it's murder.'

She was still rooted to the spot. He turned back to Tiff. She remained immobile, resolute, the syringe gripped tightly in her fist.

'Why?' Claire whispered, behind him. 'I don't understand, Tiff. Why you?'

55

It was shortly before her thirty-eighth birthday when the pain started. Sarah Craven had never felt anything like it before, and knew at once that it must be serious. It began suddenly and, rather oddly, as a tearing sensation between her shoulder blades which then spread to the front of her chest. She called her daughter's school, and then for an ambulance which delivered her to the nearby emergency department. The morphine helped to dull the pain, but not completely, and she would still grade it as six out of ten as she was being wheeled into the CT scanner. The injection of contrast – to show up the blood vessels on her scan, they said – felt like a hot flush and, for a moment, she was worried that she had wet herself. But then the sensation passed, and she was wheeled back down the corridor again.

Sarah lost track of time, but it appeared to be early evening when the diagnosis was confirmed. Her long limbs – the pride of the corps de ballet in her teenage years – were due to Marfan syndrome. This made the blood vessels prone to tearing, or dissection. The aorta, they explained, was the body's main artery, carrying blood to pretty much every organ. Her aorta had developed such a tear. It was possible that she would need an operation to repair the damage. They had called the newly appointed vascular surgical consultant for his opinion. He was on his way now.

The wall of the aorta, they explained, is made up of layers of muscle and of elastic material. If that wall weakens – perhaps due to longstanding high blood pressure or to an inherited condition – it can tear. Blood can then force itself between the layers, the inner portion blocking flow inside the artery itself. Caught early, an operation can fix the tear. Left untreated, and the tear 'runs' – blocking key branches of the aorta.

What arteries? Well, those to the arms and legs, and to organs like the kidneys – and also the brain. The brainstem was part of a twenty-watt machine, vulnerable to any interruption to its fuel and oxygen supply. And those supplies were carried in the blood of just two pencil-thick vertebral arteries which arose from the aorta.

Sarah had a vague recollection of the consultant. She could hear him talking with the doctor outside. He seemed to speak with authority. Her doctor returned. The good news was that surgery could be avoided. She would go to the high dependency ward where she would be given medicines to control her blood pressure. All would be well.

But all was not well.

Overnight, the tear extended. It first blocked the left carotid artery, removing the blood supply to the left cerebral hemisphere and, with it, the capacity to speak or to move the right side of the body. And then the vertebrobasilar artery followed. The brainstem infarcted, and Sarah's brain became disconnected from the rest of her body.

She was locked in.

For the next five years, Sarah's teenage daughter Tiffany became her carer – helping hoist her in and out of bed, changing the linen and the bags of feed which were attached to the small tube in her stomach. All this she did while studying at school, without complaint, but not without resentment. For she knew the truth.

Tiffany had received the message that her mother was unwell. The hospital wasn't far, and she went home briefly to drop off her school things and to collect a washbag and nightdress for her mother before heading for the bus stop. The weather was bad and the traffic heavy, and there was some delay before she arrived at the emergency department. Unfamiliar with hospital process, she walked in through the doors and started looking for her mother.

Just ahead of her, using a telephone, stood a serious-looking man. He was tall and handsome. A man in charge. She stood patiently to one side.

He glanced at his watch. 'About six forty-five. Yes.' He smiled. 'Of course I'm coming. Nothing would stop me. Nothing.' A pause. 'Aortic dissection. Or I'd have been there by now.' Another pause. 'No. We can take a chance on that. She won't know. It's all about priorities, right?' He smiled again. 'Then I would have been a very naughty boy and you would have every reason to express your displeasure.' He nodded, and then again. 'Seven thirty. I promise. No later. Promise. Bye.'

Sarah's daughter was just about to step forward and say something, when another man appeared.

'Sir – just checking. Prusside and labetalol infusions and analgaesia. No surgery? I know you are the consultant, but it is a type I . . .'

The surgeon smiled. 'Indeed. But this is a complex case. Marfans and a dilated root. We'd be much better placed to see if we can temporize. Much in her best interest, you know. Let it settle and review in the morning.'

And with that, he had turned his back. Off to quite a different sort of theatre, and a non-hospital bed.

In time, of course, she had looked up the correct management. Surgery would have carried its risks, but there was no doubt that this would have been the right course of action. Five years on, and her mother died. Leaving Tiffany alone. And bitter. And scarred. She lost control of her life, just as her mother had lost control of hers. But always, deep down inside, she had a plan.

'And that's why. That's why I turned myself around, after those years I had on the street, living rough. That's why I trained to be a nurse when they wouldn't take me for a doctor – and all because of who I was. That's why I studied every night and got to work as close to Michael Trenchard as I could, but not too close. The hospice was perfect: caring for other people with no hope. But I needed to be close, and I needed a uniform. Someone my size. So I found Claire, and her flat. That couldn't have worked better, too. She started going out with *you*! A pipeline of all I needed to know.

'Anyway. After that, it was easy enough. I stalked him, I suppose, until one night he was alone in a bar, a bit drunk, and I introduced myself. A man like him can be easily led. No matter how vast his intellect, there's only one thing that really matters to men like that. So I led him on. It didn't take much except enthusiasm and availabilty. Soon I was a regular at the Dorchester suite he kept, especially for fucking grateful little mistresses like me. So when it came to that night in the basement, he hadn't a clue. You should have seen him, Claire!' For the first time Tiff laughed, loud and shrill. 'Begging for it like a little puppy – and then I stuck it in him. You know, after all the planning, the waiting, I still could never have dreamed that it would work as well as it did. But just thinking about him, locked in there, just like my mother, never to get out . . . a fate worse than death – and I did it. *I did it!* You can't imagine how I felt.' She sighed. 'I'd hoped he'd suffer so much longer. But now it has to end. Thanks to you, Kash. I also hoped not to get caught. But – hey! Thanks again.' She shrugged. 'So.' Matter of fact, now. 'I'm going to kill him. Kash, get out of my way.'

Silence settled on the room.

At last there were no more secrets.

'No,' Kash said at last. 'No. I won't.' Slowly, he went on. 'What he did was terrible. He should have been locked up – *in prison*. But this is murder. I can't let you—'

'I thought if anyone would understand, it would be you,' Tiff said, looking at him.

'What do you mean?'

'Your mother, Kash. All those letters you write. Don't look so surprised – I've been in your flat, remember? I found them all, Kash, tucked away behind some books where you didn't think anyone would find them. Why did you never send them?'

'What's she talking about?' Claire asked, her eyes flitting between them.

'*You* know what it's like, don't you, Kash,' Tiff continued, 'talking to someone who can't respond, who can't answer. Someone you love. It's painful, isn't it? The most painful thing in the world.' She paused. 'How old were you when she died?'

Kash's eyes widened and for a moment, he froze. Then, his voice low, 'It doesn't matter, Tiff. It's not the same. I still can't—'

Kash didn't have time to finish the sentence. Tiff leaped forward, slapping him squarely across the face with the back of her hand to distract him while bringing the syringe to bear with the other. Kash reeled, stumbling sideways. By the time he had grabbed hold of the side of Trenchard's bed and righted himself, the syringe in Tiff's fist was about to break the skin of Trenchard's chest. Her thumb was poised over the plunger.

A blur across Kash's field of vision as Claire threw herself forwards, pulling at Tiff from the other side of the bed. She seized Tiff's wrist, forcing the syringe up and away from Trenchard. They grappled for a moment as Tiff strained towards Trenchard's immobile body, then threw herself backwards. Refusing to let go, Claire found herself dragged along with her before falling to the floor at her feet. Kash quickly scrambled around the bed towards her, making himself a human shield between Tiff and the helpless man on the bed.

'Tiff, please!' Claire begged. 'Listen! You don't have to—'

'Oh, but I do. How can I start again? How can I carry on if I don't finish what I started? I know how a life should end. That's something I've learned over the years.'

'Liz Murray,' stammered Kash, trying to throw anything at her that might put a doubt in her mind. 'You killed Liz Murray to hide your own crime. To keep this man in misery a little longer, you choked the life out of an innocent old woman.'

For the first time, a shadow of uncertainty passed across Tiff's face. 'She was on her way out. She probably had days left.'

'But those days belonged to her, Tiff. They were *hers*.'
Silence.

'You can't ignore *that*, Tiff. Everything you've done . . . and for what? For revenge? Put the syringe down, Tiff.'

Tiff seemed to hesitate, turning over his words in her mind and for a moment Kash thought she was going to give up. Then in one fluid movement she was down on her haunches, wrapping her hand around a skein of Claire's thick chestnut hair and hauling her to her feet. The syringe danced in her other fist. She wrenched Claire sideways, exposing the pink flesh of her neck, and pressed the tip of the needle to her skin.

'What the . . .? Tiff, she's your friend!'

'And she's your lover. Do you love her, Kash?'

Kash was dumbfounded. 'Whatever happened here last night, whatever happened on ward fourteen, we can put it right. Trenchard, Liz Murray. All of the rest. But she's your friend, Tiff. You wouldn't . . .'

'You haven't answered my question. Do? You? Love? Her?'

'Yes! Yes I love her!' Kash screamed.

A fleeting sadness crossed Tiff's face. She hung her head and, for a second, Kash could see the Tiff he thought he knew, the purple-haired, freewheeling pixie, a sparkle of mischief forever in her eye.

'Well, now you can prove it,' she said, pulling her head up. 'I'm leaving now, Kash. Come after me, or . . . save the woman you love.'

Before the words were even out of her mouth, the needle had pierced Claire's skin. Tiff depressed the plunger and, releasing her hold on Claire's hair, helped her fall gently to the ground. Then, without even glancing at Kash, she walked to the door.

'I love her too,' she whispered from the doorway. 'It isn't always so easy, is it? Jesus, Kash, I did my best to warn you off, but you just wouldn't listen. The road to hell being paved with good intentions, and all that. Well, now's your chance to do the right thing.'

'Tiff,' Kash gasped. 'What was it? What have you . . .?'

'Just sux, Kash. Just common or garden suxamethonium chloride.' Then her voice cracked. 'Save her, Kash. You haven't got much time.' She opened the door and disappeared into the darkness of the ward.

Kash dropped to Claire's side, cradling her in his arms. Already the sound of a fire alarm was blaring out across ward fourteen, and into every corner of the Victory hospital. Tiff had covered her escape well; nobody would remember the unfamiliar nurse joining the relatives as they hurried into the carpark.

'Claire,' he said, 'CLAIRE!'

Her muscles trembled, she willed herself to stand, but it was already too late. Her limbs would not respond. Her breathing was growing more laboured.

'No!'

She was gasping. As she slumped, finally, into his arms, she whispered one last word, 'Please . . .'

As her eyelids began to flutter and shutter-slide to obscure her failing vision, the last thing she saw clearly was Kash leaning in towards her. He locked his lips around hers and, hunched under the hammering of the hospital alarms, concentrated on one thing and one thing only – keeping Claire Barker, the woman he loved, alive, one breath at a time.

56

Nights on ward fourteen were always Michael Trenchard's favourite. The nurses hoisted him out of the chair in which he had spent his day and laid him back in his bed, occasionally turning him to keep at bay the bedsores which would otherwise be flourishing. In this position, and in the dark, he did not have to look at the other patients, could pretend that he was not one of them. A man apart.

Outside the walls of the Victory, spring had turned into summer. Sometimes a new nurse would wheel him around the ward or, if feeling generous, out into the hospital courtyard where he could feel the warm air brush his face, or take delight in the rows of potted plants and the solitary fern, otherwise abandoned with such indifference. Once, he'd been taken to a canteen and had sat while she drank a cup of scalding black tea and spoke of her father, himself a palliative care nurse from a hospital somewhere up north, and of her new job at the Victory. 'They still talk about you, sometimes. Only sometimes, mind. I've been here three months and it's only last week they told me what you did. You were a rum one, weren't you?' And that – the way she shook her head, the way she rolled her eyes, the way she'd only just heard, and even now she didn't really care – was when he knew it was finally gone: his reputation. Good or bad, there had been a time – a long time – when you couldn't ignore Michael Trenchard. This girl didn't even know who he was.

At least there was still the night-time. The solitude reminded him that, even trapped in here, his mind was still sharp. And his fingers.

The fingers had set straight enough, threaded by wires and bolted into their Meccano frames. But he didn't much care, at least for four of them. They could be hacked off and incinerated for all he cared. But that one precious finger . . . . She'd snapped the bones, not the joints, and the tendons were still intact. And that had been a mistake. And she had not known about the eye. Kash had, of course, told them. With luck, he'd soon have dual control of cursor and computer screen, language and television, lights . . . the whole world around him. Dr Jack Carney had come himself and told him that he would have an electric wheelchair of his own and one which he'd be able to drive. 'Not quite your Bentley, but it will do!' Hell, he might even go home – with a care package, of course – and control his own front door.

Yes, perhaps all that would come back one day.

But the one thing he knew he would never do was tell them her name. Oh, he still fantasized about watching the cursor type it out as it danced across the screen, propelled by his twitching finger: Tiffany Rourke. And he fantasized about what would happen to her. The trial. The public outrage. The years in *a dank jail cell. Yes, that would go some way to compensating him for what he'd lost.*

But then, of course, the truth would come out. Why she'd done it. And what he'd done – or failed to do – to her mother. Ange would scream abandonment over that boy. And that would end the rehabilitation of his reputation. He'd be even more reviled than before.

And perhaps, in small measure, rightly so. There was room for remorse, if not redemption.

It had taken him a long time to realize it. A long time to admit it. And perhaps he would never quite be able to come to terms with it. But he had finally come to understand what he was.

A man who had chosen his own fleeting pleasure over a woman's life, who had traded his few hours in a hotel for five years of a hell he had now experienced first-hand, banging and screaming in the soundproofed cell that separated her from the rest of the world.

Had he, in part, got exactly what he deserved?

If he had ever raged against her, keeping himself going in his darkest hours by vowing to have his revenge, he wasn't raging any more. The fury had burned itself out.

If he saw her again, which he didn't suppose he would, and had finally learned to turn his thoughts into words by then, he would tell her he was sorry, and that he forgave her for everything she'd done. Whether wholly true or not, it couldn't hurt him or her.

He would also tell her, in a paternal sort of way, that he admired her. It had taken nerve to do what she had done. Nerves of steel. And intelligence, too. She would have made a first-rate surgeon.

If only he hadn't screwed up her life for her.

Would she forgive him, too, then?

Probably not. But did it matter that much? Yes, he felt pity, and shame. But also pride. He had been damned good. He was damned good. How many others could have fought their way back to consciousness, to movement? How many? Yes. He had reason to be proud. He would, and should, soon regain control.

*   *   *

No longer afraid, he liked to listen to the footsteps on the ward, and had learned to differentiate the various gaits. It was a little game he played, one at which he now was expert. He could map who was where with precision. Then there was the squeaking of a trolley's wheels – supper, drug round or mortuary could all be distinguished – or the sudden flurry of footsteps as some on-call doctor was summoned from slumber to a small-hours emergency. Yes, the night-time threads could be woven into a picture, the sounds into a symphony if you knew how to listen.

The footsteps were closer now. He could tell by the pattern of the footfall, the way the sound increased as they approached. He counted: one, two . . . three people?

They'd approached from the side and hadn't crossed his window, so he could not tell who they were. The door to his private room opened, then swung shut on its heavy hinges with a muted clunk.

Who was it? Having no choice, he stared at the emptiness of the ceiling tiles, and wondered.

A hand appeared in front of his face. White cuffs on a coat. A doctor, then?

Kash, is it you? I thought you must have gone away, left the hospital, without saying goodbye. It would be understandable, of course, after everything – almost losing your lovely Nurse Barker.

He thought back to the chaos of that last night.

'Hello, Mr Trenchard. It's only me.'

Kash! It is *you! Where have you been? And who have you brought with you?*

'You must have been expecting me. You see, they say that finger's nearly ready. The technicians are raring to go. They'll have you up in a chair and scooting around the ward. They'll have you flirting with every new nurse who walks in here. They'll all think you're charming, Mr Trenchard, and so brave after everything that's happened. And that wouldn't be right, would it?'

What do you mean, Kash? What are you talking about? You're my friend, the only one who stood up for me. When everyone else was ready to believe the worst, you knew better!

'It's taken me a long time to make up my mind, Mr Trenchard. In the end, no one can really help you; you have to decide these things for yourself. I did talk to one person, though. My mother. She always knows the right thing to do.'

Damn it, Kash! You're not making sense.

'"Do no harm." That's the first thing they teach you in medical school, isn't it? The first principle of medicine. And it seems simple enough, at first. A no-brainer, if you'll excuse the phrase. But sometimes things get more complicated. As I've found out. In fact, I've learned a lot in the last few months. About all the ways of doing harm, and all the ways of trying to make things better. I suppose I should thank you.'

You're rambling like a schoolboy, Kash. Come to the point, can't you?

'I stopped her, Mr Trenchard. I stopped Tiffany from finishing it. And then I let her go. I had to, to save Claire. But now I'm glad Tiff got away. It would have been wrong for her to have gone to prison, to make her suffer any more than she already has.' He sighed. 'I don't agree with everything she did. Perhaps she wasn't completely sane. But who would be, after what she'd been through? I think she deserves peace now, to know it's over. To know she's safe. So you see, I can't let you tell anyone. And *there are others, too, who deserve resolution. Retribution. Call it what you will.'*

Something new moved into Trenchard's narrow field of vision. He recognized the silhouette of a syringe, its needle bare and glistening.

He was confused, though, by the hand. It was a woman's, with a slender wrist and long, pale fingers with nails that rose just a little at their tips.

Not her . . . then who?

'Goodbye, Mr Trenchard.'

The needle moved away. He sensed, rather than felt, a pin-prick on his arm. There was a rushing, as if a dam had been breached and water was suddenly surging over the dry land, submerging everything in its path. There followed a moment of stillness, simple and serene; then the needle withdrew. Next came the sound of the footsteps receding, the door opening and closing – and Michael Trenchard was alone once again.

*   *   *

The flood of icy water surged onwards, soaking into the parched soil, bringing moisture where before there had only been dry dust. His dessicated synapses began to come to life. It's well known that people who have lost limbs can still feel phantom pain, hovering ghostlike in the spaces where their arms and legs used to be. And that was what it was like for Michael

Trenchard now. His body had been dead for so long, but now he could feel it reviving, stretching and flexing as if it were alive again, like a balloon being blown up. It felt enormous. It rose and rose and rose until it was filling all of space, huge, strong, all-encompassing. He took a step, and the universe trembled. He was a god, golden-limbed and full of power, striding out across the void. He'd never felt so strong, so alive. So vast. He felt electricity surging round his body, crackling through his veins, fizzing and popping from his fingertips and pulsing from his eyes. For a few glorious moments he just luxuriated in this feeling of potency. Then he looked around.

He was standing in the lobby of a plush hotel. All around him were men in evening suits and women in cocktail dresses. He looked down to see that he was dressed in a dark suit, with a pink shirt and a midnight blue tie, secured with a diamond pin. On his feet were polished brogues. He'd been meticulous about his appearance, because he was meeting her. It was their first tryst. He looked up and there she was, in a red velvet dress that clung to her slim, elf-like frame. Her hair was blonde this time, and her mouth a slash of vermilion. How daring! She smiled, that twinkling, elfin smile, and held out her hand. He took it and felt another crackle of electricity at his fingertips.

'This way,' she said, walking through a door and pulling him behind her.

They were in an empty corridor now. On each side were doors with numbers. Which, he wondered was their room?

He looked forward and the corridor went on and on, receding impossibly into the distance like a funhouse illusion.

She glanced over her shoulder, pulling him onwards.

His mouth was dry with anticipation. How much further? He tried to speak but she turned again, a finger to her lips.

His legs began to feel weary, his superhuman strength starting to ebb from his limbs. He wasn't sure how much further he could go.

'Almost there,' she trilled brightly, reading his thoughts.

He dragged himself forward, forcing one foot on after the other. He hoped by the time they got to the room, he would have enough strength left.

'Here we are.'

He looked at the door. It had a shiny brass zero instead of a number.

'Are you sure?' he asked.

'Yes, this is it.' She had a key in her hand and was turning it in the lock. The door swung open. 'After you.'

He looked into the room. It was pitch black. He could see nothing. Just a dark void.

'Go on,' she said. He felt the gentle pressure of her hand at his back.

He took a deep breath and stepped forward.

57

That night, two figures exited Michael Trenchard's room. They crossed ward fourteen, past the bed where Liz Murray's life had been stolen, past the patients sleeping and the patients for whom sleep refused to come. Halfway across the ward, one of them reached out for the other's hand – and, with their fingers entwined, they reached the office at the entrance to the ward. There, lit by the light of an electric desk lamp, her face half in shadow, waited Sister Susan Vale. From her hands hung a simple yellow plastic bucket for medical 'sharps' waste. Hundreds of them were used and destroyed in the Victory each day. This one would be lost amongst them.

Dr Kash Devan barely stopped as he walked by. His eyes met Sister Vale's and something briefly passed between them. Kash reached out and the syringe that had been dangling in his one free hand dropped into the bucket. Sister Susan Vale sealed it, and placed it with all the others awaiting incineration.

The two figures walked out of ward fourteen, and down the stairs. Onwards through empty halls and on past the closed door of the mess, out into the carpark. Ambulances lay spent outside the emergency department, their crews betrayed by rising smoke from behind the fire escape as they drew furtively on their cigarettes; the ordinary business of life in the hospital went on, as it always would. Kash and his companion turned up their collars, walked briskly across the car park and disappeared into the dark. A car was already waiting.

Behind the wheel sat Dr Angela Warner. She did not turn as Kash slipped into the back seat. 'Is it done?' she asked, edging out into the traffic that, even at this ungodly hour, circled the Victory.

'Yes, it's done,' said Claire.

On the back seat she fell onto Kash's shoulder and he put his arm around her. It had been two months since they'd last seen Tiff – but, wherever she was, Kash fancied that she would soon know, and maybe understand, what they had done. Perhaps she would come back, or perhaps she was already building a new life in another place. Wherever she was, he hoped her demons were finally at rest.

Her secret was theirs now. In the morning they would find Trenchard dead. An autopsy, if they bothered to perform one, would find nothing.

Ange brought the car to a halt on a quiet street of shuttered shops in Denmark Hill. One hundred metres away, a handful of people had been drawn to the yellow light of the all-night fried chicken shop. Kash reached forward and squeezed her shoulder. 'Thank you, Ange.' He stepped out into the night. At his side, Claire clung to his arm. As they watched the taillights of the car disappearing into the traffic, they took a moment to savour the night-time air, the smell of the city's breath. Life went on.

It was a heavy burden they shared. He knew there would be sleepless nights. Moments of doubt, even. But the nightmare was over. Tomorrow Claire would tell her mother, and Kash would write his usual unposted letter to his. He knew in his heart both would give their blessing.

'Are you coming upstairs?' Claire asked.

Yes. Life went on. And it was to be good.

Kash threaded his fingers into hers, and followed her through the door.

ACKNOWLEDGEMENTS

To all my friends and colleagues, past and present, my thanks. Only the best of your traits appear, of course – the badness is all fantasy. Eddie – thanks for letting me kill you off.

To Lynda, who insisted that the book see the light of day, and to Nigel and the team, my thanks again.

To Jane and all at Walker Books, who first made me a published author all those years ago – and now to the wonderful enthusiasts at Bonnier Books: thank you for being so endlessly positive and putting up with rewrites and the constraints that a full-time job puts on meeting deadlines. Bill – you are a marvel. Kate – thank you for believing.

To Debbie, who always encouraged, even on reading a dire first draft.

And to patients past and present: please do not think that medicine is really like this, nor that I have drawn on your stories to tell my own. I genuinely have not. For those who may yet meet me, please trust that the fiction I write does not reflect my general view of the world, or of you.

Want to read
NEW BOOKS
before anyone else?

Like getting
FREE BOOKS?

Enjoy sharing your
OPINIONS?

Discover
READERS FIRST
Read. Love. Share.

Sign up today to win your first free book:
readersfirst.co.uk